"Everyone, I'd like you to meet my fiancée."

Emma closed her eyes for a moment. Had Alec Sayre introduced her as his fiancée? And he'd kissed her. Flat-out and full on the lips, as if she were the woman of his dreams. Was he blind or had he just forgotten what his finacée looked like? "Wait a minute." Emma cleared her throat and tried to look up at him.

Alec squeezed her shoulders and bent to whisper in her ear. "Don't make a scene and nobody gets hurt." Then he lifted his head and smiled. The revelers, who'd been waiting for a sign that the lovers had finished their private exchange of greetings, began to press in.

Alec's hands were firm on her shoulders. His acceptance of good wishes left her little room for denials. What was she supposed to do now?

If she was lucky, in more ways than one, she might get out of here without anyone finding out who she really was....

ABOUT THE AUTHOR

Karen Toller Whittenburg lives in the beautiful green country of northeastern Oklahoma. Her favorite pastime hasn't changed since she was a child—curling up with a good book. She divides her leisure time between a part-time job and family activities. She also scripts movies for the Narrative Television Network, a network for the blind and visually impaired. Karen and her husband love to spend weekends browsing through antique shops. He collects old cameras and she collects ideas for future books.

Books by Karen Toller Whittenburg

HARLEQUIN AMERICAN ROMANCE

197—SUMMER CHARADE
249—A MATCHED SET
294—PEPPERMINT KISSES
356—HAPPY MEDIUM
375—DAY DREAMER
400—A PERFECT PAIR
424—FOR THE FUN OF IT
475—BACHELOR FATHER

HARLEQUIN TEMPTATION

303—ONLY YESTERDAY

Don't miss any of our special offers. Write to us at the following address for information on our newest releases.

Harlequin Reader Service
P.O. Box 1397, Buffalo, NY 14240
Canadian address: P.O. Box 603,
Fort Erie, Ont. L2A 5X3

Karen Toller Whittenburg

WEDDING OF HER DREAMS

Harlequin Books

TORONTO • NEW YORK • LONDON
AMSTERDAM • PARIS • SYDNEY • HAMBURG
STOCKHOLM • ATHENS • TOKYO • MILAN
MADRID • WARSAW • BUDAPEST • AUCKLAND

For DeAnn and Terry
The Newlyweds

ISBN 0-373-16528-5

WEDDING OF HER DREAMS

Copyright © 1994 by Karen Toller Whittenburg.

Chapter One

In some other town, the red dress would have been her ticket to any party she wanted to crash. In Las Vegas, it didn't get her past the door. Emma Cates gripped her beaded evening bag as she considered the gaiety emanating from behind the closed door and the single, female sentry who blocked the entrance. The woman was close to six feet, blond, and dressed in a tuxedo that ended just shy of very long and lean thighs. With a silent and frustrated sigh, Emma admitted she had miscalculated the persuasive powers of the red dress.

"Would you consider a bribe?" she asked the blonde. "I've got two tickets to Wayne Newton."

The woman smiled. "This is a private party, hon. If I let you in, I'd get fired and you'd get tossed out on your butt, anyway."

"I told you I just forgot to bring my invitation."

"Yeah, and someone just forgot to put your name on the guest list, too." A door opened behind her and the blonde made a minor adjustment to the sleeve of her satin jacket as two men entered the hallway. For a second, Emma caught a glimpse of the party to which she had not been invited. Then the door closed her out again and the men each lit a cigarette as they walked to a smoking area a short distance away.

"You won't get fired." Emma couldn't guarantee any such thing, but no one at the Tuxedo Junction Hotel and Casino Complex had made the slightest concession to her continued complaints, and she was fed up with the whole lot of them. "I'll talk to the manager."

"So he could fire me in person? No, thanks." The blonde struck a supple pose against the door frame. "Mr. Sayre said, 'No invitation, no admittance.' If you want to argue that with him, you should make an appointment."

"If I could have gotten an appointment, I wouldn't be here now," Emma snapped. She had tried to go through the proper channels, had made several attempts to get an appointment with Alec Sayre, Mr. Tuxedo Junction himself. Crashing this party was her last resort, and she wasn't going to turn tail and run at the first obstacle. "Could you ask him to come out here? That wouldn't be breaking any moral imperative, would it?"

The blonde blinked. "I don't know. And, frankly, I don't intend to find out."

Emma sized up the troublemaker in one long look. The woman was tall, to be sure, but she didn't look like a bodybuilder. Okay, she probably had to work out to fit that body into that outfit, but that didn't mean she had enough muscle to keep a determined woman from getting through the door. Emma might be outsized in every respect, but she was scrappy. If she could catch the blonde off guard...

"Don't even think about it, hon. I have two brothers and what they didn't teach me about body slams I picked up from watching 'World Federation Wrestling' on TV."

Emma wasn't surprised. "Any chance you'll take a trip to the ladies' room before the night is over?"

"And be replaced by a man who'll take one look at that sleazy dress you're wearing and drool a path for you into the party? Not likely."

Sleazy? All right, the dress was short. And red. It clung. It boasted more spangles than "The Star-Spangled Banner." But it had cost too damn much to be *sleazy.* "For all you know, I'm a special friend of Mr. Sayre's. A friend he will be quite surprised and happy to see. Now, kindly step out of my way."

"I'm not scared of you, sugar." The blonde braced one spiked high heel against the wall behind her and examined the fine black mesh of her stockings. "Give it up. This just isn't your lucky night."

Emma glanced at the men, debating whether she was desperate enough to ask for their assistance. They were obviously invited guests. One or both of them could get her into the party. On the other hand, approaching strange men in a hotel hallway could be asking for more trouble than this whole thing was worth.

Emma caught her mind-set in midretreat. If she didn't stand up for herself, if she didn't put up a fight for what was rightfully hers, then she couldn't expect to be much of a success in her new business...or anywhere else. Overcoming her qualms, she smiled invitingly at one of the men.

He straightened and sucked in his paunch.

Emma dredged up her best female-in-need-of-assistance look. "Hello," she said, taking the few steps necessary to get within conversation range. "I wonder if you could help me. Do either of you know Alec Sayre?"

The man with the paunch smiled broadly and, even from several feet away, Emma caught a whiff of bourbon and Lucky Strikes. "Sure. We're here at a party in his honor."

"Really?" Emma said, as if the information impressed her. "Then he *is* here?"

The second smoker, a short, balding young man, gave Emma a dubious look through wire-rim glasses. "Where else would he be?"

The first man stepped forward, ready to defend Emma from a suspicious mind. "He's inside. This is a roast, you know, one of those dinners where everyone tries to embarrass the guest of honor?" He gave a little shrug. "It's difficult to embarrass Alec, though. He's pretty shock-resistant."

Emma nodded, trying her best to look knowledgeable about a man she'd never met. "I had hoped to be here sooner. I thought this would be the perfect opportunity to surprise him, but..." The sentence trailed into a misleading sigh. "I didn't receive an invitation because, of course, Alec had no idea I would be able to come. I didn't know, myself, until the last minute and now..." Her lips played with a rueful smile. "And now it seems I won't get to see him at all."

The man looked properly sympathetic. "Are you a friend of his?"

"Well...." Emma toyed with a big fat lie and ended with a slim prevarication. "I don't believe Alec would use the word, *friend* to describe me." A stranger, maybe. A name on a long-forgotten message slip, perhaps. But friend? Definitely, no. "He prefers to keep things like, uh, this, kind of quiet." She ended with a slight you-know-him shrug.

The paunch was sucked in a little more as the man's eyes rounded with awe. "Oh, my grandmother's ghost! You wouldn't...by any chance...be Alec's girl? The one he calls Lucky?"

"Don't be an idiot, Ron." The second man, the one with the receding hairline, stubbed out his cigarette. "There is no Lucky. She doesn't exist except in his imagination."

"Oh, come on, Gary. Don't be such a cynic. Just because we haven't met her, doesn't mean she isn't real." He turned back to Emma. "You are his fiancée, aren't you?" It was more statement than question. "You're Lucky."

Emma swallowed. Fiancée? Oops.

"Lucky?" She stalled, glancing at the blonde who still guarded the door. "I guess that depends on who you ask."

The man grinned. "I think I'll ask Alec. I had a feeling when I first saw you standing out here that you were someone special. And then, when you said you wanted to surprise Alec..."

She hadn't said exactly that, but if agreeing would get her past Amazon Angel, she wasn't going to argue. After all, she'd let him assume she was Alec Sayre's fiancée. It was a little late to quibble over semantics. "I believe he'll be very surprised," she said with total honesty.

"I think you can make book on that." Gary, the cynic, eyed Emma with new interest. "But this is Alec's night for surprises. A roast in his honor. What better time for his phantom fiancée to make her appearance?"

"Hey, that's right!" Ron jumped on the idea with the enthusiasm supplied by one drink too many. "Alec's roast. The speakers are all finished, but this will be the coup de grace. Man, oh, man, this is going to be great."

Emma was having serious second thoughts. A "phantom fiancée." Now, how was she supposed to carry that off? This had all the markings of a bad joke. Still, she figured, if these guys could get her inside, she could explain her way out—after she'd given Alec Sayre a piece of her mind. "I can't wait to see him," she said with perfect sincerity.

Ron nodded. "And I can't wait to see his face when he sees you."

"Yes, that ought to be something to see," Gary said in an ominous tone as he moved to open the door. "Stand aside, Bambi," he said to the blonde. "This is Alec's lucky day."

Propelled by a man on either side, Emma swept through the doorway on a wave of trepidation and sheer audacity. Behind her, she heard Bambi mutter, "I should have taken the tickets."

ALEC COUNTED twenty-six women dressed in black, clearly the preferred color for the evening, eight women wearing some variation of blue, two in lavender, one in silver sequins, and Charity, of course, in white. Not that the color didn't suit her dark beauty, but lately it seemed she wore white exclusively. *Bridal* white. The thought gave him the willies, and he downed the rest of his drink in one swallow.

"Enjoying yourself?" Charity took his empty glass.

"As usual, you planned everything perfectly." Alec slipped his left hand into his pocket. He had a bizarre superstition that if he didn't keep his ring finger out of sight, Charity would get a band of gold around it when he wasn't looking.

She cast a hostess-y smile across the crowded room. "I know you'd rather be roaming the halls, looking for some crisis or other, but it's important for the manager of a hotel like Tuxedo Junction to associate with the right people."

He shifted, uncomfortable with her superior opinions and uncomfortably conscious of how close she was standing. "I thought this dinner was supposed to be an intimate gathering of my closest friends. There must be seventy-five people here."

"Eighty-three," she corrected with a smile. "Can I help it if everyone considers you his best friend?"

"His?" Alec teased. "You mean none of these females claims a close friendship?"

"Just me."

Backfire, Alec thought. Would he never learn? He fell back on a lame observation. "Well, if this is an intimate gathering, I'll eat my white tie with melba sauce."

"Good thing you're wearing your black one, isn't it?" Charity followed his gaze with a satisfied look. "And this is intimate, Alec. I limited the guest list to the cream of Las Vegas society. And your friends, of course. All in all, I think it's a good mix."

She had gone to a great deal of trouble to plan this dinner in his honor. He did appreciate her efforts. If only he could be honest with her. Honest and friendly and unimportant to her. "A good mix," he agreed. "I'm sure each and every one of the guests will make a sizable contribution to the, uh... What foundation are we soliciting for tonight?"

"Alec." She scolded him with a pretty frown. "This dinner is in your honor. Any funds raised will go to your favorite charity."

Please, he thought, don't say it.

"And please, Alec, don't say that I'm your favorite Charity."

She'd said it. Alec fought a curt rejoinder for control of his mouth. "Maybe I'll forget about all the worthwhile causes, abscond with the funds, and run off to Mexico."

"I know you better than that," she said simply.

Which was the problem with Charity McKimber. She thought she knew him inside and out. She thought she was his soul mate, his perfect match, the woman he would eventually marry. For the life of him, Alec hadn't been able to convince her otherwise. "I suppose your father sent a generous donation."

"Daddy is always supportive. He was very disappointed that a scheduling conflict kept him from being here tonight. He's planning to visit us next week. He wants to talk to you about the upcoming board meeting, and he hopes to spend a little time with me."

"Why don't you take a few days off to be with him? I'm sure the public relations department can manage without you for a little while."

"Don't be silly. I can't take a vacation now. I'm right in the middle of the Wedding of Your Dreams contest. You know, the contest we're sponsoring in conjunction with the wedding professionals' conference? It's like planning a real wedding."

It was the tone of her voice, her proprietary touch, that made Alec feel as though matrimony was sneaking up behind him, intent on taking his scalp. "I wish

Lucky could have been here tonight," he said in self-defense.

Charity stiffened. "What a shame you couldn't give me her address, so I could have sent her an invitation."

"She moves around a lot."

"So you've said any number of times since you became engaged to her. You know, Alec, everyone is beginning to refer to your, uh, fiancée as The Phantom."

He rolled that over in his mind and liked the sound. "The phantom fiancée. She'll think that's funny."

Charity crossed her arms at her waist. "I'm sure she has a wonderful sense of humor, Alec. As do all of us who are still waiting...and *waiting* to meet her."

"I know." He tried to sound wistful. "It's frustrating for me, too."

He shouldn't be enjoying this exchange. He liked Charity and had no wish to hurt her. But she had convinced herself—and almost everyone he knew—that she and Alec was a match made in heaven and that it was merely a matter of time before he realized it, too. He had given her no encouragement and yet so strong was her conviction that he continually felt pressed to make a commitment to her, to set the date and face the inevitable.

If she hadn't been so good at her job, he would have fired her. And, considering that her father owned a sizable percentage of Tuxedo Junction, that wasn't a viable option. Alec didn't understand exactly how she was able to throw his defense mechanisms into overdrive. He liked living on the edge, courted the adrenaline rush of challenge, but Charity got too close for comfort. She even had his own mother believing that a wedding was in the offing. And with the inventiveness of a desperate man, he had plucked Lucky from his imagination and dubbed her his fiancée. His phantom fiancée.

Alec was aware of a sudden stirring around him. A rustle of animation skipped across the room, alerting him, snatching his attention.

"Alec! Hey, Alec!"

He turned, intrigued by the commotion moving his way, a little wary of the jovial energy of his buddies' approach. "I thought the roast was over," he said to Charity. "Don't tell me these guys have come up with another embarrassing moment from my wicked past."

"Your friends never seem to know when to quit. If they've hired a stripper to round off tonight's entertainment, I'll murder them. Each and every one."

A stripper? Charity spoke as if she knew what was afoot, but surely none of his friends would bring a stripper to this gathering. Why, as Charity had taken pains to point out, the "cream of Las Vegas society" was present. That thought made Alec smile, a faux pas he quickly concealed.

"Alec!" The call of a fraternity brother came again and the crowd parted like the Red Sea under Moses's rod. "Oh, Alec! Have we got a surprise for you!"

Beside him, Charity stiffened. Alec stepped forward, poised to protect the rowdies from her wrath, ready to deal with the next round of jokes at his expense. He caught a shimmer of red, a glimpse of spangled movement, before his old college buddy, Ron Taylor, moved in front of the mystery woman and blocked his view.

"Hey, Alec, you *lucky* devil!" Ron's grin was as wide as the Cheshire cat's and showed no sign of vanishing. "Guess who Gary and I found waiting outside? Guess what *lucky* lady almost didn't get into this wing-ding? Guess who is the *luckiest* man in this room tonight?"

Unless he missed his guess, Alec figured he was about to encounter a hired stripper posing as his phantom fiancée. Now which one of these yahoos had come up with this practical joke? And how in hell could he keep this situation from turning into a humiliating and truly tasteless incident?

"May I preeesent . . ." Drawing out the word like a drumroll, Ron bowed deep and backed aside, pushing Charity out of the inner circle and into the background. Alec caught her disapproving frown as she whirled angrily and walked away. "The one! The only!" Ron paused for breath, ending the suspense with an enthusiastic and slurred, "Hee-eerre's Lucky!" His silly smile was reflected on every face around him. Except the one directly before Alec.

The woman was small, with a militant sparkle in her green eyes and an impertinent tilt to her chin, and a sassy little dimple just below her mouth . . . a mouth that looked very kissable. Several wispy curls framed her face, escapee tendrils from the glittering combs that held her shining honey-blond hair upswept and off her long, slender neck. She didn't look like a stripper. She didn't look much like the Lucky he'd imagined, either. No, she looked better than the woman he'd invented . . . softer and, yes, sexier, too. And he wouldn't have thought that possible.

She took a step closer. "Alec Sayre, I presume?" Her voice was low and husky, tinged with a flirtatious overtone, and softened by threads of nervousness. Did professional dancers get nervous? Maybe she was new at her job. Maybe it was part of the act. Maybe he just didn't like the idea of that body being exposed to any eyes but his own.

Around him, the air seethed with expectancy. Some action was clearly required. Should he hustle her from the room before she began her striptease? Should he announce that he'd never seen this woman before? Should he congratulate the pranksters on their ingenuity? Should he confound them all and call their collective bluff? Alec had a mere second to make up his mind.

"Hello...Lucky," he said as he pulled her into his arms and planted a kiss in the middle of her full, and very surprised, lips. He, himself, was caught a little off guard by the flurry of sensations that ricocheted through him at the first sweet taste of her mouth.

Emma didn't put up a fight. She didn't even have enough forewarning to resist. One second she was standing in front of a tall, dark-haired, square-jawed stranger, trying to reconcile this attractive, sophisticated man with the creep she'd imagined, doing her level best to recall her well-rehearsed speech of stolen ideas and unethical business practices, and the next second she was in his arms and locked to his lips...and there was no denying that his kiss wreaked havoc. This was not at all the way she'd planned to put him in his place. And wait.... Had she heard correctly? Had he just said, "Hello, *Lucky*"?

She wanted to consider that, but his kiss was quite eloquent and she found it difficult to gather the thoughts he'd effectively scattered. They came together with amazing clarity, however, when his hand slid below her waist and pressed possessively against her hip, inducing a serious rise in her body temperature. She pulled away from his kiss, but locked her arms around his neck and squeezed. He looked her square in the eye and smiled, confirming her suspicion that Mr. Alec Sayre was too good-looking for his own good and too sure of himself by half.

"Get your hand off my hip," she said through tight lips. "I have two brothers and what they didn't teach me about body slams, I learned from watching 'World Federation Wrestling' on TV."

He moved his hand. "I didn't realize I was dealing with a professional."

"Keep it in mind, Mr. Sayre."

"Oh, please, now that we're engaged, call me Alec." In one quick move, he grasped her wrists in his hands, removed them from around his neck and turned her within the circle of his arms to face the crowd. "Everyone?" He pitched his voice to carry. "I'd like you to meet my fiancée. This is Lucky."

Emma closed her eyes for a moment, but the sounds of congratulations and good wishes didn't go away. Had Alec Sayre introduced her as his *fiancée?* Maybe she'd misunderstood the word. Maybe he'd said my...? What else could he have said? Fiancée wasn't exactly an easy word to mishear. And he'd kissed her. Flat-out and full on the lips, as if she were the woman of his dreams. Was he blind or had he just forgotten what his fiancée looked like? "Wait a minute." Emma cleared her throat and tried to look up at him. "Now wait just a minute."

He squeezed her shoulders and bent to whisper in her ear. "Don't make a scene and nobody gets hurt." Then he lifted his head and smiled. The revelers, who'd been waiting for a sign that the lovers had finished their private exchange of greetings, began to press in, wanting to shake hands, wanting to offer congratulatory kisses and happy hugs.

Emma's mind flashed frantically from how she had gotten into this situation to why she had ever conceived the idea of crashing this party to how she was going to escape. Alec's hands were firm on her shoulders. His acceptance of good wishes left her little room for denials. After all, she'd pretended to be Lucky to get in here. What was she supposed to do now? Shout that it was a case of mistaken identity?

She had lived in Las Vegas long enough to recognize faces familiar to anyone who read the society pages of the newspaper. And she was a businesswoman, trying to jump-start the economy of a floundering wedding chapel, trying to make a place for herself in this town, among this group of people. She couldn't afford to make a bad first impression. The only solution she could find was to keep quiet. If she were lucky, in more ways than one, she might get out of here without anyone finding out who she really was.

"I can't tell you how happy this makes me." Ron Taylor, the perpetrator of misunderstandings, pumped Alec's hand and bathed Emma in a bourbon-laced grin. "Gary thought this little lady was a figment of your imagination." He laughed and clapped Alec on the shoulder. "But she sure looks real to me. Damn real...and real good, if you don't mind my saying so."

"Compliment her to your heart's content," Alec said magnanimously.

"Thanks. Mind if I kiss her?"

"I wouldn't if I were you. She's into wrestling. World Federation."

Ron eyed Emma with new respect. "Wow," he said, and moved on.

A couple took his place. Alec introduced Emma. They shook hands all around. No one asked if she had a last name. Or another name, for that matter. It was as if she were famous, a pop singer or an actress, easily recognized by the one word, Lucky. In a city of gamblers. What were the odds?

She grabbed a moment between felicitations to look over her shoulder at Alec. The wicked amusement in his deep-set blue eyes evoked an odd response inside of her, an uneasy ripple of attraction that started in her stomach and swirled into a weakness around her knees. Was he enjoying this? "I can't—" she began. "This is ridiculous, you know. It's crazy. I am not Lucky."

"That depends on who you ask, doesn't it?" He gave her a smile and wondered if she made much of a living as a stripper. Her dress was made to catch the eye—and succeeded admirably—but he could see no sign of easy-open fasteners or breakaway seams. Not that he knew much about the technical side of striptease. Still, she didn't seem the type. Although to be fair, what he could see . . . and feel . . . of her body offered evidence that she packed the right equipment. And she smelled like a bit of heaven. Clean, fresh, and wonderfully innocent. Her hair, piled in loose and escaping curls on the top of her head, kept teasing his chin, caressing his skin with silky softness, catching against the beginning of tomorrow's beard. He liked the feel of her, liked the way she held herself away from him, maintaining her dignity without creating a scene. In fact, he was beginning to like the idea of having his phantom fiancée take shape. Especially the rather luscious shape of the woman in his arms.

And unless he was mistaken, one of the advantages was approaching in a rustle of indignant white. "Charity," he said smoothly. "I want you to meet someone very special. This is my fiancée. Lucky, this is Charity McKimber, my business associate."

"Hello." Charity hid her anger with perfect composure. "How nice to finally meet you. I'd begun to think that Alec was having a little fun with all of us and just pretending to be engaged. But..." She paused to give a soft laugh, as if Alec had never been able to fool her. "I suppose I was mistaken."

"I'd say that is an understatement." In his arms, Lucky bristled like a black cat on Halloween.

The sudden tension caught Alec by surprise, like so many other things this evening. "Have you two... met?"

"Of course not." Charity was quick to release her facade of control. "How could we when you've kept her such a secret?"

"Yes," Lucky snapped back. "You couldn't take a chance on meeting me face to face, could you, Ms. McKimber? Then you would have been forced to admit what you stole from me."

Charity looked astonished and then slyly amused. "I can't imagine, Alec why your fiancée has taken an instant dislike to me...unless she's jealous of our relationship."

Alec felt he should nip this in the bud before it bit him on the butt. "Lucky? Why, there isn't a jealous bone in her body." He gave her shoulders a warning squeeze. "Is there, sweetheart?"

"*Don't* call me that!" She shrugged off his hands and jerked the slender strap of her evening bag from her shoulder. "I have some papers to show you, Alec.

I've been trying for some time to get these to you. No thanks to this . . . person."

Sensing calamity, Alec grabbed the bag out of her hands and set it aside. "Now now, sweetheart." He took her by the shoulders and turned her from disaster. "We'll have time for that later. Right now, there are other people I want you to meet." He nodded to Charity. "You understand, I'm sure."

"Don't I always, Alec?" Charity said softly.

"Wait a minute," Emma protested as Alec propelled her away from the woman and the battle she'd come to fight. "Do you know who that woman is?"

"What kind of question is that?" He kept walking and she had to keep pace. "I just introduced you, didn't I?"

"Yes, but—"

"Look, why don't we get out of here? We'll go up to my suite, I'll order drinks or something and you can tell me who put you up to this."

"Up to what?"

"Impersonating my fiancée."

"You mean there really is one?"

Alec stopped cold and Emma would have stumbled if he hadn't kept hold of her elbow. "Why is that so surprising to everyone?"

"Well, for openers, what kind of a name is Lucky?"

He looked offended. "A nickname."

"Sure." Emma glanced around, checking for privacy. "Look, I don't care if there is or isn't a Lucky. I mean, you just said she's not jealous and besides—"

"I lied," he interrupted. "She's extremely jealous. There's no telling what she'd do if she found you here in her place."

That was a sobering thought, but Emma ignored it in favor of getting to the point. "Mr. Sayre, I came here tonight because—"

"I know why you came."

"You do?"

He frowned at her and placed a hand at her waist as he moved forward. "It wasn't hard to figure out. I have some very immature friends."

Emma tried to understand the relevance. "And?"

"And when we get to my suite, you can tell me which one of them hired you. And maybe then, I'll let you earn your money and strip for me."

This time Emma stopped cold. "I beg your pardon?"

"Strip," he repeated distinctly. "Take your clothes off and dance. That's what you came here to do, isn't it?"

Words failed her.

"Oh, no." Alec looked past Emma's shoulder. "It's Uncle George. I forgot he was here. The only one of my family foolish enough to want to attend this debacle. Well, it looks like more introductions are in order. Watch out, he'll undoubtedly try to kiss you."

Emma had no interest in Uncle George. She was too busy imagining scenarios in Alec's hotel suite...none of which included him listening to her complaints about the Wedding of Your Dreams contest. All things considered, this seemed like a good time to end this impulsive masquerade...and get the heck out of Dodge. "Uh, Alec," she said. "Would you get me a drink? I'm suddenly very thirsty."

"Wouldn't you rather wait until we get to the room?"

"No!" She tried to disguise her sudden panic. "No, I need it now."

"All right." He seemed a little surprised by her insistence. "I guess I can understand that. A little alcohol can really loosen up the inhibitions. So, what do you want?"

Out of here with my clothes on. "Oh, anything," she said. "How about a...a double Scotch? On the rocks."

His eyebrows lifted. "A double? Are you that nervous?"

She smiled, willing him to move out of her path to the door. "Better make it a triple."

"Now, look, I don't want to have to carry you out of here."

Emma shot him an impatient glare. "You bring it, I'll drink it. Now, will you just go and get me the drink?"

Alec raised his hand in peace. "I'm out of here. Keep an eye on Uncle George. I'll be back in a minute."

Alec had barely taken two steps before Emma whirled and ran for the door. "Hey, there!" someone called behind her. "Lucky lady! I'm your Uncle George."

Emma hit the door and raced past Bambi to the stairs at the end of the hallway. She made it to the main lobby and through the casino in record time...if, of course, anyone had bothered to keep records on that sort of thing. She didn't breathe easy, though, until she reached the street and hailed a taxi.

"Golden Glow Wedding Chapel," she instructed the driver.

"Don't worry, lady," he said as he flipped on the meter. "I'll get you to the church on time." He laughed. "I've always wanted to say that."

Emma decided that if he burst into song, she wasn't going to tip.

Tip. Her purse. Left behind in her hurry. Left, along with her name, her address, and all of her evidence against Charity McKimber, Alec Sayre, and Tuxedo Junction.

Bambi had been right.

This was not her lucky night.

Chapter Two

"What do you mean, you don't know if you can find her? Honestly, Alec, I've never heard of anyone who has this much trouble keeping up with a fiancée."

"It's an unusual situation, Mother."

"You'll get no argument from me." Her sigh came clearly over the phone line. "I just can't decide if it's unusual because she doesn't want to meet your family or because you don't want her to. Either way, this does not bode well for your marriage."

"Lucky and I aren't married. And she wants to meet the family. The timing just isn't right."

"The timing will be right next Thursday night at nine, dear. You'll bring her here to the house. I'm having an engagement party for you and—" here, the sigh was resigned "—Lucky."

Alec wished he had chosen a nickname like Moonbeam or Daisy Mae, something his mother would have really hated. "We don't want an engagement party," he explained. "We prefer a minimum of fuss."

"This is the minimum, Alec, and I'm taking no more excuses. You grab Lucky by the hand and be here Thursday night at nine or you'll see just how much of a fuss I can make when I put my mind to it. Understood?''

There was no talking to her in this mood. "I understand, Mother.''

"Wonderful. I'll see you both then. Goodbye, son. Have a lovely day.''

"Goodbye, Mother," he said, but she had already disconnected and all he got for his good manners was an annoying buzz.

He put down the phone receiver and picked up the beaded evening bag. Turning it over in his hand, as he had done several times every day for the past three days, he leaned back in his office chair and contemplated the identity of his runaway fiancée.

Her name was Emma Cates. She was the owner of the Golden Glow Wedding Chapel. As a rule, he avoided anything connected with weddings, but he admitted to being very curious about Emma Cates.

Someone had hired her to pose as Lucky. "Persuaded" was probably a better word, because after looking at the contents of her purse, Alec didn't believe any money had changed hands. Which pretty much, and regrettably, ruled out the idea that she was a striptease dancer. No wonder she'd asked for a triple Scotch.

Setting the purse on his desk, Alec riffled through the papers he'd found inside. Emma Cates wanted something from him. More precisely, she wanted a piece of the Wedding of Your Dreams contest. The papers she had left behind made that obvious. It was an enterprising idea on her part, but obviously Charity hadn't been interested in sharing Tuxedo Junction's resources.

Considering the numerous publicity possibilities she'd sketched out on these papers, he was glad he hadn't taken her to his suite. He could have spent the rest of the night listening to her sales pitch. Wouldn't that have been a great way to end the evening? Alec made a face. Almost as great as having the woman he'd just introduced as his fiancée run from the party as if the hounds of hell were at her heels.

He'd taken some serious teasing over that. The phantom fiancée had appeared . . . and disappeared, leaving him with a barrage of questions he couldn't answer. And a mother who insisted on throwing an engagement party...now that Lucky had finally taken a recognizable form.

It would be simple enough to divert his mother. He could end the charade altogether, say Lucky had broken the engagement, run off to marry another man. Then again, he could take Emma to meet his mother. Alec settled back in the big leather chair and picked up the evening bag again, turning it end to end in his hands as he contemplated that bit of mischief. He knew where to find her. He had something to bargain with. It could be done.

After all, turnabout was fair play and fair play was fun, and if Emma Cates could pose as his fiancée, why couldn't he pose as hers?

"I THOUGHT YOU SAID you knew a couple of professionals who would do this as a favor to you." Emma pulled Harry Lukinbill into the cubicle she fondly called an office. She had to move the lone chair in the room to close the door and she clipped Harry's shoulder in the process, but finally she was out of leering range of the man Harry had hired.

"That...that ape out there is not a model. He has stared at me from the moment he got here. And, Harry, I'm sure I saw him drool."

Harry settled his trim, fifty-eight-year-old body on the corner of her desk and unfastened the stiff clerical collar he wore when he performed wedding ceremonies. "You're a pretty girl."

"He's caught the scent of a female," Emma stated flatly. "I could be as ugly as a toad on a lily pad and he wouldn't be able to tell the difference." She paced three steps, which brought her to the wall, and then three steps back to the door. "We'll have to find someone else."

Harry began doing his facial exercises. One set of a-e-i-o-u mouth stretches, a half dozen smiles into frowns, ten eye squints, and a finale of twenty chin-toners. Emma was beginning to get accustomed to the idiosyncrasies of her right-hand man and adopted uncle. She had adored him ever since she could remember and appreciated his help and advice more than she could say. But there were times, like now, when she wished he didn't have so many "friends" looking for a little extra work on the side.

"Harry, are you listening to me? The photographer will be here any minute. We have no bride and the groom we do have could pass for Cheetah of the Jungle."

"He's not so bad, Emma. He won a local body-building contest, so keep your eyes on his biceps and you won't notice if he drools a little." Harry put one hand behind his head, one beneath his chin, and began pulling his neck into elongated stretches. "And Cookie will be here. Unless she got that job at Circus Circus, which frankly I hope she did. Poor thing's been unable to find a place in any show. And her with two babes to support.''

''Children? She has two children? How old is this model?''

''Not kids, Emma. Babes. A couple of babes in the woods. Thought they'd come out here, work in the casinos and get rich. Cookie took them under her wing.''

''Harry, did you give her money?''

''Now, Emma, she needed a little cash. She'll be here . . . unless she got the job.''

Emma could see her plans for inexpensive publicity disappearing into the generosity of Harry's oversized heart. ''Harry, I want professional models who look like they might actually be a bride and groom. I want good publicity shots so that the new brochures for the Golden Glow won't look like they were made at the penny arcade. Is that too much to ask? Business is down. We need to advertise. Professional photographs might do the trick.''

''The whole Las Vegas economy is down, Emma girl. You're not going to wipe out all the red ink with a few pictures.''

''I've got to do something, Harry. And a few *good* pictures is a start.''

''What happened to that contest you thought up? That dream wedding thing?''

A sore point, and after last Saturday night, an embarrassing one, as well. ''I, uh, shelved it. Too much competition.''

''Since when did that stop you?''

''Since the competition got tougher.'' Emma had thought she might hear from Alec Sayre. She'd worried over that possibility for the better part of two days before she realized he wasn't interested in her contest or in her. She was just a woman he'd been engaged to for one disastrous half hour. "Back to the problem at hand, Harry. What are we going to do with Jungle Boy? I'm not sure we have a tuxedo in our rental inventory that will fit him."

Harry paused in mid-stretch and frowned out of sequence. "I hadn't thought of that. The boy is massive. Wait, I've got it. He can wear my studded jacket, the one from my Elvis collection. It's always been too big for me."

What a picture that would make. "Never mind, Harry. Call off the photographer. See if he can come some other time." Some time when *she* had made the arrangements.

"I don't know, Em. It isn't easy to coordinate something like this."

"I'll handle it. The chapel is my baby, now." She paused. "You haven't said anything to Julian about me buying the chapel, have you?"

He chucked her under the chin. "If I had, would we be having this conversation in private?"

Good point. Her father had a penchant for putting his nose where it didn't belong. Someone knocked and Emma opened her office to another of Harry's freelance friends. She recognized him by the camera hanging around his neck. "Hello," she said. "You must be the photographer."

"Bill Willis." He nodded and looked pleased as punch to be standing outside her office door.

"Bill, my boy." Harry maneuvered past Emma to shake hands with the newcomer. "Good to see you. And right on time, too." He slapped an arm around the photographer's shoulders. "Problem is, Bill, we have a little problem. We're short a bride."

Bill looked at Harry and then his mouth broke into a gap-toothed grin. "She can't be that short. How many places can you hide a bride in a wedding chapel?"

Emma did her best to appear appreciative of his humor. "I'm afraid we're going to have to postpone the photo session."

Bill looked alarmed. "We can't do that. I'm ready. I'm primed. I bought film for my camera and a new charger for the flash. I've studied up on the proper angles. I know I can do a good job for you. And besides, tonight is the full moon."

Oh, of course, Emma thought, a truly sensible reason for taking publicity shots. "But, Bill," she explained patiently, "we don't have a bride."

"Couldn't you be the bride?"

"Absolutely not."

"That's a great idea." Harry's eyes took on a gleam. "You can pose as the bride. Put on that new rental gown and we'll have your publicity pics for you in no time."

"Harry," she protested. "You forget. The bride isn't our only problem. The groom—and I use the term loosely—doesn't have a tux."

"Sure, he does." Bill began adjusting the settings on his camera. "I passed through the chapel on my way in. He's got it on."

"What?" Emma squeezed into the hallway and peered into the chapel. "Oh, my...." she whispered. The model had changed from sweatpants and shirt into a blue velvet tuxedo. Bill was right. A full moon was the only explanation for this. "Harry, you'd better see this."

He whistled as he came up behind her. "I haven't seen an outfit like that since the last time Elvis was in town."

"I'm not going through with this, Harry. I don't care if he needs the work. I do not need this kind of publicity."

Harry tapped her shoulders lightly. "Relax, I'll handle this. Don't worry about it. Everything will be fine."

Emma wished she had a nickel for every time a male had assured her that *he* would handle her problems. She wished she had a dime for every time she'd tried to explain that *she* could do it herself. "Harry, I don't want..."

"Time's a'wasting." Bill buzzed past them as if he had to work in these few publicity shots before rushing off to photograph Jackie. "Let's do this shoot."

Harry restrained Emma from going after him and giving him the boot. "He's only charging us a hundred dollars, Em. That's dirt cheap. And Curtis, the model, is doing this almost free of charge. As a favor to me. Well, actually, I had to give him a fifty-dollar deposit, but I think we should run with what we've got. Otherwise, we'll have to pay now *and* later."

Emma wished she'd never mentioned this idea to Harry. "I don't want to be in these pictures."

"Put on a veil. No one will know it's you. And be positive. This will be fun. You'll see."

"This will be disastrous."

"Now what makes you think these pictures won't turn out great?"

"Blue velvet?" she suggested.

"I told you I'll take care of that. I'll get him into something more suitable while you change. Now run on."

Emma hesitated. "A hundred dollars? Whether he takes the pictures or not?"

Harry fastened his clerical collar. "Actually, two hundred."

"*Two* hundred?"

"Okay, two-fifty, but he'll come back and reshoot if we're not satisfied. He needs the money, Em. He's an out-of-work photojournalist."

The way things were going, they were all going to be out of work. "I don't know how you do this to me, Harry, or why I let you. But I can't afford to give away two hundred and fifty dollars, plus what you've already given out as deposits." Before last Saturday night, the Wedding of Your Dreams contest would have cost less and been of greater benefit, but the price had gone up and she could no longer afford to think about it. Unless she wanted to take off her clothes for that arrogant Alec Sayre.

"Quit stewing about the money, sweet cheeks, and get into your duds. I'll get rid of the blue jacket."

Emma could only hope.

ALEC NEARLY DIDN'T get out of the limo. Once out, standing in front of a scene fresh from his nightmares, he almost turned tail and ran. A neon bride and groom loomed larger than life above a sign that read:

GOLDEN GLOW WEDDING CHAPEL
Flowers! Gowns! Tuxedos! Rings!
Photos of your special ceremony!
Loveknots tied tight—we do the job right!

And around the front perimeter and lining the primrose path was a white picket fence. He debated whether he would rather face a walk down lovers' lane or his mother's wrath if he failed to produce a flesh-and-blood fiancée for her little engagement party.

Curiosity weighted the scales in favor of going inside. He wanted to find Emma Cates, wanted to discover if he'd imagined the impact of her impertinent green eyes and sassy dimple. He also wanted to make absolutely certain she wasn't a stripper...and that he hadn't missed out on anything other than a sales pitch the other night. After asking his driver to wait, Alec squared his shoulders and walked decisively past the white pickets and through the golden portals.

The reception area was large, with pictures of smiling newlyweds on every wall. A white desk, edged in gold trim, took up one corner of the room. White wicker chairs with eyelet cushions were scattered along either wall. On the far side of the room, two plump cherubs graced either side of a curved archway. White, gossamer curtains looped from one cherubic foot to the other and draped together in the center of the arch to form a gauzy bow above a pair of golden wedding bells. Beyond the entrance, he could see into the chapel where a bride and groom were posing for pictures. A camera flashed every two seconds, like machine gun fire, as the photographer moved from one angle to the next.

Alec stepped through the archway, the ends of the sheer curtains gliding across the shoulders of his tuxedo jacket like ethereal attendants. A bolt of white satin lined the aisle and ran to the altar between six neat rows of four chairs each. All the seats were empty. Two candelabra, six lighted candles apiece, illuminated either side of the chapel and shed a flickering touch of atmosphere over the happy couple.

"Will you stop that?" The bride slapped the groom's hand before putting an appreciable distance between them. "I hired you to pose for publicity photos, not to take my measurements."

"You've got to stand close to him," the photographer complained. "I didn't bring my wide-angle lens."

The bride provided equal opportunity glares for both men. Undaunted, the groom tried to see down the front of his beloved's wedding gown. And on the grand piano in the corner, someone was playing "Moon River."

Alec cleared his throat.

The scene froze like a snapshot from a Chaplin film. The bride flipped back the netting of a veil that sat askew on her honey-blond hair and wrinkled her nose and forehead in a charming squint. "Alec?" she whispered.

She was even prettier than he'd remembered, and he made up his mind then and there to play out this charade. He smiled, noting that she was surprised to see him. The small "o" of her lips was a dead giveaway. "Emma Cates, I presume?" He paused for effect. "Or are you Lucky tonight?"

"What are you doing here?"

"Emma...darling. Tonight's our engagement party. We're already late." He took a couple of purposeful steps down the aisle. "How could you even think about marrying another man on the night of my mother's party?"

"Moon River" ended abruptly in a clash of discordant notes. Emma stared in thunderstruck silence. The photographer lowered his camera. The groom couldn't tear his eyes from Emma's cleavage. Alec thought someone should teach the guy a lesson.

"You know how insanely jealous I am." Alec walked confidently to the altar in a plethora of inspiration. "I don't know why you insist on flaunting these little flirtations in my face. We both know they mean nothing to you." He stopped in front of her and took a moment to enjoy the way shock deepened the color and widened the shape of her very lovely green eyes. He could almost interpret this as a sign that she was glad to see him. "Once we're married, I'm going to put my foot down. You'll have to concentrate on me, exclusively."

Her mouth worked for a second before the words found their way out. "It's the full moon," she said.

Alec couldn't hold back his smile. "Is that why the Wolfman can't get his snout out of your bodice?"

"Hey!" The Wolfman tapped Alec on the shoulder. "Who are you?"

"I'm Emma's fiancé. Who are you?"

"I'm Curtis, the groom."

Alec stepped up onto the dais. "Impossible. I just told you I'm her fiancé. Now, who are you really?"

Curtis stuck a thumb inside his cummerbund. "Curtis Levy," he said. "I'm Mr. Las Vegas Biceps."

Alec arched a wicked eyebrow in Emma's direction. "A professional associate?"

"He's a—he's *supposed* to be a professional model. I wanted new publicity photos for the chapel. For the new brochures I'm having made."

Alec frowned as he assessed Mr. Biceps. "Is this the best you could get?"

Emma felt there was little point in explanations. "He needed the money."

"Excuse me." Harry approached from behind the piano, his clerical collar lending him a stern authority. Emma sighed in relief. He would tell Alec Sayre to go to hell and that would be the end of this. "I don't believe we've met." Harry extended his hand. "I'm Harry Lukinbill."

Alec shook hands. "Alec Sayre, Emma's fiancé. No doubt she's told you about me."

Harry sent an accusing glance her way. "No, she's been very secretive about you. In fact, this is the first I've heard of an engagement."

"Emma," Alec said in a voice of tender disapproval.

Panic stole over her. "Harry, I don't even know him!"

"Are you trying to tell me you've gotten yourself engaged to a perfect stranger?"

"I am not engaged!" The veil slipped forward again and she tossed the bothersome netting over her shoulder. Click-flash-whir. Emma realized the camera was no longer silent. Click-flash-whir. Click-flash-whir. "Bill," she said politely, "save your film for my publicity shots, please."

Click-flash-whir. Bill lowered the camera, but only slightly.

"Hey!" Curtis stepped forward. "Are we through shootin' pictures? If we are, I've got other things to do."

"Don't let us keep you." Alec nodded in the direction of the exit. "Emma has to leave, anyway. We can't keep my mother waiting much longer."

Curtis looked at Emma for confirmation. She didn't want to bow to Alec's autocratic commands, but she didn't want an extra witness to this insane conversation, either. "Thanks, Curtis. I'll let you know how the pictures turn out. Bill, you may as well go on, too."

"That's okay, Ms. Cates. I can stick around for a while longer."

Great. Just what she needed. An out-of-work journalist with a loaded camera. "Harry," she said, desperately trying to get the correct message to Harry without giving information to Bill. "Do you remember the wedding contest? Well, Alec is the owner of Tuxedo Junction."

"Is that so?" Harry seemed inordinately pleased. "Then I'm doubly happy to meet you. And to find out you're engaged to Emma. She's like my own child, you know. I practically raised her." Harry lifted his hands and smoothly dispersed of the clerical collar. "You have quite an operation over there at the Junction. Especially in the Silk Stocking Lounge. I, uh, am something of a performer, myself. I'd be happy to give an audition when you have the time." Emma's SOS floated away as Harry's ambition rose to the surface. "I could play a little something for you now, if you'd like. I have an extensive repertoire."

Alec managed to look sincerely grateful. "I am sorry, but I promised my mother I'd bring Emma to this party tonight and, as I've said, we're late already."

Harry nodded, his eyes shining with possibilities. "Another time, then. When will you be bringing her home this evening?"

"I am not going anywhere with this man," Emma stated to thin air.

"I'm afraid we'll be very late getting back." Alec took her hand and stepped off the platform.

Emma remained where she was, fastening a defiant gaze on her tormentor. "I am positive," she said, "that this is simply a bad dream and that when I wake up, you will be gone."

Alec took advantage of his position and pulled her off balance with a slight tug. She fell forward. He caught her and scooped her up into his arms, wedding gown, crooked veil and all. "You, my love, are going with me."

Emma grabbed his neck to maintain her equilibrium and then made the foolish mistake of looking into his eyes and losing it, anyway. She wondered why the really good-looking men always seemed to be intellectually flawed. "This is kidnapping," she protested. "A felony, pure and simple."

"So, sue me." He turned and started down the aisle, nearly knocking over Bill who was snapping pictures fast and furiously. Click-flash-whir. Click-flash-whir.

Emma closed her eyes, trying to find a bit of reality to grasp. "I have a headache," she said.

"There's aspirin in the limo and Perrier for a chaser." He kept walking.

"This is my business. I can't afford to leave the chapel unattended."

Alec glanced over his shoulder. "Harry, you're in charge." Back to Emma. "Now, it's not unattended."

"I'll take care of everything," Harry called from the altar. "Thursdays are never busy, anyway, and Sanchee and Dan are still here in case we get any drop-ins before closing time. We'll be fine. Don't worry about a thing."

Emma waved goodbye to her last hope and wondered why she wasn't afraid of Alec Sayre. He was obviously crazy, but undeniably attractive. Her body was behaving like a wanton woman's in his arms, despite her brain's legitimate protest. Maybe she was the one with the flawed intellect. On the other hand, if she went along with him, she might be able to turn this situation to her advantage and resurrect her shot at the Wedding of Your Dreams contest. "I don't want to go anywhere with you," she said.

He never slowed his pace. "You're perfectly safe with me, Emma. Think of this as an adventure. Relax. Enjoy yourself. I promise you'll have fun."

What was she supposed to say to that? Hooray for fun? The veil slipped and Emma grabbed it, clasping it to her head as they walked beneath the archway and out of the chapel. "I can't meet your mother dressed like this."

"You look beautiful. Like a blushing bride. My mother will be ecstatic...and delighted to discover you're not really named Lucky." Alec pushed open the front doors with his shoulders and carried Emma outside.

A group of people were gathered around the limousine, talking to the chauffeur and trying to see through the darkened windows. A woman looked up as Alec and Emma approached. "Oh, look, somebody just got married!"

"Congratulations!"

"What a beautiful bride."

"Isn't he romantic?"

"This man is kidnapping me," Emma informed the well-wishers.

"Lucky you," a woman called out.

"Yes," another woman said. "We should all be so lucky."

Alec's laugh caressed her ear with warmth and pleasurable sensations. "See," he said. "Even the tourists think you're Lucky." His arms were strong and protective. She wondered if she ought to struggle. "Put me down," she commanded.

Obediently, he set her on her feet. The chauffeur, a grizzled but friendly looking man in a natty uniform, opened the car door and touched the brim of his hat as Alec took Emma by the hand and pulled her into the limousine after him. A cheer went up from the spectators.

As she tried to maneuver the flounced train of the wedding gown into the limo, the veil slipped forward and the netting fluttered in the breeze. The chauffeur began to close the door and, seeing the expensive veil flirting with disaster, Emma jerked back in an attempt to save it. At the same moment Alec reached around her to grab the ethereal fabric, bringing her back against his chest and his cheek against her temple. Heat flared in Emma's face and curled around her in quicksilver awareness. She turned her head, her lips parting in surprise and an invitation she did not mean to give. And, Alec, being a man of opportunity, seized the moment and a kiss.

As his lips claimed her compliance, the door closed with a soft *whuff*... but not before Emma registered a faint and familiar sound.

Click-flash-whir.

Chapter Three

If he'd thought about it beforehand, Alec would have been more cautious about kissing a woman in a wedding gown. No matter how tempting she looked. But here he was, wrapped in white tulle, and thoroughly enjoying the very soft, very luscious taste of Emma Cates. Something about her expressive eyes mesmerized him, had him doing things he could live to regret. Her lips, he was discovering, were not without fascination, either. He was savoring this kiss a little more than he should...considering how much she resembled a bride. On the other hand, maybe, by avoiding all things matrimonial, he'd been missing out on something special.

As the limousine pulled away from the curb, he pulled away from Emma, slowly, unsure of her reaction.

She drew a long breath and released it in a rush as she attempted to straighten the wayward veil. "For a woman who, two weeks ago, couldn't get an appointment to talk with you on the telephone, I have made amazing progress."

Alec had to admire her recovery, even though he was a little disappointed that she'd immediately recognized her advantage. His thoughts were still lingering on the way she tasted, the pleasurable scent of her, and the warm curves of her body. He had to search through the sensual reminders for a cohesive answer. "You should have thought of posing as my fiancée sooner."

She slanted a green-eyed and indicting gaze at him. "Oh, please, I can't take all the credit. If you hadn't been so cooperative, introducing me as Lucky the way you did, I might never have been able to carry it off."

Alec ignored the sarcasm in her voice and settled back with a smile. "We were magnificent."

"Is that the reason for tonight's encore performance?" She paused. "Assuming, of course, that you weren't lying about the engagement party."

"Oh, no, the party is for real and, for tonight, so is our engagement."

"And what makes you think I'll agree?"

"The Wedding of Your Dreams contest." He put the chips on the table, turning her advantage into his. "You want something from me. I want something from you. It's really quite simple."

"Is it?" she said. "First, you steal the contest from me and then you expect me to barter to get it back. I don't consider that a simple trade. Or an ethical one."

"No one stole your idea."

"Oh, give me a break. That woman, that McKimber person, asked me to send her everything I had on the contest. When we spoke on the phone, she said the idea had possibilities and that we should work out the details before we met to discuss making it a joint publicity venture. I—foolishly, I admit—dropped off the plans I'd drawn up." She shrugged and swatted at the errant veil. "A week went by, then another, then two more. During the following three months, I made several attempts to reach her. Finally, in response to repeated phone calls, I received a snippy letter informing me that Tuxedo Junction had no interest in a joint promotional venture with my wedding chapel. She returned my original paperwork without comment. And then, just when I'd decided to take the idea to another hotel and casino, I see a preliminary ad for a wedding industry conference and there, in black and white, is my Wedding of Your Dreams contest.''

Alec rubbed his jaw with one hand as he considered her story. He had no reason to doubt her, but then, he had no reason to question Charity's integrity, either. ''I'm sure there's a simple explanation.''

The lift of her brows informed him that one had occurred to her.

''I'll check into the matter, ask Charity to reconsider a joint venture with your wedding chapel. I'm sure something can be worked out. In the meantime, we'll continue our engagement.''

''Why would *we* do that?''

''Maybe because you placed me in an awkward position in the first place by impersonating my fiancée.''

''Excuse me, but I believe you had a hand in shaping any awkwardness.''

''For whatever reason, I want to continue the engagement until I can find a graceful way to end it.''

''Engagements never end gracefully, Alec, and I fail to see how perpetuating this mistake will help.''

''Humor me, Emma, and I, in turn, will help you get the publicity you want. Monday morning, you can come to my office. I'll explain the situation to Charity, in your presence, and we'll clear up this misunderstanding.''

"Oh, I'm sure she'll be pleased to cooperate, especially if you ask in *my* presence."

"Emma, I assure you, you won't have any further problems with Charity or any of the staff at Tuxedo Junction. As my fiancée, you will naturally be treated with the utmost courtesy and respect."

Emma crossed her arms just below her breasts and looked at him long and hard. Alec felt the impact all the way to his toes. His Lucky was turning out to be a surprise in more ways than one.

"Alec, this may be hard for you to comprehend, but I do not have to pretend to be your fiancée in order to get courtesy and respect. The original idea for the wedding contest was mine and, if necessary, I'll sue Ms. McKimber, Tuxedo Junction, and you, to prove it."

"Come on, Emma, what can you possibly gain in a lawsuit? Spend your money on the contest and target the publicity at potential clients. The only notoriety you'll get from legal action will be buried in the local newspaper. I've just offered you the opportunity to participate in the contest. What more can you expect?"

A little courtesy and respect, Emma thought but didn't say. Why bother? Alec's attitude was very much like her father's . . . a little bit patronizing and a whole lot "Father Knows Best." And that attitude wrapped up in the sexiest male she, personally, had ever set eyes on was a dangerous combination, indeed. She stared out the window at the famous strip passed in a splendor of excess. This wasn't a bargain she particularly wanted to strike, but refusing the publicity was an extravagance she couldn't afford. "Tell me," she said without looking at him. "Why don't you get out of this 'awkward position' by taking the real Lucky to the engagement party? I'll bet she could explain this simple misunderstanding to everyone's satisfaction.''

Alec cleared his throat. ''Lucky is no longer in the picture.''

Relief flowed over her like a refreshing shower, relief she had no reason to feel. Emma sifted the emotion into a proper response, sympathy for his broken heart. ''She broke your engagement?''

''No, you showed up.''

Her heart jumped and ran and she had to force it back to a normal, sensible rhythm. Turning from the window, she met his eyes and wished she didn't get wobbly every time she looked at him. ''Are you saying you broke your engagement because of me?''

He pursed his lips. ''This may sound a bit odd, but I was never engaged in the first place. Lucky is a . . . figment of my imagination.'' He shrugged. ''At least she was until you came along.''

''You invented a fiancée?'' Emma thought she probably ought to be shocked. Or appalled. What gall. What absolute, unmitigated nonsense. And yet she admired his chutzpah in doing such an outrageous thing—and then admitting to it with a straight face. Her sense of humor blindsided her composure and she began to laugh. In a moment Alec was laughing with her. He didn't seem in the least chagrined. She liked that. Almost as much as she liked the deep, throaty rumble of his laughter.

''It seemed like a good idea at the time,'' he offered. ''And there are extenuating circumstances.''

Emma had been afraid there might be. ''She must be very special if she has you running scared.''

He lifted an eyebrow as his smile waned to a wry curve. "You're very perceptive. Or was that just a lucky guess?"

"A little of both, I suppose. Am I right?"

"About the running scared part, I'm afraid so. She's determined. Very determined. But then, so am I. I won't be trapped into a commitment."

"Really?" Emma's laughter bubbled again. "So that means our engagement is, in effect, a commitment to avoid commitment. Right?"

"You make it sound more absurd than it is. My phantom fiancée, silly as it may seem, saved me from a disastrous situation. Inventing Lucky wasn't a perfect solution, but it was working just fine until you got the bright idea of taking on the role."

"Believe it or not, being any man's fiancée is not a role I've studied for all my life." She sat straighter to add emphasis. "In fact, I've spent most of my life trying to climb down from my pedestal and seize the responsibility for making my own decisions."

He stretched one arm along the top of the seat cushion behind her, allowing his fingers to brush against the silky softness of her hair, giving his thumb permission to skim the creamy curve of her shoulder, letting the tempting warmth of her seep into and under his skin. Her sudden stillness told him she was aware of his touch and studiously determined not to show it. And he, just as studiously, decided to keep his hand where it was. "I can see why a man might want to put you on a pedestal. There's a certain fragility about you, Emma, a look of innocence and a touch of vulnerability. Men tend to feel protective toward a woman like you." She stiffened and he lifted a hand, palm out, to ward off her protest. "But you have nothing to fear from me. I wouldn't know how to get you onto a pedestal if I found one. In all truthfulness, my only aim in continuing our fictitious engagement is to avoid the marriage trap being set for me."

Emma didn't try to conceal her surprise. "It's hard to imagine that you couldn't just step around it, Alec."

"We all have our blind spots." He frowned slightly, then allowed his good humor to return. "So, here's the deal. You get the publicity you want in return for continuing the engagement. There will not be a Wedding of Your Dreams for us, but we are the only two people who will know that. As far as the rest of the world is concerned, and this especially pertains to my mother, we are wildly in love and anxiously planning to be married. Agreed?"

Put like that, Emma thought she'd be crazy to agree. But she had done crazier things for much less of a reason. And if it would benefit the chapel, an enterprise she was banking on, she'd be crazy not to. Her agreement had nothing, nothing at all, to do with the scintillating stroke of his thumb as he absently brushed it across her shoulder. She shifted slightly away from that gentle touch... just to prove to herself that she could. "This doesn't involve anything physical, does it? Because, contest or no contest, I am not taking off my clothes."

"I was afraid you'd say that."

"I beg your pardon?"

"I owe you an apology. When you came into the party the other night, I got the wrong impression and thought someone had hired you to, uh, entertain me. But I realized later that I must have been mistaken."

"Oh, I see," Emma said with feigned politeness. "Another simple misunderstanding. Your life seems overly complicated with them, Alec."

"Well, at least we're clear on one. You're not a stripper. And it's obvious you never have been."

"Never." She frowned. "Why is it obvious?"

His smile was not reassuring. "I'm going to plead the Fifth Amendment, here, and go back to the physical demands of our relationship."

Her chin came up. "What physical demands?"

"We're engaged, Emma. I think a few kisses will be unavoidable. But that's not to say you have to enjoy them."

He said it as if it were a challenge. *I dare you not to enjoy them.* Emma could read between the lines. She could also recognize a healthy male ego when she ran across it. "Thank you," she said. "It's a relief not to be under pressure. There's just one problem I can see at the moment."

"What's that?" He was all solicitousness now that he'd accomplished his goal.

Emma played her ace. "For tonight, Alec, I won't deny being your fiancée, but I am not going anywhere in this getup. Together, we look like the topper on a wedding cake."

"I have no objection if you want to take it off."

She shifted her position to award him a don't-be-stupid look. "We just covered that topic, Alec."

"And uncovered it, as well."

"And I'm staying covered. Now, why don't you just take me back to the chapel so I can change my clothes."

"That would take too long." He looked at the flounces of tulle and lace, touched the yards of netting that composed the headpiece. "We could get rid of the veil," he suggested. "That would make you less conspicuous."

"True, but carrying your fiancée, kicking and screaming, into your mother's house may call some attention to you."

"You won't do that," he said confidently.

"I will," she assured him.

"You talk pretty tough for a woman wearing lace." His smile mocked her gently. "I think you're bluffing."

"Only one way to find out, isn't there?" Her smile matched his, tit for tat. She was calm, collected, and determined to hold her own. "How long before we reach your mother's house?"

He considered for almost a minute before he pressed a button on the side panel of the car. The smoked-glass partition between the front and the rear of the limousine lowered with hardly a sound. "Buzby?" Alec said. "Pull over in front of one of the hotels. Pick one with a lot of people milling about outside."

Emma's curiosity surged to the fore. "Are we stopping?"

"You said you wanted a new outfit."

"I'm not going shopping dressed in this bridal gown, either," she warned.

"Okay." He reached for the door latch. "You stay in the car. I'll pick something for you."

When he returned a few minutes later, he was empty-handed and Emma felt a twinge of disappointment that she had won the match so easily. "Emma," he said as he opened the door nearest her, "give me the veil."

"What?"

"The veil. Give it to me."

Mystified, Emma removed the hairpins that held the headpiece in place. She handed it through the door and wondered if he was going back to his original idea of eliminating the most conspicuous item of apparel. He closed the door again and walked toward the Lady Luck Casino. She lost sight of him in the influx and departure of hotel guests. In a moment he was back, but this time he had company—a young woman, dressed in a black sequined dress, who tottered slightly on a pair of very high heels. She held Emma's veil in her hands, and her expression was that of someone waiting for the punchline of a long and involved joke.

Alec opened the door with a flourish and gestured the woman into the limo. "Emma," he said. "Meet Pam. Pam, Emma. Buzby and I will stand guard outside while you two change clothes."

"C-change—?" Emma sputtered. "Alec, you can't do this."

His smile had winner written all over it. "You're right. Neither one of you is my size and sequins aren't my style. Luckily, though, my tuxedo goes anywhere. Now, ladies, you've got ten minutes to swap clothes. Emma, may I remind you, we are very late already." He closed the door with finality.

On the facing seat, Pam eyed Emma with caution and the bridal gown with envy. "It's even prettier than he said it was."

Emma couldn't believe this. "Did he just stop you on the street and ask you if you would exchange clothes with me?"

"Well, he didn't mention you specifically." She extended her hand to display a chip of a diamond. "He noticed my engagement ring and asked if I was interested in a wedding gown.''

''And you agreed?''

''After he showed me the veil.'' Pam's big blue eyes reflected a miracle of naiveté and innocence. ''I paid a hundred and twenty for my dress, but this...'' She touched a finger to the lace on the bridal gown. ''Well, it must have cost ten times that.''

''Yes, and frankly...'' Emma stopped, realizing that Alec had dealt her a lousy hand. But she, in turn, could hand him the joker. ''Are you positive you want to do this? You think it's a fair trade?''

''Are you kidding? I think it's a great trade.'' She reached for the side zipper of the sequined dress and kicked off the shoes. ''Do you want the hose, too? He said I should give you the whole outfit.''

Emma swallowed. ''No, thanks, we'll stop with the outer garments and call it even.''

In five minutes they were stripped to undies and, by the time Alec tapped on the darkened window, Emma was zipping the side opening of her new dress. She had to hand it to Alec. The dress fit her perfectly, even if it needed another yard of fabric at the bottom. She adjusted the short skirt, gave it a self-conscious tug, and lent Pam a helping hand with securing the gown.

''I'll just carry the veil with me.'' Pam reached for the door latch and then suddenly threw her arms around Emma's neck. ''Oh, thank you so much. I could never have afforded to buy anything this nice. Enjoy Little Black. The first time John saw me in it, he proposed.''

Wonderful, Emma thought. A dress that came with sentiment attached. ''Thanks for the warning. I'll wear it with extreme caution.'' But Pam was gathering the flounces and lace and gingerly stepping out of the limo. "If you're looking for a wedding chapel," Emma called after her, "try the Golden Glow."

Pam smiled over her shoulder and then was gone, replaced by a smug and smiling Alec.

"You look nice," he said. "Does it fit?"

"Perfectly." She resisted giving the hem another futile tug. "I don't believe I could have done better myself. How much did you have to pay her?"

"A token." He summarily dismissed monetary considerations as he ran his gaze over the sequined sheath, leaving Emma warm in places she would rather have kept cool. "And worth every penny."

"I'm glad you think so." She slipped one high heel on her foot and winced as it pinched her instep. "Because you'll have to pay for the bridal gown, too. It was the newest gown in the chapel's rental inventory and will have to be replaced."

His wince was not as painful as an ill-fitting shoe, but Emma enjoyed its brief appearance. "Oh, and Alec, I had to give her my earrings, too, in exchange for these black baubles. That's another twenty-seven, ninety-five."

He reached into his breast pocket and, for a moment, she thought he was going to bring out his checkbook. But when he extended his hand to her, it was closed. "Here, you might as well put this on, too." He opened his palm and something winked at her.

She picked it up carefully, turning the emerald-cut diamond in a sparkling circle. "An engagement ring?" she asked. "Where did you get this?"

He leaned back.

"On second thought, don't tell me. I don't want to know." She slipped it on the fourth finger of her left hand and told herself it was okay to admire the diamond—which was undoubtedly cubic zirconia in a good setting—without wondering what poor woman had sold it to him. And why. Whoever she was, she had excellent taste and was now probably confiding to her friends how she'd fleeced Las Vegas without going near a slot machine. "It's a little big. I hope it won't slip off my finger and get lost."

"You know, Emma, as a fiancée, you're turning out to be very expensive."

"Yes." She smiled, oddly content. "But worth every penny, Alec. Every penny."

"I HAVE TO SAY, ALEC, Charity seems more your type."

He returned his mother's comment with a tolerant smile. "As usual, Mother, we must agree to disagree. I think Emma is perfect."

A sniff signaled her opinion. "I suppose I'll become accustomed to her," she acknowledged. "Eventually."

"I'm sure you'll grow to love her like a daughter."

Another sniff, louder this time. "Her dress is *very* short, Alec."

"I know. I picked it out. She has great legs, doesn't she?" Across the room, Emma crossed one leg over the other as she leaned closer to hear whatever Uncle George was saying to her. Alec's throat tightened and his stomach knotted with a curious tension. She was gorgeous, despite the sassy tilt of her chin, and he was enchanted. "Uncle George seems quite taken with her."

"He would be. Your uncle thinks she's a stripper. Lord only knows where he got that idea." Millicent

Sayre waved to someone at the hors d'oeuvre table. "Oh, there's Joyce Barrett. The woman is chronically late, always arriving just as everyone else is preparing to leave. I suppose she wants to meet Emma." Millicent drew a lace handkerchief through her slender fingers and dabbed the tip of her nose. "And I suppose I should be the one to introduce them."

Alec patted her ramrod-straight back. "No one does it better, Mother."

"Humph. Thank God she has a real name and I don't have to introduce her as 'Lucky.'"

Alec grinned as his mother marched off to do her duty, a graceful welcome shaping her lips as she approached the dilatory guest. Millicent Sayre was a slave to convention, critical of anyone who didn't fit her rigid standards of what was proper and what was not. She said what she thought and meant what she said, however graciously she said it. He had never understood her, but he'd learned to accept her and knew that, in her way, she accepted him, too.

"Are you going to drink the rest of your champagne?" Emma came up on his left, eyeing the nearly full glass in his hand. "Because if you're not, I need it for Uncle George."

"Let him get his own. There's plenty of it around."

"Believe me, he is well aware of the fact." Emma wrinkled her nose as she swirled the last swallow of champagne in her glass and then lifted it to her lips. "Your uncle has quite an imagination." She set the empty glass on the table behind them. "Not to mention an amazing agility for his age."

"Tried to kiss you, did he?" Alec glanced at his fool of an uncle, too old to be taken seriously, too young to stop trying. "I believe I warned you about him."

"Not sufficiently, it seems. It was all I could do to keep his hand off of my knee."

"Why, that old devil. I should have warned him that you're not as helpless as you look."

"One more incident of roaming hands and he'll find out for himself. I finally decided the only thing that would cool him off was a glass of bubbly poured over the part of his anatomy that has the most vivid vision of grandeur."

Alec laughed. "Quite a family, isn't it? My mother has someone else for you to meet. An old family friend."

Emma sighed and reached for his glass. "Being engaged to you is hard on my nerves, Alec."

"But fun. You have to admit, Emma, that you're enjoying yourself. I've heard you laughing." The memory of that pleasant sound made him smile. "And aside from Uncle Octopus, no one else has propositioned you, have they?"

"Only you." She lifted the champagne flute in mock salute and her eyes sparkled mischief at him over the rim of the glass as she drank. Her saucy manner and the quick wink of the dimple in her chin tempted him to kiss her and taste the flavor of her laughter for himself. "However, considering that you propositioned at least two other women tonight, I can't really say it was any great honor."

"Two other women, huh?" He raised an eyebrow. "How do you figure?"

She made a sweeping gesture from neckline to hem. "You propositioned Pam to get the outfit." She flipped her hand in front of his face. "The ring came from someone's finger." She frowned as she balanced on one foot, peeled off a shoe, and massaged her stockinged toes. "If you were half as clever as you think you are, you would have put the moves on someone with a size seven shoe, instead of this miserable little six and a half."

Alec caught her elbow in his palm as she tottered on one high heel. "Steady. Don't the shoes fit?"

She tossed him a glance that was just shy of coquettish. "As if you couldn't tell by the way I've hobbled around this evening."

"I thought you were just uptight." Actually, he'd thought she had the sexiest walk he'd ever seen, but it seemed a bit early in their engagement to tell her so.

"Emma?" Millicent Sayre approached with another woman in tow. "I've been looking for you. I want you to meet Joyce Barrett, a dear family friend."

"So happy to make your acquaintance." Ms. Barrett extended her hand, forthright and proper, and Emma realized she had a faux pas in progress...a champagne glass in one hand, irritated toes and a dangling shoe in the other.

"It's, uh, nice to meet you." Just as she wobbled on one high heel, Alec reached down and took the shoe from her hand. She put her toes to the floor and balanced precariously, one shoe on, one shoe off. "Alec bought the wrong size shoes." She offered the lame explanation along with the handshake. "Normally, I can stand without any assistance. And truly, I haven't had too much of this wonderful champagne." Not yet, anyway, but the idea was holding out more and more appeal. "Have you known Alec since he was a child?"

The dear old family friend waxed nostalgic. "For years and years, sweetness. He was, of course, the most adorable boy, full of piss and vinegar, as the saying goes...."

The saying did not go. Emma could see Alec's mother bristle at the impropriety before she brought the reminiscing to a quick closure and led her guest away.

Alec twirled Emma's shoe by the heel as he watched the older women join another group of guests. "In case you haven't noticed, my mother has a low tolerance for even the most remote form of vulgarity."

"She must have had a heart attack when I arrived wearing this outfit."

"You're a long way from vulgar, Emma."

"But only a couple of inches removed from being very embarrassed." She swayed like an unsteady stork and he braced her with one hand. "This dress is very short, Alec."

"And you have the legs to make every man in the room appreciate it, too. Ignore my mother. You look terrific."

For a moment Emma basked in the compliment before she remembered that this was all a silly masquerade, anyway. "Of course, you'd say that," she said. "Considering you paid a premium price for this outfit."

"And it's going to cost considerably more if you fall and break your leg. Here, give me the other shoe."

She looked at him and nearly lost her balance, although this time it had nothing to do with being unsteady on her feet. "You're not going to trade them for another pair in this room, are you?"

"No, you'll have to go barefoot for the rest of the evening. But when the time comes, I'll carry you to the car. You see, I plan to fulfill my part of the physical demands of this engagement." He teased her with a smile and she had to place her hand on his arm to remain upright beneath the wave of heated response that melted through her like hot fudge over vanilla ice cream.

"You're going to fulfill the role of hospital patient if you keep carrying me around." Without hesitation, though, she shifted her champagne glass to one hand, her weight to her bare foot, and then slipped off the remaining shoe with a sigh of relief. "Here," she said as she handed it over, "I'll walk to the car, but you can have the shoes, anyway. And next time, get sevens."

"Size seven. I'll remember." He slipped her a wink as he slid the high heels, toes first, into his jacket pockets. "And now that I have the glass slippers, are you going to change into a pumpkin?"

Her right hand repossessed control of the champagne flute, and she took another full sip. "The night is young, Prince Charming, and for your information, my fairy godmother works overtime. I mean, look at me. I began the evening in bridal white trying to get some inexpensive promotional pictures and, poof, suddenly I'm in abbreviated black, drinking a very fine wine, and in line for some premium publicity, thanks to you and Tuxedo Junction." She toasted his health with a wave of her glass. "So tell me, Mr. Sayre, is this a fairy tale or what?"

"It may be one of Aesop's fables." His gaze slid past her and his voice dropped to a private whisper. "Watch your rear. Uncle George is approaching at top speed."

Emma glanced over her shoulder to see the old man bearing down on her. "I'm out of champagne, Alec," she said. "I guess I'll just have to walk across the room and get some more. 'Bye."

Without shoes to hinder her, she was on the other side of the room in seconds, well ahead of Uncle George's advance. Alec noticed, however, that she still had the sexy walk, high heels or not.

"Damn, she's fast." Uncle George huffed with the exertion of moving a few feet. "Fine-looking girl, Nephew. Heard she does a bit of dancing."

Alec didn't bother to tear his eyes from Emma. He already knew his uncle was no substitute. "She can't dance at all, Uncle George. Has two left feet and no sense of rhythm. Whoever told you she was a dancer didn't know what he was talking about."

"That's a disappointment." The old man sighed. "Bet she could be taught, though. She's got a re-markable...figure."

Alec overcame a nearly irresistible impulse to punch his relative. "Let me give you a word of advice about Emma, Uncle George. She knows all there is to know about wrestling and, if you should ever try anything, like putting your hand on her knee for instance, she'll have you in a half nelson before you can holler uncle. Get the idea?"

Uncle George paled a little. His eyes became round blue agates set in his pasty face. "Oh, my," he said. "Mud wrestling, you say? Hmm. I never would have guessed it. What a pity. Well, I wish you joy of her, Nephew."

"Thank you, sir." Alec smiled as he watched Emma laugh and point to her shoeless feet. "I'm going to do my damnedest." He saw no reason to tell his lecher-ous old uncle that he had already had the joy of Emma. She had taken an evening at his mother's and turned it into an enjoyable experience, given him someone with whom to share a little laughter, made the time fly past. She had flirted with him and captured his interest. She had handled the extraordinary and bizarre events of the evening with a wry and winning sense of humor and won his admiration in the process.

He liked Emma Cates, liked her despite the knowledge that she had nothing to lose and much to gain by accompanying him through this charade. There was no doubt in his mind that Emma recognized the benefits of an alliance with him. Not only the publicity she could receive from a joint-venture promotion with Tuxedo Junction, but the additional benefits, as well. A wedding chapel needed referrals and contacts. And in this town, the hotels and casinos provided a wealth of both. He had offered Emma a golden egg and she had seized the goose who'd laid it. In fact, he'd probably played right into her hands by insisting on continuing their pseudoengagement.

The thought should have made him uncomfortable. It took too much control from his hands and placed it too readily into Emma's. However, he stood to reap some reward from the arrangement, himself. And watching her now, watching the sexy way she stood, the sensual way she moved, the seductive tilt of her head, he thought there might be a few unexpected benefits, as well. Benefits he was inclined to explore at the first opportunity.

"YOU KNOW, ALEC," Emma said through a lovely haze of good will and premium champagne. "Being engaged to you isn't half as bad as I thought it would be. I could get accustomed to riding around in limousines. This beats pumpkin shells all to pieces."

"Will it break your fairy godmother's spell if I tell you it's after midnight?"

She yawned prettily, closed her eyes, and leaned her head against the cushioned seat, exposing an expanse of slender, ivory neck. "You can tell me it's noon tomorrow, just please, do not put those high heels back on my feet."

"I wouldn't dream of spoiling the evening that way." Morning, actually, he thought. Early morning. And he didn't want the night to end. He wanted to stay with Emma for a while longer, gaze at the smooth, rosy glow of her cheek, analyze the contented curve of her lips, touch her, kiss her. . . .

The impulse was too great. He leaned closer to claim her lips. Her response was slow, but satisfying. A throaty sigh escaped as she turned toward him, accepting his kiss and granting his arms permission to gather her closer. Alec wondered if she'd had one too many sips of champagne and if she realized how warmly uninhibited her body felt pressed tightly against his. He could feel the fullness of her breasts, recognized the itchy insistence of his palm to touch and explore the twin temptations. When he felt the tip of her tongue brush the inner curve of his upper lip, he decided her action would suffice as a nonverbal invitation. The sensations shooting through him felt too good, too natural, and he wasn't about to object to them on a technicality.

He cupped the back of her neck and allowed his fingers to steep in the tactile delight of silken skin caressed by the feathery curls at her hairline. Deliberately, he deepened the kiss, seducing her tentative tongue thrusts into a playful and sensual dance. Desire kindled inside him and surprised him with the heat of its fire. He wanted to lie down, pulling her with him, covering himself with the warm blanket of her body. But even as he made a move in that direction, he felt her slight resistance and stopped. He was a man of opportunity, but he never took unfair advantage.

Emma released him slowly, and with more reluctance than she cared to admit. What a night, she thought. What a ridiculous, fantastic, exhilarating night. How much champagne had she had? Two glasses? Four? Pushing her hair off her forehead with one hand, she puffed a breath of air past her lips, lips still heavy from the too good taste of Alec. How many times had he kissed her? Once? A thousand? She hadn't kept a careful count. Or maybe she had looked at him, wallowed a little in the sensual pleasure of his smile, and forgotten where she'd left off counting. He had a powerful effect on her, that much, at least, she didn't deny. But she had to put a stop to this. Business and pleasure did not mix. Someone very wise had once said that. Shakespeare, maybe. Or had it been Elizabeth Taylor?

"Alec." She kept her eyes closed, because she knew if she looked at him, it would all be over. "I must advise you not to trifle with my emotions. I like kissing as well as the next person, but you and I have a business arrangement and we don't want the, uh, physical demands of our engagement to interfere." She felt his breath, warm and seductive against her ear, and experienced a little shiver of wanton pleasure as his tongue circled the lobe. "Besides..." Her voice dropped like a rock to a sensitized whisper. "If...if my father...ever finds out about this—this engagement, there will be...complications. Some serious complications."

Alec's chuckle caressed her skin from ear to temple. "What's he going to do, Emma?" He kissed her forehead, her eyelids, the tip of her nose. "Hold a shotgun to my head until I marry you?"

The words drizzled through the champagne mist in her head and she imagined Julian Cates holding a bazooka. "If you knew my father, Alec, you wouldn't be laughing."

"Oh, no?" He nuzzled her neck, starting a scuffling sensation along her nerve endings and sending a slow sweet shiver moving through her veins.

"No," she confirmed, her head clearing with each progressive thought of Julian. "Julee has a way of convincing people to do what he wants."

"Julie?" Alec stopped nuzzling. "Your father is named Julie?"

"Julian, but some people call him Big Julee."

Alec almost choked. "Your father is Big Julee Cates?"

"Yes." Emma opened her eyes. "Do you know him?"

A cold shower couldn't have cleared his head any faster. Alec straightened, slowly, so as not to encourage the dull headache beginning above his eyes. "Damn," was his only comment. He had known of Julian Cates for a number of years. Rumors about him scurried through town like rats in an alley. Unsubstantiated rumors about "connections" and high-stakes poker games. Big Julee was practically a legend in Las Vegas. No one actually knew him. No one had ever actually sat in on a game in which he had played. But the stories went on, faded out for a while, then returned to make the circuit one more time.

And Emma was his daughter?

"Damn," Alec repeated. "How long have you known about this?"

Emma sent him a quizzical look. "I've been his daughter now for a little over twenty-nine years."

Alec tried to counterfeit a grin, but it was a puny attempt. "Of course you have," he said, as if that made any sense. What had he gotten involved in here? As a casino owner, he had to maintain a squeaky clean reputation. The standards for conduct were absolute and inflexible, black and white. At best, Big Julee Cates fell into an area of murky gray. And, by association, so did his daughter. This pseudoengagement would have to end, gracefully and immediately. Alec couldn't take a chance on it becoming more public than it already was. He felt no small relief when the limo stopped in front of the wedding chapel.

"Returned to your chapel, as promised, and none the worse for wear." He tried not to hurry as he escorted Emma out of the car and up the white-picketed lane to the golden doors. "Thank you, Emma, for a lovely evening. It was fun and..."

She looked at him, all wide eyes and questioning frown, and he thought maybe one last kiss would satisfy him. But her arms slipped around his neck, her lips touched his with sweet hunger, and he wasn't satisfied at all. He wanted to pursue this attraction, take her home, take her to bed.

He drew back quickly, conscious of warring factions inside his head—and other parts of his body. "Good night, Emma," he said quickly, before he did something he truly would regret. "Sweet dreams."

He felt her eyes on him as he walked away, back to the limo, back to safety, feeling guilty, as if he had given her a Roman Polanski ending to a Charlie

Chaplin film. Maybe, if he were lucky, she'd had just enough champagne to sleep deeply and awaken with only a foggy memory of how he'd left her standing, shaky and shoeless, and thoroughly kissed, beneath the crackling brilliance of a neon bride and groom.

Chapter Four

The picture splashed across the society page of the *Las Vegas Sun* the following morning made Alec want to crawl back into bed. But as he was already in his office, he drank a cup of black coffee, instead. So this is what happens when you get engaged to a woman you don't know, he thought. Disaster in black and white. And in all probability, a serious round of questions from the gaming commission. Maybe Julian Cates had retired from his career as a gambler. Maybe the rumors about his "connections" weren't true. Maybe Emma had been mistaken about who her father was.

Alec raked a hand through his dark hair and examined the picture more closely as he sipped coffee. The photograph could have come straight from a wedding album. He looked like an adoring groom, drowning in the eyes of his beloved, savoring the kiss that hovered a breath away. Emma was looking up at him, lips slightly parted, her expression more inviting than even he remembered. That particular moment, captured for all time and all Las Vegas, had occurred inside the limo just before the door closed . . . just before he'd kissed her.

A particularly difficult moment to explain if anyone asked. There wasn't a doubt in Alec's mind that no one would believe this photograph was strictly a publicity shot. *Authentic* was written all over it.

"You cannot go in there without an appointment!"

He looked up from his desk as his secretary did her business-school best to bar the uninvited visitor.

"I don't need an appointment." Emma swept past the other woman with a smile and an attitude. "Do I, Alec?"

He bore, in stoic guilt, the accusing glare of his secretary, who'd been with him for five efficient years. "This is Emma," he explained to his assistant. "She doesn't need an appointment."

"Really?" The woman clicked her heels, like Dorothy in Oz, before she left the room. Alec would have sworn the temperature climbed ten degrees when the door closed behind her.

"I see you've met Sheryl."

"Oh, we're practically best friends." Emma dropped her purse on the red leather sofa and crossed to one of the two navy print cushioned chairs in front of Alec's desk. She settled into the one nearest the window and smoothed the hem of her straight black skirt, revealing an enticing length of shapely leg in the process. "I've hassled her for weeks trying to get an appointment with you. The little power play you just witnessed is my reward for not punching her lights out now that I have political immunity."

"You must have had Wheaties for breakfast, champ." Picking up the folded newspaper, he moved from behind the desk and perched on the corner. "Or are you just flexing your muscles in preparation for a tag team match?''

"Take your pick," she said pleasantly. "But I enjoyed doing that. And it was not undeserved. So, I'm here and ready to get to work on expanding the Wedding of Your Dreams sweepstakes to include the Golden Glow. I hardly slept a wink last night for thinking about it."

Alec acknowledged a pinch of regret that she hadn't spent the night—what was left of it after he'd left her on the doorstep—thinking of him, and a twinge of relief that she hadn't lain awake dwelling on his brusque departure. "Well, take a look at this." He unfolded the paper and offered it to her, picture out. "You may never sleep again."

Emma took it. With one look, her smile faded like denim after a hot wash. Her gaze flicked to his and then back as she read the caption aloud. "'Local casino owner, Alec Sayre, and bride, Emma Cates, as they leave the Golden Glow Wedding Chapel.' That makes it sound as if we got married!" She dropped the paper into her lap. "This is not the kind of publicity I had in mind, Alec. But I'd be an idiot not to recognize that it will probably be great for my business."

The thought of what it could do to *his* business reeled through his mind. "I'll get the paper to print a retraction, but I'm afraid the damage is done."

A rueful curve framed her full lips. "No, the damage will occur when Julian sees this picture."

"The dreaded shotgun wedding." Alec couldn't keep from smiling at the one bit of humor he could still see in the situation. "There has to be a way to explain this."

"To Julian?" Emma's laugh was not funny. "Forget it. I'm his baby, his only child. He's going to go nuts."

"I remember distinctly your mentioning two brothers."

"You had your hand on my hip. I didn't want you to think I was bluffing."

"Were you?"

She didn't blink.

"Remind me not to get into a card game with you." Alec shifted position, squaring one knee against the desk for balance as he leaned forward to get another look at the picture. "I'm sorry I ever involved you in this pseudoengagement, Emma. I never meant for it to be so public."

"Julian's on the east coast. There's a chance he'll never see this issue of the *Sun*."

There was a good chance, however, that someone else would. Someone who could create more problems for Alec than the threat of a wedding at gunpoint. "Maybe we should stage a fight. Break the engagement in public."

"You should read the newspaper, Alec. In the past few hours, we've progressed from being engaged—although we're really not engaged—to being married—although we're really not married. I don't think we can move on to 'not really being divorced' by choking each other in the lobby."

"I had something a little more civilized in mind, Emma. Something along the lines of you yelling at me and throwing the engagement ring in my face."

"Why don't you wrestle me for it? That would be civilized."

"But an uneven match."

When had she gotten so at ease with him? he wondered. And when had he become so taken with that flirtatious flash of a dimple in her chin? He wanted to kiss her, then and there—to hell with the consequences. He leaned a little closer and was pleased to see her lean back, ever so slightly, but enough for him to know she was aware. Tantalizingly and cautiously aware of his every move.

"Is that a challenge, champ?" He watched the movement of her fingers as she toyed with one of the oversize buttons of her tailored pink jacket...the second button from the top...the button between her breasts. He wondered what he would see if she unfastened a button—any button...but preferably the top two.

"No," she said. "Probably just a double dose of Wheaties." She dropped her hand to her purse and opened it with a snap. "Here's the ring you stripped from some poor woman's finger last night." She handed him the ring. "I hope you can get your money back."

He held the diamond in his palm, admiring its old-fashioned charm. "I didn't strip anyone's finger. This was my paternal grandmother's engagement ring." He tucked it into his breast pocket. "I wanted you to wear it last night because I knew Mother would question its absence."

Emma felt suddenly a little sorry that she had given the ring back without a fight. His grandmother's ring...and she'd thought it was cubic zirconia. "So, Alec, are we officially no longer 'not really engaged'?"

"I'm afraid—"

"Alec!" After the briefest knock, the door swung open to admit Charity, wearing virginal white and a flush of angry red. "What is the meaning of this—?" Her sentence vanished into a humming silence as she caught sight of Emma. "Well, well, well. If it isn't the blushing bride."

"Hello, Charity." Under the circumstances, Emma didn't find it difficult to be gracious.

"What is it, Charity?" Alec's tone was not nearly so accommodating. "Emma and I are busy at the moment."

"Oh, I'm sure there's never a dull moment when *Lucky* is around." Charity's mouth formed a lifeless smile. "I suppose you've seen the paper?"

"First thing this morning," Alec said.

"You do realize who she is, don't you?" With a toss of her dark hair, Charity threw a challenge to Emma, without once looking in her direction. "Do you have any idea what my father's going to say when he sees this?" She held out the paper, society page exposed, her fickle finger of guilt pointing at the picture. "I hope you can explain this to him, because I certainly can't."

Emma didn't like the feeling that she was a fence post in the room. "Explain what?" she said as she rose from the chair. "It's a publicity photo . . . for my wedding chapel. It turned out well, don't you think?"

"For you, perhaps. It could be hell for Alec."

Emma stepped forward and slipped her hand around Alec's arm, feeling his tension, wishing it were a simple, uncontrollable response to her touch. "On the other hand, it could be heaven."

"Charity, Emma is here at my invitation." He placed his hand over hers on his arm and sent a rush of warmth spiraling through her. "And now that you've joined us, there's a little matter I would like to discuss."

"No, please." Charity covered her heart with her hands and rolled her eyes to the ceiling. "Don't tell me. It's the thrill of a lifetime. I get to be a bridesmaid at your next photo session." She shed the artificial sweetness, but held on to the sour smile. "I am not as naive as you might think I am, Alec. I know what you're doing and why. This person—Emma." Her name had never been pronounced with such venom. "She is nothing but a convenience for you, a way to keep a barrier between the two of us, to save you from making a commitment. I understand that. What I can't understand is why you would take such a stupid risk."

Alec straightened slowly. "This is not your concern, Charity."

"I disagree."

Emma felt the muscles in Alec's arm flex.

"Let's see if we can agree on the Wedding of Your Dreams contest," he said. "I want Emma's wedding chapel included in any future publicity."

Charity's expression turned frosty. "She seems to be getting plenty of publicity without any help from me. And, I might add, at the expense of Tuxedo Junction."

"Now just a minute." Emma took up her own defense. "You stole the contest idea from me in the first place."

"How ridiculous. I don't need to steal. We may have had similar ideas at the same time, but that is merely a coincidence."

"Coincidence or not, I intend to rectify the matter right now." Alec moved behind his desk. "Charity, Emma will work with you through the end of this publicity campaign and you *will* treat her with the utmost courtesy and respect."

"I'll quit first."

Alec lifted his head, and Emma was chilled by the look in his eyes. "I'll be sorry to lose you as an employee."

"You'll be sorry in more ways than one." It was a standoff of no small proportions and Emma thought for a moment that Charity would back down. But with another toss of her head, she turned to the door. "My father will be in touch. He has friends on the gaming commission. If I were you, I'd watch my step . . . and hers."

"Clear out your desk, Charity. I'll have security escort you from the hotel."

She sashayed to the door, unfazed by her dismissal, untouched by his cold anger. When she turned in the doorway, the curve of her mouth was oddly tender. "I know you, Alec. You need me and you'll beg me to come back before the month is out. So, I won't say goodbye. I'll just wish you the best of luck in winning the wedding of your dreams."

The door closed behind her with a click. Emma turned to look at Alec and assess the damage. His knuckles were white and his jaw tight as he stared long and hard out the window. The idea occurred to her that there was more to this encounter than she had seen and heard. Something below the surface. Something that ran deep and was of long standing. Was he in love with Charity? Was she the woman who had him on the run from commitment? The thought was unpleasant, but seemed all too possible, considering that she could still feel the ricochet of emotions left in the room. "Does she know that I'm just a figment of your imagination, Alec?"

"Charity knows everything. That's her problem." His laugh was strained. "But she's gone now and that's my problem. Do you think you can take charge of the contest, Emma? At least, you have an idea of the concept. I know it's a lot to ask since you have your own business to run, but I'll make sure you have as much help as you need."

"Are you kidding? I'll love doing the contest. I am sorry, though, that you had to lose an employee because of me."

"You had nothing to do with it, Emma. Charity and I were overdue for that confrontation. It was inevitable."

Emma didn't want to see, or understand, the turmoil in his blue eyes. But the clues pieced together to spell out a broken love affair. "She's the reason you invented Lucky, isn't she?"

Alec directed his anger out the window. "Let me notify security," he said after a pause. "Then I'll take you to Charity's office and we'll see what we have to work with."

"What are you going to do about the picture in the paper?"

He glanced at the desk, at the newsprint and the photograph. "I think I'll have it framed as a gift for my mother. It's the closest she's ever going to get to having a wedding photo with me in it."

And that, Emma thought, pretty much put the whole thing into perspective.

"WHAT DO YOU HAVE against weddings?" Emma asked a few days later. "You stutter every time you say the word."

Alec looked up from sorting through Charity's files. "Wedding. Wedding. Wedding," he said with perfect articulation. "I don't have a problem with the word. It's the ceremony and everything that comes after that gets to me."

Emma bent over the papers spread before her on the floor. "Is this an inborn aversion or have you just had a bad experience with marriage?"

"Thirteen, at last count."

She sank back on her heels and looked at him over the rim of her reading glasses. "You've been married thirteen times?"

"You said experience, you didn't say anything about personal ordeals. Over the years, I've watched family and friends step up to the altar, take the plunge, and sink like stones. Fortunately, I was born with a healthy fear of investing too much of my resources on one big gamble. I don't have to jump off a cliff to know that it's not something I want to do."

"Hmm."

He closed the file drawer with an easy push. "*Hmm*. What does that mean?"

"Oh, nothing. I was just wondering how many of the couples who've been married at the Golden Glow Chapel would appreciate your jumping-off-a-cliff analogy."

"All of the bridegrooms. None of the brides. Women have too much fantasy riding on the wedding. They never look beyond the ceremony."

"Really? And how did you come by such insight? Considering your natural aversion to matrimony?"

"Six stints as best man, eleven bachelor parties, nine divorces, three separations and one no-show." He pulled out another drawer of the filing cabinet and began to flip through the folders. "The no-show was my father on his third attempt to find happiness and marital bliss with my mother."

"Your parents married three times?"

"Twice and one near-miss. Mother planned a wedding, went to a great deal of trouble in preparing for the ceremony only to learn that my father had discovered, at the last minute, that he had other plans. My mother took the attitude that he'd saved her from committing a terrible mistake. She said murder would have been the ultimate social blunder."

"My mother died of pneumonia when I was a baby, but I've sometimes thought that if she'd lived, she might have murdered Julian." Emma picked up a stack of contest pamphlets and set them aside, then with a sweep of one hand, she spread out the remaining papers. "Don't get me wrong. Julian's a dear, but he can be overpowering. When I was a teenager and all my friends were dreaming about falling in love, I spent hours daydreaming about how it would feel to be independent."

"So, how does it feel?"

Emma caught the edge of his smile and returned it with a touch of laughter. "I don't know yet. Ever since I bought the wedding chapel, I've been so busy there hasn't been time to think about how I feel. And there is one small blemish on my autonomy—Julian doesn't know I bought the Golden Glow Chapel."

"Are you afraid to tell him?"

"Of course. He has this way of butting in and taking over. One minute, I'm on my own, making my own decisions, plotting out goals, taking responsibility for myself. The next minute, he's whipped through my life like the Great Emancipator, freeing me from having to make a single decision on my own." She sighed as she bent over the scattered contest material. "I haven't found anything of value in this stack of papers, Alec. I know Charity must have sent this list of rules to contest participants, but there isn't so much as a penciled note about to whom or where the information was mailed."

He closed the file drawer with a metallic clunk. "I think we've been sabotaged. Even with the escort of a security guard, she obviously managed to get out of here with enough paperwork to undercut our efforts. Have you found anything at all you can work with?"

"Well, in the material I so foolishly handed over to Charity, there was a list of publications I'd planned to use for advertising the contest in each state. There's a copy here, so we can start by contacting each magazine or newspaper on the list and seeing if Charity placed the ads with them. She could have put together a list of her own, but maybe we'll be lucky and discover she used mine. I'm sure she received tear sheets or some other confirmation of publication, but I can't find any evidence of it. And there's nothing to indicate how many responses she received. Without her files, we're flying by the seat of our pants."

"Not my favorite way to fly, either. I'll get someone started on the contacts right away. Any other ideas?"

"You might ask Charity's secretary to check the computer files again, just in case she missed anything the first time."

"Done." Alec came to stand above Emma. "Leave that. It's time for a coffee break." Reaching down with one hand, he pulled her to her feet.

Her eyes met his. Her fingers lingered in his palm for the space of a heartbeat...and then another...before she slipped free of his touch and his gaze.

She dusted carpet fuzz from the seat of her slacks and stretched a little to loosen the tension in the backs of her knees. Alec watched the lithe movements, the graceful arch of her back as she stretched, and wondered how he'd managed to keep his hands off of her for the past three days. And, more importantly, how he was supposed to convince himself to end this platonic engagement. The *Sun* had printed a correction, stating that the photo was a publicity stunt and had been run with the wrong caption. Alec figured that was as good a defense as he deserved, if and when the gaming commission came around. His mother had clipped the photo and sent it to him with a terse reminder that not inviting the mother of the groom to the wedding was highly disrespectful. He'd sent her the notice of correction without comment. After all, what more could he say?

There was no longer any reason to continue the engagement. With Charity gone, he didn't have to resort to subterfuge. But somehow, he hadn't gotten around to telling Emma yet. He was waiting for the appropriate moment...a moment when he wasn't so fascinated by the delicious and completely random appearance of her dimple. A moment when he wasn't thinking about how she would look between the black satin sheets on his bed.

"I've got to get back to the chapel," she said, breaking the moment into separate and distracting pieces. "We've got four weddings scheduled this afternoon and there may be a drop-in or two, although that's more common on weekends." She looked up at him with curiosity darkening her eyes. "Are you still thinking about Charity?"

Hell, no. His thoughts were closer to the moon than to Charity. It was hard to believe Emma didn't feel them embracing her, seducing her, luring her to make the first move so he wouldn't have to. But, of course, he wouldn't even if she didn't. Emma Cates came with a small disadvantage—her father. And although, after some reflection, Alec had decided the gaming commission couldn't reasonably infer any taint in his brief association with Julian Cates's daughter, he knew he should heed his gut feeling and keep this relationship at arm's length. Which wasn't turning out to be easy.

"When are you coming back?" he asked like a lovestruck idiot. "To work on the contest again?" As if there was any question as to why she would return.

"Tomorrow, probably." She paused before giving him a slanted smile. "You can come to the chapel later today, if you'd like. I might have time in between weddings to go over some of the contest rules with you."

He considered it, but not for long. "I don't think so. Something about being sandwiched in between weddings makes me uneasy."

"I understand." She turned toward the door, and he came within a breath of going with her. "It's like having to watch helplessly as someone jumps off a cliff."

He couldn't have said it any better.

"WE HAVE A REAL problem on our hands here, son."

Alec settled back in his chair, prepared to listen to the "problem" as interpreted by Charity's father, Sam McKimber. Clasping his hands behind his head, Alec swiveled toward the window and waited for Sam's gravelly voice to rumble through the speakerphone.

"Charity has explained the matter to my satisfaction," Sam said. "I'd like to know how you're going to handle it."

"I'm going to hire someone to replace her." Alec measured his words, keeping his voice low but tough. "Just as I would with any other employee who quit."

"You fired her."

"She quit, Sam. She refused to do something I asked her to do and when I insisted, she quit."

"You can hardly blame her for that, Alec, when you were the one who involved another woman in a private matter between the two of you. And the woman you chose, Alec—a professional gambler's daughter...." Sam's opinion was transmitted clearly through the slight chastising click of his tongue. "Well, it's no wonder Charity lost her composure, and she only did that after being accused of outright theft. Charity is concerned for you, Alec. She has your best interests at heart, you know."

Alec held on to his temper. Barely. "Charity has given you some misinformation, Sam. There is nothing even remotely resembling a private matter between the two of us. And if she told you there was, she lied."

The pause that came through the speaker was as audible as anything Sam had said aloud. "You know, son," he continued, "I'm trying to do the right thing here. I like you. I had hopes that you and Charity would work out your problems and you and I would someday be in-laws. But regardless of the outcome of this unresolved and *private* matter, I'm not going to sit by and let you slander my daughter. I know she's a good employee, one of the best PR people the hotel's ever employed. If I thought otherwise, we wouldn't be having this conversation. So, in light of what you've both told me, I'm convinced Charity's dismissal is a result of a personal conflict between the two of you and upholding it is not in the best interest of the business.''

This time Alec took charge of the pause and used it to his advantage. A minute ticked past, and then another, and the tension across the phone lines became almost palpable. ''The last time I checked, I was in charge of running this hotel and casino, Sam. If you want to fight me for control, we'll take this matter to the board for a vote.''

Sam's chuckle echoed hollowly in the room. ''Don't get into a mudslinging contest with me, son. You won't like my aim. We'll talk again, once you've had time to reconsider the matter.'' And with that and a final click, the conversation was over.

Alec stayed where he was, not bothering to reach across the desk and turn off the speakerphone, which was now filling the vacuum left by Sam's vague threat with an annoying dial-tone buzz. He was surprised, but not really shocked by the call. Sam McKimber was a tough guy and an overprotective parent. Alec should have expected him to defend his daughter. Still, facts were facts. No matter what Sam did or said, Alec did not intend to rescind his decision. Charity had left of her own volition, and Alec was not about to ask her to come back. Especially not after what she'd done to Emma's contest.

Emma. The thought of her relaxed him and he smiled, despite the energy he'd lost in dueling with Sam. Maybe he would reconsider her offer. Sam had put a new spin on the situation, turned the whole incident into a matter of principle. As if a couple of hours with a professional gambler's daughter could ruin his reputation, as if his association with Emma was a scandal in the making. And all the while, Emma was burning the candle at both ends, trying to save the contest Charity had sabotaged. The least Alec could do was to take a few hours from his own schedule to help her cause. Even if he had to spend those few hours at a w-w-wedding chapel.

"COME ON, ALEC. This will only hurt for a minute." Emma took his hand and tugged him toward the altar. "This couple wants attendants and, since we're the only two available, we're elected. All you have to do is stand there and hold the ring until Harry asks for it."

"You don't know what you're asking, Emma."

"Let's call it a favor. And, Alec, please don't make any comments to the groom. He's nervous enough already."

"I wish you hadn't told me that."

The scrawny young man standing before the altar did look nervous, but he showed no fear during the ceremony and spoke his vows with the fervor of conviction. Alec played his part well, handing over the ring at the precise moment, bolstering the bridal couple with his presence, ready to catch bride or groom in case of a dead faint. He made one too many faces at the maid of honor and was denied the pleasure of seeing even a glimpse of her dimple. When it was over and Harry pronounced the life sentence, Alec was surprised to find himself wearing a smile.

"Thank you," Emma said after the couple left the chapel.

"It wasn't so bad," Alec answered. "You'll notice I didn't pass out once during the ceremony."

"I admire your fortitude." She sank onto a front row seat and muffled a yawn with her hand. At the piano, Harry began to sing a snappy version of Sinatra's "My Way." He never missed an opportunity to impress Alec with the range of his repertoire. "There'll be another couple here any minute," Emma said. "You might want to slip out the back door before your services are called on once again. Or before you sign Harry on the dotted line and force me to find someone else to officiate at the weddings."

"I wouldn't dream of stealing Harry away from you, Emma. Even though this is one of my favorite tunes."

"He really wants a shot at the Silk Stocking Lounge. Don't lead him on if there's no chance, okay?"

"I'm a straightforward kind of guy. I never lead people on, especially not performers. Now, can we talk about the contest?"

"Oh, I can't think about that now."

"But we haven't had a chance to talk about the letters I brought over. Or the fact that the contest is in the homestretch and we're short a hundred couples. Or the more pressing matter of whether to cancel the whole thing, conference, contest, and all."

She looked at him with some surprise. "Alec, I first thought of this contest nearly a year ago. For the past week, I've been working night and day to salvage what little of it Charity left for us. I won't agree to cancel it. Not even if it means I have to personally phone every engaged couple in all fifty states to find the winners."

He took the chair across the aisle and sat sideways to face her. Resting his forearms on his thighs, he leaned toward her. "You're working too hard. You need a day off for R and R, Emma."

She laughed. "I can't afford a day off. There's not enough time as it is."

"Monday," he said firmly. "I'll pick you up at eight. In the morning."

"You won't be out of bed then, Alec. You're just like most of the people on the strip. Up all night, sleep the day away. You won't pick me up at eight."

Alec smiled, as much at the thought of having a whole day to enjoy with Emma as at the idea of showing her he wasn't just like other people in Las Vegas. "Wear something comfortable. Something easy to get on and off."

"Forget it, Alec. You'd have to kidnap me, and I won't fall for that stunt again."

"You will, Emma, because you're in desperate need of adventure. You're craving a break from routine, an activity to get the blood pumping and the adrenaline flowing. Lucky for you, I know just the thing."

One expressive eyebrow arched as she leaned across the aisle and patted his cheek. "Well, I'm not going to strip for you, so don't bother to ask Harry to play his rendition of 'Let Me Entertain You.' "

"'Fly Me to the Moon' would be more appropriate." Alec settled back in the fold-up chair and watched for the dimple to make an appearance. "Because I'm going to take you skydiving."

Chapter Five

"There is no way I am jumping out of this plane."

"You won't have to jump," Alec assured her. "I'm going to push you."

Emma tried to look at him over her shoulder, but they were rigged for a tandem jump and she was strapped to him like a sausage to a skin. Her backside was aligned so closely to his front side that she couldn't make a move without his cooperation. She could barely breathe...a fact she attributed to the open door in the side of the plane and the vast expanse of sky beyond rather than to his proximity. Her heart threatened to pound a hole through the wall of her chest, and she dared to hope she would die of a heart attack before she hit the ground.

"Relax." Alec's voice in her ear was meant to soothe her fear...as if a voice alone could do that. "You'll do fine. Just remember everything we practiced. Cross your arms, placing your hands shoulder to shoulder. Tuck your head, chin to chest. Bring your legs up. When we've cleared the plane, you'll feel a jerk. That will be the drogue chute, which will slow us down to about the same speed as a single jumper in a free-fall. From there, you can put your arms out and we'll fall in the frog formation to about forty-five hundred feet when I'll deploy the main chute. Remember, I'll hold your head when the chutes open to keep you from clonking me in the mouth, so don't let that alarm you. About fifteen feet from the ground, I'll tell you to raise your feet, then I'll yell *flare* and you'll pull your set of toggles straight down to your sides. Clear on everything?''

She nodded, even though his instructions were bouncing around her brain like water droplets in the hot grease of apprehension.

"Relax and enjoy the experience. You're going to love this, I promise. And, Emma, I'll be right behind you all the way down."

"Why do I feel like Coyote waiting for the boulder to fall on top of the Roadrunner?"

"You're nervous. That's understandable. Jumping out of an airplane at thirteen thousand feet can be a bit unnerving."

Really? she thought. "Were you nervous your first time?" she asked.

"I shook so badly the instructor thought we were having an earthquake—and that was before the plane left the runway." Alec's lips pressed against her ear as he spoke so she could hear above the inescapable noise of the small plane barreling through the atmosphere. "The first time is the worst. And the best. You won't ever be this scared again."

Of that much, at least, Emma was certain. She wasn't ever doing this again. Period. "Let's go back," she said, but the last word was whipped from her mouth and tossed aside when the plane rattled through a pocket of air.

Alec squeezed her shoulders. His breath warmed her temple...at least it would have warmed her if she hadn't been cold from the inside out. "That's my girl," he said. "Not afraid to take a chance."

No, Emma thought. She wasn't afraid. She was terrified. No amount of adrenaline rush could be worth this anxiety. How Alec had talked her into going this far, she couldn't understand. But he was exhibiting a likeness to Julian she found disturbing. One minute she heard herself clearly saying no, and the next minute she was doing exactly what she'd said she was not going to do. And being patted on the head for doing it, too. *Good girl,* Julian always said. *That's my girl,* Alec echoed the praise.

Well, she was not his girl. She had no desire to be his girl. And she was not jumping out of this airplane. "Alec?"

"Ready?" he yelled, and began a forward shuffle, moving with the awkwardness of a woman pregnant with a hundred and five pounds of baby.

Emma frantically tried to recall the instructions he'd given her over and over again before they'd gotten on the plane and on the way up to jumping altitude, but her mind was mush. She couldn't think. Her voice, even if it could be heard above the roar, came out as nothing more than a thin squeak of denial. She could feel Alec's excitement, the tightness of his body against hers, the tension of anticipation, the eagerness with which he approached the idea of risking it all.

His mouth covered her ear one more time. "Are you sure you want to do this? It's not too late to call it off."

The fear left her like water spiraling down a drain. It was too late. She did not want to do this, but more than that, she wanted to experience Alec's excitement, to discover, if she could, the source of his zeal for taking chances. She could feel the strong, rapid throbbing of his heartbeat as it pulsed from his body into hers. They hovered at the door of eternity, and Emma closed her eyes as she gave the fatal nod.

"Trust me, Emma. You'll live to thank me for these next few moments." His words came as clearly as if there were no competing sound, as if they came straight from his thoughts into hers.

The airplane cut its engine, and the roaring sound in her ears was nothing more than her blood wailing like banshees through her veins. Heart in her throat, Emma crossed her arms, hands to shoulders, tucked her chin, and placed all of her trust in the man who assured her she'd live to thank him. She felt the harness straps pull taut and then she was hurtling into open air.

The rush of wind caught her breath and battered her ears with a howling nothingness of sound. She instinctively wanted to fight against the sensation of falling, but Alec's instructions kept her still. She felt his hand against her head and then a jerk as the drogue deployed. Great, she thought with some minuscule amount of relief. At least now, they wouldn't die any faster than a single parachuter on his way down.

Cautiously, she relaxed her grip on her shoulders and let her arms spread apart. More of Alec's instructions came flooding back, as clear as a summer day. *Relax. Arch your back. Keep your eyes open. Enjoy the view. Free-fall.* And he was falling with her, sharing the same risk, bearing the added burden of parachute and responsibility. Emma watched the mottled brown earth rise with a curious fascination but no real fear. Her fate was packed inside the parachute. There was no point in being afraid now. There was only the sting of the air, the hard pump, pump, pump that was her heartbeat, and the parade of seconds that seemed both fleeting and infinite.

She decided the experience was a little like dreaming, falling fast through a limitless range of emotions and sensations into a cushion of illusion. She wasn't going to die. The day was too beautiful. She was a bird, a butterfly, dropping on the air currents, light as a sunbeam. Intense color surrounded her. Blinding color. Blue...green...white.

The straps slammed across her chest and the jolt grabbed her breath as the parachute deployed and opened into a marshmallow canopy. She could feel Alec's body again, sheltering and safe against her. She *wasn't* going to die. The day *was* too beautiful. She *was* a bird, a butterfly, floating gracefully to the ground. The colors softened and blended into recognizable forms. Sky blue. Spring green. Cloud white. A glorious Mother Earth brown.

And Emma knew why Alec took the risk.

"Grab your set of toggles." His voice in her ear was heavenly, warm and reassuring. She reached for the toggles and felt a thrill of discovery as she realized she could guide their direction by pulling from one side or the other. She knew Alec was allowing her to control their drift and appreciated the fact that he wouldn't let her take them too far off course.

"Look." Below her, the landmarks of Las Vegas assumed shape and identity. She nodded as Alec pointed out the twin towers of Tuxedo Junction. She looked for the Golden Glow and thought she could just make out the spire on top of the chapel before it was blocked from her view. Time seemed limitless as the canopy caught first one air current and then another. The earth moved closer, but Emma was lost in the experience and was caught by surprise when Alec told her to raise her feet.

"Flare!"

She jerked the toggles to her side, forcing the parachute to flare and catch a full canopy of air, further slowing their descent. Alec absorbed the shock of landing and ran with the last gust of air in the parachute. Emma put her feet down too quickly, stumbled and fell, taking Alec down with her. When they stopped rolling, she was lying on top of him, face up, like a turtle turned on its shell. A giggle started low in her chest and bubbled into her throat. "The sky is falling! The sky is falling!"

Beneath her, Alec released a grunt. "I believe you, Chicken Little. Now, let's coordinate our efforts and get Turkey Lurkey on his feet." Alec wrapped his arms around her and rolled to the right, picking up momentum that propelled them over and onto his left side. From there, it was only a brief struggle with gravity and the parachute lines before they were on their feet and Alec was releasing the clamps that held Emma against him. She turned immediately and threw her arms around his neck. "Thank you," she said through barely contained laughter. "I have never been so thrilled to be alive in my entire life."

He picked a blade of grass from her hair and tossed it over his shoulder before his hands came to rest at her waist. "Your cheeks are flushed and your eyes are sparkling. Skydiving is very becoming, Emma."

The flush on her cheeks deepened—she could tell by the rush of warmth beneath her skin. She lowered her lashes so the stars in her eyes wouldn't start winking at him, betraying her secret knowledge that he was in part responsible for their shine. She removed her hands from their compromising position around his neck and took two discreet steps back. "Anyway, thanks."

Alec's smile was slow and satisfied as he pulled on the lines to drag the parachute toward him. "I hate to say 'I told you so,' but I believe I did say you'd live to thank me. Skydiving is an exhilarating sport. Are you ready to go again?"

"No." She laughed because she couldn't help it. "No, no, no, no, no, no, no." She shook her head for emphasis. "No. I never, ever, want to do that again."

"It's like falling off a horse, Emma. You should get right back on."

"It is nothing like falling off a horse, Alec, and don't try to talk me into it. I did it. I parachuted out of a plane. And now that we're on the ground, it was great. Really great. But I'm not doing it again."

He laughed and began bunching the parachute into a transportable bundle. "Famous last words."

"Alec, don't say that. I'm not like you. Taking chances is something I try to avoid. I don't know why I let you talk me into jumping in the first place, unless it was to prove that I'm not a coward. I don't enjoy life on the edge. And I don't have to jump out of an airplane again and again to know that."

He regarded her as he gathered the last folds of parachute and tucked the bundle beneath one arm. "Is that why you haven't jumped off the cliff into matrimony?"

"Julian is the reason for that bit of caution. It's taken me years to gain my independence. I'm not about to turn around and blithely hand it over to another man."

"Maybe it would be like skydiving, Emma. Not nearly as bad as you expected."

"Skydiving was worse than anything I imagined." She began undoing the clips that held her harness in place. "I will admit, though, that it turned out much better than I ever expected." For a moment, she thought about doing it again . . . but the thought was quickly vetoed. "Of course, since I was sure I was going to die, 'turning out better than I expected' isn't saying a heck of a lot."

"I warned you that the first time is the worst and the best." Alec led the way to the van they had parked earlier in an area beside the landing field. "Are you positive you don't want to try another jump? The experience gets better each time."

"I'll take your word for it."

"And nothing I do will persuade you to change your mind?"

"Nothing." She shrugged free of the harness and unzipped the flight suit, pushing it off her shoulders and shimmying until it skimmed past her hips, leaving her in the jeans and cotton shirt she'd started out in that morning. "You can get me something to eat, though. I am starving."

"Abject fear does wonders for your appetite." Alec tossed the equipment into the back of the van, then removed his harness and flight suit and added them to Emma's bundle. "Hop in the van and we'll see if we can find a bite to eat."

"I think it's going to take more than a bite." Emma walked around the end of the van. She looked up as the plane from which they'd jumped circled overhead, dipped a wing, and buzzed away. "Is that a congratulations dip?" she asked. "Or is he checking to make sure we're not splattered all over the—ow!" Her right foot twisted sharply beneath her, and she crumpled to a sitting position on the ground.

"Emma?" Alec ducked his head around the rear door. "Are you all right?"

She rubbed her ankle. "I turned my foot."

He was kneeling beside her in an instant, wrapping one hand about her ankle, resting the other hand on her shoulder, sending a spiral of awareness through her, making her momentarily forget the pain in her ankle in favor of the sweet warmth of his touch. "Does this hurt?" He pushed at the injured area with his thumb.

Emma winced. "No. Well, maybe a little. It feels sort of numb, actually."

He untied the laces and slipped off the shoe, then the sock. He cupped her heel in his palm and probed the area from arch to calf, pushing his fingers beneath the leg of her jeans, massaging her skin and sending her heartbeat into shock with the impact of his touch. "You could have a fracture, but I think it's just sprained. How did you do this, anyway? I told you how to land so you wouldn't injure yourself."

"I landed on top of you, if you'll recall. And I just did this. I must have stepped in a gopher hole or something."

Alec raised his head and flicked his gaze across the flat, Nevada landscape. "I can't believe you jumped thirteen thousand feet without harm only to twist your foot on a little patch of ground."

The ache in her foot swelled to a throb. "Can we skip the lecture along with lunch and go straight for some aspirin?"

"Put your arms around my neck."

"I only need a hand up."

"What you're getting is a full carry and a fast trip to the nearest doctor. Put your arms around my neck."

"Don't be ridiculous, Alec. I can walk." But she did as he asked, allowing him to lift her close to his chest. His strong, solid chest. He gathered her against him and held her tightly as he stabilized his center of gravity before attempting to stand upright with her in his arms. For the first time since the start of her morning, she felt secure. She could feel the warmth of his skin beneath her palm and the heat of the desert sun on the back of her hand. Two different heats. Two different sources. Each warming her in its own way.

Emma enjoyed the solid strength of his arms around her. She wanted to tuck her head beneath his chin and listen to the steady rhythm of his heartbeat. A tremor began in her fingertips and raced through her body with alarming urgency. Delayed reaction to stress, she explained patiently to the fanciful voice inside her head that was running everywhere and shouting, *What a man! What a man!*

She had no business appreciating anything about Alec. He'd just pushed her out of a plane. Or pulled her. Depending on perspective. Either way, if she'd died, it would have been his fault.

"A couple of aspirin will take care of me in no time," she said as he set her gingerly on the passenger seat. "There's no need to see a doctor."

Alec slid his arm from beneath her knees, his other arm from around her shoulders, stepped back, and closed the van door. A moment later, he climbed into the driver's seat and turned the key in the ignition. "Do you have a preference?"

"I'm not picky. Aspirin is aspirin."

He smiled with the utmost patience. "You're going to the doctor. Do you have a preference?"

"Yes. No doctor."

He smiled. "Your independence stops short of my better judgment, Miss Fourth of July. Now, do you have a physician in mind or do we drop in on my preference, Dr. Arnold?"

On another day Emma might have beat her head against the brick wall of his "better judgment", but her nerves were shot and her ankle was throbbing. "Dr. Arnold," she said tightly. "But there is nothing wrong with my foot."

"SPRAINED," Dr. Arnold pronounced.

"Sprained," Emma grudgingly repeated to Alec a few minutes' later, back at the chapel.

"Sprained," Alec informed a hovering Harry as he carried Emma through the chapel, past the office, and into the two back rooms that Harry called home. "She's supposed to stay off of her foot for a few days. Can you keep her down?"

"With a tire tool, maybe." Harry followed the procession into the room. "She's not exactly what you'd call biddable."

"She's not even what I'd call reasonable at the moment." Alec looked around the small, neat room. The bed took up most of the space and was made up with a puffy, peach-colored coverlet and brightly hued throw pillows. Obviously, Emma's attempt at redecorating Harry's humble abode.

"Will you stop pretending you're He-Man and put me down?"

"My pleasure." He dumped her unceremoniously—but with due concern for her injury—onto the bed. "Now, what needs to be done?"

"What do you mean by that?"

Alec shrugged easily. "I'm here to help."

Emma frowned...and he felt the full impact of her dimple. Until that moment Alec thought it would only appear when she smiled. But he realized he'd been wrong. Even in annoyance, the dimple packed a walloping charm.

"Maybe you can ask Harry if he needs to be carried someplace," she suggested. "That will give you something meaningful to do."

Hands on hips, Alec looked from Emma to Harry. "She's going to be hard to handle these next few days."

"You ain't just whistlin' 'Dixie,' boy." Harry shook his head as he turned toward the door. "Are you planning to stick around?"

"Someone's got to help. This business won't run itself. And with Emma out of commission, how can you be minister, manager, and piano man?"

"We have Sanchee and Dan, our florist and chauffeur, to help." Emma struggled into a sitting position.

"That still leaves you shorthanded...and one foot short. I'll stay."

"No, you don't." Emma swung her feet off the side of the bed and immediately wished she hadn't. Grabbing the headboard, she balanced on her good foot. "You are not taking over my wedding chapel."

"This isn't a revolution, Emma. I'm not attempting a coup." Alec looked at her bandaged foot, but didn't make a move. He was half afraid she'd try a body slam if he got any closer. "You're overreacting."

"Oh, well, forgive me," she said sharply. "It's been a harrowing morning."

"It will be less harrowing if you'll get off of your feet."

"He's right, Em," Harry said in Alec's support.

"Harry, I know he's right. I'll put my ankle up as soon as I've hobbled into the office. I can do plenty of things while my foot is propped on a chair." She adjusted her grip on the headboard. "Now, stand back and let me by."

The older man exchanged glances with Alec. "I think I'll get back to the chapel. We've got a wedding scheduled for two-thirty and I still have to put on my collar."

"I'm right behind you," Emma called to Harry's departing back.

"You are not going anywhere but to bed," Alec informed her as he moved just close enough to catch her if she fell. "And don't give me any lip. I have business experience. You've been giving Tuxedo Junction and the Wedding of Your Dreams contest a lot of your extra time. It's only fair that I return the favor. So, plant your cute little butt on that bed, prop some pillows under your ankle, and relax, dammit."

She wavered. He could almost see her throbbing foot communicating a plea for acceptance to her stubborn brain, but obstinacy won. "I can handle the wedding chapel without your help, Alec."

"This doesn't have to be difficult, Emma. Why are you being so bullheaded?"

"Why are you so concerned?"

"Damned if I know." Alec took a couple of exasperated steps away from her before he spun around, picked her up as gently as his irritation allowed, and put her on the bed. "Now, stay put—or else."

"Or else what?" She looked up at him with green eyes that glistened with challenge. "Are you going to push me out of another plane?"

Alec felt a little like an innocent bystander shouldering the blame for crimes his accomplice had committed. And then, abruptly, he saw the problem, understood Emma's reaction. She wasn't afraid he could take control of her business, she was afraid he could take control of her.

All the signs were there... the overconfident lift of her chin, the I-dare-you smugness in the curve of her lips, the uncertainty she couldn't quite mask, the sexual awareness that sparked the challenge in her eyes, the physical attraction that closed around them like a cocoon. She was afraid she couldn't handle him...and he found that idea far more exciting than skydiving had ever been.

"Or else..." He placed his hands on her upper arms and pressed her down and into the puffy coverlet. A topaz blue throw pillow popped up as her head slipped between it and another pillow of multicolored stripes. Keeping her pinned with one hand, Alec grabbed both pillows with his other hand and placed them under her injured foot. Deliberately, slowly, he planted a knee on either side of her thighs and straddled her on top of the bed. His theory was further strengthened by the sudden shadow of desire that slipped into her expression. "Or else, Emma, I'll have to take whatever action is necessary to make sure you stay where I put you."

Her tongue darted across her upper lip in a giveaway gesture that belied the defiant, and belated, arching of her brows. "I think you have better things to do," she said in a voice just this side of breathy. "I think you're bluffing."

"Why don't you call the bluff and find out?"

A moment ticked past as he watched her weigh her options...of which there were none. But he didn't tell her that. He didn't have to. He knew she was fully aware that this time he held the winning hand and meant to accept her challenge. Her eyelids drifted down, shading her eyes with thick lashes, and her lips parted. Moist and full, they invited him to sample, to taste, to take. But he wanted a real invitation, an acknowledgment that she wanted to sample him, too. He wanted an admission that this round went to him. He brought his face close to hers, let his nearness signal his intent, then touched the tip of his tongue to her earlobe. "What are you going to do, Emma? Raise the ante? Or call?"

She opened her eyes as he pulled back to look at her. He watched for the dimple to signal approval...or the end of the game. "I'll call," she said softly. "Let me see what you've got."

Alec's lips curved with pleasure in the instant before he rose to her challenge and then sank his mouth over hers. No more Mr. Nice Guy, he thought. She had asked for this, baited him, tried his patience, tested his resolve, and then to cap it off, she had dared him to prove he was more than bluff. He'd show her what he had and gain the upper hand with sheer animal magnetism, if nothing else.

He parted her lips with his tongue and sought dominance with a couple of deep thrusts. But she wasn't to be tamed so easily and met his aggression with a tantalizing defense. She surprised him, as much with the intensity of her kiss as with the way she quickly reduced him to a mass of quivering desire.

Alec told himself the shakiness was the result of his awkward positioning on the bed. It would be gone the moment he stopped bracing his weight with his arms. And the desire was easily explained . . . Emma was an attractive woman, and the thought of making love with her was a delicious proposition. He wasn't a saint. On the other hand, he wasn't a sadist, either, and her foot had to be causing her enough pain without being jostled around by him.

But when he tried to pull out of the embrace, Emma refused to let him go, looping her arms around his neck and plying his lips with another seductive kiss. After a moment or two, he decided that either her ankle wasn't really bothering her or else *he* was the antidote she needed to take her mind off of the pain. In either case, who was he to argue?

He rolled to his side and gathered her close, softening the pressure of his lips and letting the kiss take on added sweetness. She threaded her fingers through his hair and moved her mouth in a lazy and deadly sensual response. His heart began to thrum faster than it had in the airplane, beating a persistent, exciting rhythm against the wall of his chest. He tugged the hem of her cotton shirt from the waistband of her jeans and slipped his hand inside to touch the warm, hidden pleasures of her silken skin. With scarcely a pause, he traced the planes of her stomach and breached the security of her lacy bra, to cover and cup the round firmness of her breast in his palm.

Emma's sigh was one of acceptance and of alert. Her breathing came more quickly against his lips. She placed her hand on his arm, but didn't move to stop him. His thumb circled the peaked tip of her breast, and she made a soft, low sound of arousal. And then, again, he felt the seductive slow dance of her tongue against his, the rising fire of a raging passion.

This was getting beyond his control, Alec realized. He had initiated the kiss to prove a point and to satisfy his exasperation with Emma's stubborn behavior. But he wasn't at all sure he'd proved anything, and he'd certainly created more needs than he had satisfied. And the upper hand? He wasn't fool enough to think he'd won *that*.

But he didn't want Emma to think that she had won, either. It would have to be a draw, a tie, an unfinished hand, and they each should leave the table with their own particular illusions.

And with new awareness, he thought as he raised his head and let himself down in the shadowed, secret depths of her steady gaze. "Are you satisfied?" he asked softly.

"Are you?"

"Give me your hand and I'll show you how dissatisfied I am at the moment."

She blushed, deeply and with utter grace. "That isn't what I meant. You intended to teach me a lesson. I wondered if you thought you had."

His lips curved lazily. "Well, you are lying on the bed, off of your feet. And I haven't heard a complaint for the past five minutes. I think it's safe to say I achieved my objective.''

Emma's smile made him think twice about being overconfident. "You, Mr. Sayre, are a master of bluff. But I am a gambler's daughter. Don't expect me to fold and throw in my cards in the first round of play. The moment you get off this bed, I'm out of it.''

"What if I stay here for days?''

"You'll be very lonely, because one way or another, I'm going to run my own business.''

He shook his head. "You're a stubborn woman, Emma. Luckily for your ankle, however, I am the most stubborn person ever born. Just ask my mother.''

"Uh-huh.'' From the doorway, Harry cleared his throat. "I hate to barge in like this, but I'm afraid there's a slight problem in the chapel.''

Emma jerked into as straight a sitting position as she could with Alec straddling her. "What's wrong?''

"I'll handle this.'' Alec levered up and off the bed. "Don't worry about a thing.''

Harry ran a finger under his clerical collar. "There's a couple out there who want to be married in the buff.''

"Naked, you mean?'' Emma asked.

"As the day they were born,'' Harry confirmed. "And that's not the worst of it.''

"They're already *un*dressed for the occasion?'' Alec suggested.

"They had clothes on when I left 'em in the chapel.'' Harry glanced nervously over his shoulder, as if he were afraid of seeing two nudists in their natural state. "What are we going to do, Em?''

"Well, Harry, if they want to get married in the nude, I suppose we can deal with that."

"Harry and I will deal with it, Emma." Alec took a step toward the door. "You stay put."

"Actually," Harry clarified, "they want everyone to be nude, right down to the piano player."

"That's it, Emma," Alec said. "It's time you got out of bed."

Chapter Six

"Have I ever told you I have a low tolerance level when it comes to weddings?" Alec whispered to Emma over the ukelele twang of "Blue Hawaii," as played for the bride by the groom.

"Shh. You don't want to get picked up by the Camcorder." She shifted her foot on the pillow, prompting Alec to make an adjustment in the positioning of the chair that held the pillow and her foot.

"Better?" he asked.

"Fine," she mouthed, wanting to keep distractions to a minimum. Marrying two people who insisted on "baring" soul and body for the ceremony was not without its charm. True, Emma had lied through her teeth when she invented a city ordinance prohibiting a justice of the peace from performing a wedding ceremony in the nude. Alec had supported her by saying that business owners were also prohibited from public nudity within the city limits. It was a little-known law in Las Vegas, he'd added for authenticity.

Emma improvised a curtain, which Alec and Harry hastily rigged, to shield the couple's exposed charms from any less open-minded individuals who chanced to walk into the chapel. Sanchee came up with the floral arrangements, a bouquet of thornless daisies for the bride, a boutonniere attached to a spare clerical collar for the groom. Alec thought the boutonniere should have been worn much lower than the neck, but Emma's dimple flashed in disapproval at the comment and he didn't share his suggestion with the groom.

"I hope they brought plenty of sunscreen with them," Alec commented after the newlyweds had departed, fully clothed and with a videotape of their very own nudie musical wedding. "Did you notice how pale they were?"

"I tried not to let my gaze drop below the neck." Emma entered the couples' names into a ledger. "I though the ukelele was a nice touch."

"Frankly, I found it a little difficult to enjoy the music for wondering if he was going to get splinters in his navel." Alec settled into a chair across the aisle from Emma and propped his feet beside her cushioned ankle. "So, now that the excitement is over, what do we do for entertainment?"

Amusement tipped the corners of her mouth. "We get ready for the next wedding."

Alec, manfully, managed a smile.

"Do you, Walter, take this woman, Torchie, to be your lawful, wedded wife?" Harry turned the sixty-four-thousand-dollar question to the bespectacled and nervous groom, whose Adam's apple bobbed up and down in obvious distress. "Say, 'I do,'" Harry prompted in a whisper.

Walter took one look at the buxom redhead beside him and fainted dead away, collapsing into the watchful arms of Alec, the best man.

"DON'T ANYBODY MOVE!" Halfway through the ceremony, the bride, a petite brunette, threw her arms out to her sides, bouquet in hand, in a warning gesture to the rest of the bridal party. "I've lost my contact."

Alec moved from his seat beside Emma to take command. "Contact lens," he said. "Clear or colored?"

"Clear."

Of course. He figured the lens had fallen according to Murphy's Law, which meant it was nestled somewhere amidst the thousands of shiny sequins and shimmers on her white bridal gown.

"Stand still," he instructed the bride and caught, from the corner of his eye, a glimpse of Emma's laughing smile... a smile that she quickly, and astutely, hid behind one hand.

"Maybe, you should check the dress, Alec," Emma suggested from her supervisory position in the front row.

He returned her smile with tight-lipped patience. "I'll do that," he said, and bent close to the bride's bodice.

"Hey! That's my wife! Don't be looking down her dress!" The groom popped Alec in the jaw. It was a light punch, as punches go, and there was never any danger of losing teeth over it—a positive note that did very little to evoke Alec's sense of humor.

"Oh, wait," the bride intervened just as Alec regained his bearings. "I found the contact. It was in my eye all the time." She giggled. "Now we can go on with the wedding."

Alec rubbed his jaw and wondered how he'd wandered into this Twilight Zone of bridal bliss. It seemed like days rather than mere hours since he and Emma had parachuted from the plane. It seemed like a lifetime since he'd branded Emma as his fiancée and consequently forsaken his vow to avoid weddings, and the accoutrements thereof, at all costs. At the moment he regretted that particular decision with all the fervor of an aching jaw.

"Alec? Are you all right?"

He turned to tell Emma he'd had enough, he was through with weddings, whether in full regalia or birthday suit. But with one look at her expression, wide-eyed and concerned, his regret faded. It vanished altogether with one fleeting glimpse of her disarming dimple.

"I'm okay," he said, trying not to notice the soreness settling along his jawline. "Just a case of sticking out my chin at the wrong time and in the wrong place." He looked at the groom, who still stood in fighting stance with fist clenched. "Take it easy, fella. I was only trying to help."

"If you'll take your places . . . ?" Harry, his clerical collar in full display, tapped the young man on the shoulder. "Where was I, son?"

And from there it was but a hop, skip, and two "I do's" to congratulations, an embarrassed apology from the groom, and a special send-off from the Golden Glow—a shower of birdseed. Alec returned to the chapel and sank onto the seat beside Emma. He slumped in the chair, laid his head back and closed his eyes. He smelled the soft, fresh scent of her hair a second before he felt the sweet apology of her lips against his jaw.

"I'm really sorry about that," she said. "People sometimes get so nervous they do really stupid things. Do you want me to get an ice pack?"

Alec opened his eyes. "Your kiss seems to have amazing healing powers," he said. He reached up and ran a fingertip across his lips. "You know, I believe he hit my mouth, too. My lips are really beginning to ache."

"You may have a concussion," Emma said.

"Brain fever," Alec concurred. "Brought on by unhealthy exposure to too many—" he shuddered "—w-w-w-ed-d-d-dings."

"It was your idea to stay around and help out."

"Don't remind me." He rubbed his jaw. "I'll probably have nightmares for years. Honestly, Emma, do you like this business? All the goo-goo eyes and slack jaws? All the crazy, ukelele-playing nonsense?"

"This hasn't exactly been a typical day, Alec. And honestly, I do love it. Ever since I was a little girl and stayed here with Harry while Julian played the strip, I've loved the excitement and the sense of new beginnings that a wedding brings. I used to sit over there by the piano and watch the brides. I thought each one looked so pretty. Now I realize they were simply happy and in love."

"Or thought they were at the moment," Alec said. "Marriage has a way of ruining the illusion."

"Maybe so, but the part I get to see is the hope and promise of the beginning. And I like that." Emma pulled her hair away from her face with a sweeping gesture and Alec watched as it swayed back into place in a lustrous, burnished gold shower. "I also like to think the couples married in the Golden Glow Wedding Chapel beat the odds."

"Funny, I had the idea you weren't much of a gambler."

She smiled, easily winning a bit of his heart. "Actually, buying this chapel was the biggest risk I've ever taken. And these happy, crazy couples are paying my mortgage. God bless them all, even the naked ukelele player and his blushing bride."

"I didn't notice her blushing."

"That's because you were looking below her neck."

He grinned and closed his eyes again. "No, that was the fully dressed bride. The one whose husband tried to break my jaw. You know, I should be getting hazardous duty pay for this."

"You forget, Alec, this is volunteer work. You're not getting paid at all."

"You were right. I must have a concussion."

"It's the only explanation. Why else would you be spending so much of your time helping poor, unsuspecting bridegrooms jump over the edge of the matrimonial cliff?"

"I've been asking myself that same question, and I can only come up with one answer."

She looked at him expectantly.

"I'm a martyr, willing to sacrifice myself for the cause."

"And what cause would that be?"

"The Wedding of Your Dreams contest, of course."

"That would be the contest you want to cancel altogether, wouldn't it?"

"Did I say that?" he asked calmly. "I must have been talking out of my head. A result of the concussion, probably."

Emma nudged the pillow, pushing his feet off the chair. "Sorry," she said. "My ankle's acting strangely. A result of skydiving, probably."

"It was a gopher hole."

"Oh," Emma said, and looked over her shoulder. "I wonder what's keeping Harry."

"I DO," Randy, the groom, said eagerly, with eyes only for his bride. "I do. I really do."

"Not yet, son," Harry whispered. "Wait till I cue you."

"I do, too," Brandie, the bride, sighed, her gaze locked with her lover's.

Emma exchanged a look with Harry, who shrugged and skipped to the end. "By the power vested in me by the State of Nevada, I pronounce you husband and wife." Finishing his lines with the speed of an auctioneer, Harry stepped aside as Randy swept Brandie into as enthusiastic an embrace as her pregnant belly would allow.

"And another one bites the dust," Alec commented from his observation post behind Emma.

"Whew!" Harry stepped from the dais and began doing a few neck stretches. "I wasn't sure I was going to get those two married in time. She looks like she's about to give birth any second."

"To quintuplets." Alec moved into the aisle and prepared to do the closing ceremony—the presentation of the marriage certificate folder and the subsequent departure of the newly wedded. After three days of helping out at the chapel, he had the routine down pat. He did his best to pump sincerity into the weary congratulations already halfway out of his mouth. But before he could get his lips around the word, the bride slipped from her new husband's arms and crumpled to the floor, holding her stomach.

"Oh," she moaned. "Oh, Randy!"

The groom knelt beside her and took her hand. A tender scene, Alec thought, but not very practical. "Call 9-1-1," he snapped over his shoulder. "Tell them we have a woman in labor."

"She's overdue," Randy said, as if that explanation were necessary. "We wanted to get married before the baby came."

"And you made it right under the wire." Alec did his best to make the bride more comfortable, although he didn't have the faintest idea what should be done. "Did the pains just start?" he asked, for lack of a better question.

"I've been having cramps for days, but I thought it was false labor. This is my first baby, you know, and even though it's past my due date, I didn't want to go to the hospital and get sent home. And Randy and I, well, it seemed like a good idea to get married before we became parents."

"A good idea," Alec agreed, although he wondered why it hadn't occurred to them before the nine-month deadline.

"Ohh-hh." She clutched her stomach and squinted up at Randy, who was looking deathly pale. She turned to Alec. "I think this is really it. Do you know how to deliver a baby?"

Alec patted the hand that clung to his like a lifeline. "Oh, there's plenty of time. First babies always take hours to be born." Please, God, he thought, let that be true. "The paramedics will be here any minute." He glanced at Emma, hoping for a helpful suggestion or at least some clue that she knew what to do. She picked up a seat cushion from one of the chairs next to her and tossed it onto the dais. Alec caught the cushion and pillowed it beneath Brandie's long, dark hair.

"Thank...yoo-ooh-hh-hhh!" A contraction crumbled the word, and her grip on Alec's hand became a vise he couldn't have escaped if he'd tried.

"We're going to have a baby," Randy said in a voice chock-full of amazement. Then he let out a low moan. "Ohh-hhh! I don't feel so good."

Alec looked over just as Randy's eyes rolled and he fainted, collapsing with a hollow thud on the carpeted floor.

Brandie turned her head to see her groom sprawled unconscious beside her. "He must be having sympathy pains."

Alec hoped the man was in pain. How could he pass out at a time like this? His baby was about to be born, for Pete's sake. No, wait. Alec grimaced. Not yet. The baby wouldn't be born for hours yet. In a hospital. With trained professionals who knew what to do and when to do it. The father would be awake by then and Alec would have no further part in this blessed event. Please, let it happen that way, he thought. Somewhere else. Not here. Not now.

Brandie cried out again and Alec focused all of his energy on holding her hand, giving her strength, doing something to help. "Harry called for an ambulance." Emma knelt beside him and laid a damp rag on the young woman's forehead. "It'll be here any minute."

Alec's relief at Emma's nearness was tangible. "Good," he said, and they exchanged a silent communication of hope that any minute wouldn't be too late. "Be careful of your ankle," he said. "I can't handle another patient."

"It's fine," she assured him.

Harry walked up, dumped a set of sheets on the floor, and observed the scene for the length of the next contraction. "We may have to deliver the kid ourselves. It won't be the first time I've had to play midwife."

"You've done this before?" Emma asked in a tone of measurable relief.

"I've helped deliver dozens of puppies and kittens. How hard can one baby be?"

Emma looked at Alec. He looked at her. "I'll go see what's keeping the paramedics," he said.

He'd hardly reached the gauzy curtains at the chapel entrance when he heard the ambulance wail. Within seconds, help had arrived in the form of two uniform-clad paramedics. Calm descended on the Golden Glow, despite the chaotic activity it took to get the new bride and mom-to-be onto a stretcher and out the door. The comatose groom came wide awake the moment the professionals pronounced everything under control. "Hey, thanks," he said to Alec and Emma as he followed the stretcher outside. "We couldn't have done it without you."

"Do you think they'll name the baby after me?" Alec asked as the ambulance pulled away from the curb.

"No." Emma balanced on her good foot and the crutch Alec had bought for her to use. "They don't know your name, Alec. Besides, it could be a girl."

"Then they should name it after you." He raked his hand through his hair, feeling as drained as if he, himself, were having a baby.

"Another kind of new beginning," Emma said softly as the ambulance disappeared into traffic. "Just think, Alec. We came very close to witnessing the birth of a new life. Isn't that exciting?''

He took one look at her face and felt something wonderful and frightening stir inside him.

"YOU'RE GETTING pretty efficient with that crutch." Alec sat on the altar and braced himself with his hands. "You should enter the peg-leg olympics."

Emma hobbled up the aisle as Harry turned an arpeggio into "Peg O' My Heart." Harry never missed a chance to audition for Alec. During the past few days, the old piano had been beaten nearly to death in between weddings. Luckily, there had been little time during Alec's week-long tenure as her employee. Emma preferred to contribute the increase in business to the promos being run for the Wedding of Your Dreams contest, but she knew some of it was a direct result of the misleading newspaper photo of her and Alec. Even the retraction printed later had only served to put the Golden Glow Wedding Chapel in the newspaper again. Free publicity. Worth its weight in gold.

"I'll have you know I can swing this baby, too." She balanced on her good foot before she swung the crutch in a loose circle to demonstrate. "I can activate a lazy employee at, say, three feet or less."

"But you could never catch him, Emma. Harry and I can both outrun you, although we would never do that." He reached out and grabbed the end of her crutch and she had to reset her equilibrium accordingly. "We'd trip you first."

"You could try." She tugged on her end of the crutch.

He held fast. "If I trip you, Emma, you'll fall."

Nothing changed in his tone of voice. It remained teasing and mellow. The corners of his mouth held the same good-humored smile. But his eyes... Something changed there, something that reached out to touch her, something that ruffled her easy acceptance of his presence in her wedding chapel.

"Peg O' My Heart" gave way to a slow-moving and sappy version of "When I Fall in Love." Alec's smile deepened, became more assured and infinitely more seductive. Her heart skipped a beat before she scolded it into steady submission. He was playing with her, nothing more, nothing less. And she was an idiot to waste a heartbeat on him.

"Harry," she said without allowing her gaze to stray from Alec's, "I'm tired of romantic melodies. Play something else."

"Name your poison." Harry ran a series of scales up and down the keyboard. "Any song, any key."

"How about 'Frankie and Johnny'?" Alec suggested smoothly.

"'Mack the Knife,'" Emma countered.

The scales metamorphosed into minor chords and progressed to Rachmaninoff. With a grin, Alec released his hold on the crutch and on Emma. "This is my last day as indentured servant, Emma," he said over the crashing waves of the music. "I've got to get back to the real world before all these 'new beginnings' warp my cynical nature."

Despite her best resolve, she was disappointed...and determined not to show it. "Thanks for your help," she said. "Don't let the door hit you on your way out."

He clucked his tongue. "Is that any way to treat a good samaritan?"

"You're only covering your rear, Mr. Samaritan. Making sure the contest takes place without a hitch."

"Actually, I'm hoping for a hundred hitches, otherwise we've done some false advertising."

"Hello?"

"Anyone here?"

Two tremulous voices preceded the timid entrance of an elderly couple. Emma turned, regretting that she'd abandoned her post at the front desk, even though it was after ten and business had been unusually slow all evening. The music switched from Rachmaninoff to romantic, minor to lilting major, with hardly a break. Alec pushed to his feet and smoothed the creases from his slacks.

"May I help you?" Emma positioned her crutch under her arm and made her way to the back of the chapel. "Do you want to get married?"

The lavender-haired, sweet-faced old woman nodded. Her partner, a gravel-voiced, George Burns lookalike, glanced over his shoulder. "Yes, and make it fast."

Emma resisted the impulse to share a quick, almost irrepressible grin of amusement with Alec. "Do you have the license?"

Their expressions fell in simultaneous dismay. "License," the man repeated. "I didn't think of that."

The woman clutched his sleeve. "They'll be here any minute."

"I know." He patted her hand. "Now, don't worry, Lizzie. Can we get one here?" he asked Emma.

"I'm sorry, but you have to go to the courthouse for that. We can't issue a license."

"It's over, Pete." Lizzie's lower lip trembled. "They've won."

"It ain't over till it's over." His sharp gaze pulled Emma to attention. "We want to get married tonight. We haven't got time to waste. We got cash money. Two hundred dollars, and it's all yours if you help us."

Emma wished she hadn't already sent Dan home for the night. "I let our driver leave early," she explained. "Otherwise, he could drive you to the courthouse and bring you back here for the ceremony. All in all, it only takes a little over an hour."

Pete took Lizzie's hand in his and offered her a regret-filled smile. "That's about an hour more than we have."

Lizzie turned sad, pleading eyes on Emma. "You see, our children don't want us to get married. They say we're senile and silly. My son is going to move me into another nursing home, away from Pete. We've just got to stop them from separating us."

"Do they know you're here?" Alec came up behind Emma.

Lizzie looked down. Pete coughed. "We ran away from the nursing home," he admitted with a tinge of embarrassment. "I thought we'd have a couple of hours' lead time, but Lizzie saw her son's car outside the first wedding chapel we came to, so they're on to us."

"It's that snippy old woman next door." Lizzie's chin quivered with new defiance. "I told you she was eavesdropping, Pete. Remember? I said, that snoopy Marie Upjohn is spying on us. I bet she ratted to the night nurse the minute we snuck out the window."

"Now, Lizzie. That isn't important now. We've got to figure out a way to get our hands on a marriage license without getting caught."

"Come on. I'll drive the limo." Alec assumed command. "Harry, you come along and perform the ceremony. Emma, you and I will be the witnesses. Let's go before Lizzie's son decides to drop in on us."

"You mean, we can get married?" Lizzie asked. "Now?"

"We're going to give it our best shot," Alec declared, motioning Harry to hurry. "Let's go out the back, just in case."

"Just in case this isn't a good idea?" Emma caught his sleeve on his way out the door a moment later and held him back. "Alec, I don't know if we should be doing this. I could get sued for this kind of thing."

"You could get sued for refusing to do it, too. Take the risk, Emma. You're the romantic. How can you send Pete and Lizzie back to the nursing home without giving them a chance for this last shot at living? What possible harm could it do to try and help them?"

She could think of a great many possibilities. "I'm just afraid we're rushing into a situation we know little about."

He tapped her chin with his finger. "Be daring. Be brave. Rush in where angels fear to tread." His smile was quick and devastatingly persuasive. "We'll get Harry to sing 'Fools Rush In' on the way to the courthouse. Now, lock up and let's get out of here."

With misgivings, Emma complied and in less than five minutes they were careening through traffic at a healthy clip. "Do you have an operator's license?" she asked Alec through the open partition between the front and rear of the limousine.

"What a foolish question."

She felt foolish when she looked across the seat at Pete and Lizzie's anxiously hopeful faces and wondered what the next forty years would hold for her. Not Alec, of course. He would be out of her life in a matter of weeks. The contest would end. Their engagement would be forgotten and she would become someone whose name he barely recalled. Chances were she would forget all about him, too.

Pete whispered something to Lizzie, who giggled like a schoolgirl.

Emma sighed. Chances were she would remember Alec Sayre for many years after she was older than either Pete or Lizzie. She was totally, completely, in lust with the man. With any luck at all, she'd get through the contest without falling into bed with him and with her pride still intact. Not that the experience wouldn't be worth a small sacrifice of pride, but Alec was the wrong kind of guy for a relationship, and she was the wrong kind of gal for a one-night stand. And there was no reason to fool herself into thinking otherwise.

Alec parked the limousine and opened the door with a flourish. "All right, young lovers, into the courthouse. Let's get that license and get out of here."

The deed was done quicker than Harry could do a complete set of facial exercises. Alec held the door as a triumphant Lizzie settled in. "We got it," she said. "And we didn't even have to give our ages."

"They didn't even ask why we had the same address, neither." Pete stepped inside with a big grin. "We're set now, Rever—"

"Hey! You, there! Stop!" A man's voice came from across the street and Emma looked out the window to find the source.

Lizzie's hand flew to her mouth. "It's my son. He's found us."

Alec slammed the car door and jumped behind the wheel. He was entering traffic before Emma could suggest that perhaps they should confront the man and, at least, listen to his side of the story. "Harry," Alec directed over his shoulder, "get on with it. The guy's going to be on our bumper in about three seconds."

"Oh, my," Lizzie said.

"Make it short and sweet." Pete grabbed Lizzie's hand as he gave the license to Harry.

One glance at the document and Harry snapped on his collar. "Do you, Elizabeth, take this man to be your lawful, wedded husband?"

"I do." The limo picked up speed and Lizzie cast a nervous glance out the darkened window.

"Do you, Peter, take Elizabeth to be your lawful, wedded wife?"

A flash of whirling red glanced off the rearview mirror and into the backseat.

"I do."

The wail of a siren clipped the night.

"Is the deed done?" Alec asked. "They're bringing in the big guys."

Emma rubbed her forehead as Harry rushed his final lines.

"I now pronounce you man and wife." He closed his Bible and looked at the excitement outside the window. "And," he said softly, "what God hath joined together, let no man put asunder. Amen. Kiss her, for Pete's sake. Alec, you'd better pull over. Here, Emma, sign this."

She witnessed the license, handed it back to Harry, and looked up in time to see a burly officer tap on the driver's side window. "Don't open your door," Alec growled over his shoulder as he pushed the button that controlled his window. "Is there something wrong, Officer?" he asked.

"You got a license to operate this vehicle?"

"I have my driver's license right here." Alec reached into his back pocket.

Emma knew what was coming next, and she was torn between wanting to stop it and hoping she was wrong.

"This is not a license to operate this limousine, Mr. Sayre. Would you step out of the car, please?"

"He's the one," a familiar voice said. "He's the one who aided and abetted the nursing home runaways."

"He makes it sound like we're Bonnie and Clyde," Pete said.

"My son," Lizzie said apologetically. "He's forty and thinks he knows everything."

"Mother? Are you in there?" A man with Lizzie's nice blue eyes opened the limousine door and looked inside.

"We're married," Pete announced proudly.

"To each other," Lizzie added with a sweet smile.

"Mother, what are you doing?" Her son leaned in the open door. "That idiot driver could have killed you."

"He did us a favor."

"I'm sure he'll be justly rewarded. Now, both of you come with me. It's time we talked about the practicalities of this... marriage."

"We're not getting a divorce." Lizzie ignored her son's proffered hand and climbed out of the limo on her own. "I am not senile, addle-minded or too old to know when I'm in love. So, don't think you can change my mind. And if you don't stop badgering me, I'll write you out of my will."

"Thank you." Pete shook Harry's hand and gave Emma a peck on the cheek as he pressed a roll of bills into her hand. "You made this a night we'll never forget." He nodded toward Alec, who was still leaning against the hood of the limo, talking to the policeman. "And there's a little extra there—a tip for the driver. Tell him whatever happens, I appreciate what he did."

Whatever happens? Emma thought. She spun around to get a good look at Alec and heard the officer's voice as clear as a bell. "I'm sorry, Mr. Sayre, but I'm going to have to take you downtown. You may have to spend the rest of the night in jail."

Chapter Seven

Emma scrambled out of the limo, nearly forgetting to favor her ankle. "Officer? Excuse me, Officer?"

The policeman, a beefy, flat-nosed fellow, turned.

"Officer, I demand to know why you're arresting this man."

His shaggy brows drew together in a frown. "Who are you?"

"I'm, uh, the owner of the limo."

"Have you got a license to drive it?"

"Well, no, but Harry does."

"Is he here?"

"He's inside."

"If he has an operator's license, why wasn't he driving?"

Emma tried to look around the officer's burly form to see Alec. "Because he had to perform a, uh, marriage ceremony."

The officer nodded and squinted at the darkened windows of the limousine. "And Harry's in there now?"

"Yes."

With a second nod, the policeman sauntered over to the rear door and poked his head through the opening. "Harry, you old geezer, what are you doing mixed up in a kidnapping?" The limo bucked and settled as the officer climbed inside.

Emma limped to Alec's side and leaned against the car. "Kidnapping?"

Alec shrugged. "When I'm making car tags in prison, can I count on you to provide the cakes with hacksaws?"

Her eyes widened. "You were only driving the car."

"The *getaway* car."

"Without a proper license, I know." She looked across the street to where Lizzie and Pete were standing with her son. His arms were crossed and his head bent as he listened. "I hope he lets them stay married."

"I hope he lets us go home. Stan, the policeman, says the guy is really mad and wants to press charges against us for aiding and abetting."

"That's ridiculous."

"Hmm." Alec reached over and tucked a strand of shining hair behind her ear, letting his fingertips linger against the downy softness of her hairline, wondering at the shiver of pleasure he felt at the contact. "Maybe they'll let the two of us share a jail cell."

"I am not going to jail and neither are you. And if they try it, I'll scream 'false arrest' all the way to the supreme court."

"It's nice to know you're on my side, champ." He touched her indignant dimple with a fingertip that then moved to her lips in an unerring and sensual path. He traced the outline of her mouth slowly and felt her give the slightest tremble beneath his touch. "Just promise me you won't pull any body slams on poor

Stan. He used to wrestle some in college, but he's no match for a professional like you."

Her breathing came more quickly as she drew away from his touch, and the dimple deepened with a frown. "No promises." Her voice began with a betraying quiver, but she steadied it and went on. "If you take the fall for this, I'm going down with you."

Alec laughed easily, enjoying the thought that his touch evoked a response she couldn't hide. It was there, in her eyes, in the moist, self-conscious tilt of her lips, in the provocative flash of that damned dimple. He savored the moment, being here with Emma in the midst of the glittering, noisy chaos that was Las Vegas after dark, delighting in her company, wanting to touch her lips again, wanting to kiss her, wanting so much more. "Where have you been all my life, Emma?"

"Trying to stay away from men like you, that's where. 'Come on,' you said, 'I'll drive the limo.' And against my better judgment, I went along. And look at us now. Standing on the street, highlighted by an official strobe light, and waiting to be arrested."

"Aren't you having fun?"

She looked at him, and he decided to go for broke and kiss her—right here, right now—under the flash of the red light and the eyes of a thousand passing strangers. He leaned toward her slowly, making her aware of his intent, giving her time to pull away, knowing she wouldn't even if she could. And then he took her lips in a kiss that lasted only a moment, a kiss that was more casual than he liked, but that he knew conveyed more than a dash of desire.

She responded with surprise and unmistakable interest in the few seconds before she remembered to disallow his impulsive move. "Be careful," she said as she drew back. "You'll get us arrested for public display of affection."

"We're already up for kidnapping, as well as aiding and abetting a couple of runaways. If we're going to get an additional charge, I think we may as well go for indecent exposure." He reached for her again. "Something worth doing time for."

"Alec!" She sidled out of range. "This won't be so funny when we're behind iron bars."

"This is an adventure, Emma, and more fun than you've had since the night you decided to impersonate my fiancée."

Her chin came up. "What about the night you kidnapped me and pretended to be *my* fiancé?"

"See how much fun you have when you take a few risks?" He smiled and, after an indecisive moment, won the reward of her smile in return.

"You're a dangerous man, Alec."

"Don't kid yourself. You're the dangerous one. You, with your innocent eyes. And that stubborn chin with its sassy little dimple. And the kind of mouth that makes a man dream of kissing it, again and again and again." He paused, drinking in her stillness, the quiet shimmer of uncertainty in her eyes. "You are very dangerous, Emma, and altogether too tempting. If I had one ounce of good sense left, I'd get myself arrested here and now and spend the next couple of years behind bars, until you're safely married to the man of your dreams."

She met his gaze and then, too quickly, looked away. But he heard the long, shaky breath she drew before she managed to get her chin back up to challenge level. "I guess that means we won't be sharing a jail cell, after all."

He couldn't resist her slender smile. "You *are* a dangerous woman, Emma. I think you should stay away from me."

She looked at him from beneath a sweep of feathery lashes. "Do me a favor. Once we're in jail, don't tell me about any escape plans you may make."

He grinned. "I'll let you rot in prison."

"I'd appreciate that."

"BUT SHE'S MY MOTHER!" Stephen Fites, occasionally referred to as "Buster," was beginning to sound like a broken record and a warped one at that. "I have every legal right to demand that the people responsible for this . . . this ridiculous marriage should be suitably penalized."

Sergeant Thomas drew a handkerchief from his pocket and blew his nose. He stuffed the cloth back into his pocket and clasped his hands on top of a ten-inch stack of paperwork on his cluttered desk. "What do you want me to do? Take away their birthdays? Ms. Cates, here, and her people get paid to conduct weddings. Your folks asked for a wedding and that's what they got. A wedding. As far as I can see, son, you haven't got a legal leg to stand on. Now, go. All of you. Get out of here."

"I will see you tomorrow, Mother, at the nursing home." Fites stalked out without saying goodbye to anyone. Emma thought he was very rude and a bad sport into the bargain.

"Hey, Sayre?" Thomas stopped Alec at the door. "Get a chauffeur's license or drive your own car."

Alec tipped the sergeant a salute and took Emma's elbow. "Let's go before they decide to book us for contributing to the delinquency of our elders."

"What a night." Emma limped through the doorway of the police station and paused outside to get her balance. Lizzie and Pete were huddled together on the sidewalk. Harry lingered to finish a conversation with Officer Stan. "Alec?" Emma pulled him close enough so that she could reach his ear and whisper in it. "What are we going to do about Lizzie and Pete? We can't leave them here. They just got married."

"I can take them out to the nursing home."

"Not without a chauffeur's license, you can't. Besides, don't you think it would be nicer if they could go somewhere else? One night at Tuxedo Junction, maybe?"

"And to think I accused you of not being romantic." Ready to lend a helping hand if needed, he walked beside her as she limped toward the waiting limo. "I'll give them the suite I use at the hotel."

"And where will you stay?"

"With you."

She gave a slight start before she met his innocent look with an arch of her brow. "You forget, I'm a dangerous woman."

"Now, who told you that?"

"A dangerous man."

"You shouldn't believe everything you hear." He looked at Pete and Lizzie, who were holding hands and staring into one another's eyes like the newlyweds they were. "I know several places where I can get a bed for the night. Don't worry about me."

"I am not worried. I just wondered, that's all." A slow warmth crept into her face. "Frankly, I don't care where you sleep."

"Good, that opens up all sorts of possibilities." He left her to approach the newlyweds with outstretched hands and an offer they couldn't refuse.

"Tuxedo Junction," Lizzie said in a whisper. "Oh, my, I can play the slot machines."

Pete nodded with satisfaction. "And I can watch the women."

Lizzie elbowed him and he kissed her on the cheek. With a round of thank-you's and several excited "I can't believe this," Pete and Lizzie got back into the limousine and Harry took control of the driver's seat. Emma started to join the two older people inside, but Alec grabbed her elbow and held her back as he slammed the door. "That's it, Harry. Drop the happy couple at the hotel and take a turn at the piano in the lounge. Talk to Bruno. Tell him I said it was okay."

"You mean it?" Harry slapped his palm against the car door, his grin growing as wide as a boy with a brand new BB gun. "Thanks, Alec. You won't regret this." And with that, the limo turned on a dime and sped away like a sports car fresh off the lot.

Emma cleared her throat. "Excuse me, but I believe you're standing on my toes."

Alec stepped back quickly and looked down at his feet, which were in no position to threaten hers. "I am not."

"My mistake," she said tightly. "But I was sure I heard you tell *my* limo driver to take *my* limo and drive off without *me*."

"I'll make sure you get home safely." Confidence straddled the charming tilt of his lips. Mischief sparkled in the deep, dreamy blue of his eyes. "I have a plan" was written all over his face.

"Did it even once occur to you to ask if you could take me home?"

"If I had thought to ask, you'd only have argued, so I saved us both the time and aggravation."

She shook her head and wished she had brought along her crutch so she'd have something to swing at him. "I'm going inside and call a cab."

"I'll go with you."

"Why don't you make the call for me?" Annoyance was becoming anger. He was maddening, so much like Julian. Always one step ahead of her, always so infuriatingly sure that his plan was superior to hers. "But that would be too simple. You're such a hero, tonight. Why don't you just pick me up and carry me home?"

He stood very still. Only the tightening of his jaw and the hard pulse in his neck revealed his tenuous grip on control. "As you wish."

He moved faster than her instinctive protest and pulled her roughly up and into his arms, sending a wave of excitement rolling through her, stealing the sting from her anger and leaving her breathlessly aware of him. She clasped her hands around his neck and told herself, quite sternly, this was not the time to bury her face in his shoulder and fly the flags of surrender.

"And if I were you," he continued, "I would not say 'put me down' because, sprained ankle or no, you'll hit the ground faster than an amateur wrestler up against Hulk Hogan."

She believed him. His strength was wrapped in his displeasure, and the tension vibrated through her like a flare of electrical current, sharp and stimulating. She tried to grab her retreating resentment, but it faded beneath the erratic thrumming of her pulse and his nearness engulfed her. And her anger was quickly nonexistent, replaced by a deliciously wicked spark that tickled her skin like pinpricks.

She didn't want to feel attraction. She didn't want to recognize the awareness that flicked at her every thought, chipping away any lingering indignance, leaving behind an undignified and stirring ache. She didn't want to want this man.... But she did, against all the arguments of her better judgment. And as he strode into the street with her in his arms, every footstep jostled her, titillated her senses, and made her tantalizingly aware of his muscular and manly form. He stopped halfway across and shifted her weight as if she were a troublesome bag of laundry.

Emma waited for him to move on and when he didn't, she looked him full in the face. "What are you doing?" she asked. "We could get killed, standing in the middle of the street like this."

"You forget. I'm a hero tonight." His smile was of the thin variety. "I can stop cars with my bare hands."

He flagged down a taxi and, somehow, managed not to drop her in the process. He had the door open and her in the backseat before she could think of a suitable and succinct protest. As he climbed in beside her, he pulled the door shut and looked at her expectantly. "Tell him where you want to go, Emma. I wouldn't presume to suggest a destination."

"You make me angry," she said.

"And you graciously return the favor." He turned toward the window.

"Hey, excuse me, but I ain't got all night." The taxi driver looked at them in the rearview mirror. "You got someplace you want to go? You tell me and I take you there. Otherwise, I got places to be and fares to get."

Emma glanced at Alec, but his attention was directed out the window. With a sigh, she gave the driver her home address and settled back in the seat, scooting further away from the strong, silent hero beside her. "You could have asked," she said stiffly some long minutes later.

He turned an enigmatic blue gaze to her. "Asked what?"

"If you could take me home." It sounded petty even to her, but she lifted her chin as if she hadn't noticed.

"We got engaged the first time we met, Emma. I just assumed we were past the point of 'Please, may I see you to your door?'"

She folded her arms and wished she hadn't started this. "We're not engaged and we're not past the point of common courtesy."

"We are, however, past the point of rational discussion, and there is only one way for this to end."

"I'm glad you finally see it my wa—"

He smothered her words with his mouth, jerking her across the imaginary dividing line and into his arms. Her heart stopped, then slammed against her chest in a frenzied rush of adrenaline. His lips held firm, giving her no room to breathe deeply and restore calm. He allowed for only one response—surrender to the pressure of his lips, to the anticipation that arced like lightning from his body into hers and then fanned into dozens of burning sensations beneath her skin.

She told herself that if the night hadn't already been packed full of roller-coaster emotions, she would have struggled . . . would have done her best to cool his ardor with a professional body slam. But her body was uncooperatively pliant and so melded to the shape and pattern of his that she knew he'd already won the round. And with a TKO, too. One kiss, one taste of him, and she was on the ropes . . . and sinking fast.

He pushed open her mouth with his own as he pressed her back and down into the shadowed darkness of the rear seat. She slid under him and felt the rough friction of his clothing against hers. This was a good way to start a fire, she thought through a haze of rising, heat-filled sensations. A good, hot fire. A fire that could singe her pride and scorch her heart. She had better sense than to fan this flame—but somehow the kissing went on and she couldn't seem to make the slightest move to stop it. Instead she reveled in her own utter abandonment to his embrace, basked in his willful disregard for everything except this moment. And her.

When his hand covered her breast, she gathered her arms around his shoulders and cupped the back of his head with her hand. His hair was thick and wiry and coupled with her fingers in a sinuous tangle. Her skirt rode up on her thigh and his hand was at the hem, his fingers stroking her silk-stockinged leg in small but meaningful circles. Emma moved her hand to stop his progress and found, instead, that she simply moved with him, her hand on top of his, circling, stroking.

His lips left hers to follow a delicate path of longing along her chin, up to her ear, down to the pulsing hollows of her throat. She opened her eyes and watched the blur of lights flicker through the car windows. She had never been kissed in a taxi before and had never given the omission a thought. But there was something to be said for the sound of spinning tires mixed with the noise of her rapidly beating heart. And the danger of it...why, they might be thrown to the floor at any moment. All it would take was one good stomp on the brakes....

"Open your mouth." Alec's command against her lips spun her rambling thoughts into compliance. She traced the outline of his lips with her tongue. He kissed her with rough magic and sensual wizardry, taking her participation and turning it into a mystic and mortal desire. They were going somewhere fast. Of that much she was aware. Their premature arrival at that destination was of more concern to her. He stroked her tongue with his, teasing her, tempting her, and Emma surrendered to the seeking heat of his seductive kiss.

Alec cupped the back of her head, pressing her lips against his, holding her firmly in a position where he could taste her mouth, her chin, her throat, every sensitive place his lips could reach and all at his discretion...or lack of it. He wanted to hear her cry uncle, wanted to make her want him, wanted to kiss her until she sighed with pleasure and forgot to insist that he ask permission first. She was maddening and so tempting that he forgave her for making him mad. They had been heading for this for days now and he, for one, had every intention of playing out the hand.

But not in a public conveyance.

He withdrew slowly—teasing her with nibbling kisses, deriving satisfaction from the tiny, aching sigh that escaped her throat—somewhat nonplussed by his own accelerated pulse beat. He sat up, pulling her with him, keeping her cloaked within his arms. And he watched as her dreamy expression faded into a mysterious smile. Her lashes graced her cheek with a thick line of modesty, then lifted to reveal green eyes, darkened by the smoke of the fire he'd started and then deliberately banked.

She gave her composure, and the hem of her skirt, a couple of firm tugs. "That is no way to end an argument."

He straightened his shirt sleeves, but left his collar open and appealing. "Want to try another tactic, champ?"

"Maybe—" she drew a shaky finger across her lips "—later."

"Uh-uh-uh. Never put off until tomorrow..." His breath caressed her as he brushed her lips with a tenderly persuasive kiss. She clung to the touch, unwilling to lose the sweet craving for more.

"Hey! Romeo and Juliet!" The taxi driver's voice was a grating intrusion. "Hark, it is the lark! And you are home." He made a sweeping gesture with his hand and Emma noticed that the cab was, indeed, parked in front of her house. She felt disoriented and not at all steady. But she reached for the door handle, anyway.

"Thank you," she said, not knowing which man she addressed or why. She stepped out of the car and wobbled slightly as her injured ankle demanded attention. "I think I can make it from here."

"Is she drunk?" The driver pushed back his cap.

"Only on moonlight." Alec pulled several bills from his wallet and passed them over the seat as he climbed out of the taxi.

The driver took the money and eyed Alec suspiciously. "I don't see no moon. Moonshine, that's closer to the truth. You ain't plannin' to take advantage of her, are you?"

"Certainly not without her permission."

The man nodded and put the taxi in gear. " 'Good night, good night! Parting is such sweet sorrow, that I shall say good night till it be morrow...' " The words trailed off into the night as he drove away.

"He probably does summer stock." Emma strove for a normal tone of voice, but she met Alec's gaze and knew the flimsy, breathy quality of her words gave her away. She could feel the heavy throb of her heart and hoped he couldn't hear it in the still midnight.

"With his talent, that cabbie probably came straight to Las Vegas from Broadway."

Emma smiled and hoped he'd assist her to her door. Her door. Her house. They were alone. After midnight. Wait a minute. Had Alec simply assumed he would be invited in? "You sent the cab away."

His eyebrows drew down at the inside. "Yes. Did you want to know if he could recite *The Tempest?*"

"You don't have a way to get home."

This time the accusation in her voice was unmistakable. Alec pursed his lips. "So what's your point, Emma?"

"I was simply stating the obvious."

"No, you weren't. You were trying to start an argument."

"I wasn't."

"You were." He cupped her chin in his hand. "And furthermore, you were hoping I'd kiss you to prevent it."

She swallowed hard. "I wasn't."

He smiled as he held her gaze captive and very much aware of his intentions. He bent his head, coming so close to her lips he could feel the moisture as she ran her tongue across them in preparation for his kiss.

And then, just as he sensed her slight sway toward him, he drew back. "Sorry," he said, "I forgot to ask. Would it be all right if I kissed you?"

Her lashes swept up as a new irritation set a sharp glimmer in her eyes. "If I had two good ankles, I'd kick you in the shin."

With a throaty laugh, Alec scooped her up into his arms and carried her to the front door. "Key?" he asked.

"In my purse."

"Which is?"

"In the limo." She adjusted her grip on his neck and smiled sweetly. "For some reason, I didn't get a chance to get it. But I'm not worried. You're a hero. What's one solid-steel door with a double-bolt lock against your superhuman powers?"

He let her slide to her feet, keeping his arm positioned so that her descent was one continuous body stroke. From his upper chest to his lower torso, Emma didn't think she missed an inch. Her breathing came in soft, quick puffs, but she met his eyes and upheld her challenge. This round, she decided, went to her.

With meticulous purpose, he propped her against the wall and reached into the flowerpot hanging beside the door. Taking the key he found hidden in it, he unlocked the door and pushed it open. Then he turned to her and, with a slight bow, presented the key. "No applause, please. Your eternal gratitude is my reward."

Scratch round two. Emma sighed. "Would you settle for a cup of coffee?"

"Don't be silly."

She drank in the sight of him painted with the nightbrush of shadows and etched by the streetlight's glow. She could smell the faint scent of his cologne mingled with the fragrant desert night. His breathing was a soft, low rhythm scored by the midnight quiet. He seemed mysterious and distant and so desirable that she wanted to discover his every secret. "You don't want to come in?" she asked.

"Not for coffee."

She tipped her head to one side. "It's a long walk from here to Tuxedo Junction, and you must be tired from carrying me around." He said nothing. Emma knew the decision was hers. At least, it was in his mind. To her way of thinking, she should have realized she was a goner that first moment he'd smiled at her and called her Lucky.

"You'd better come inside, Alec. I don't think I can hop into bed without some assistance."

He crossed his arms but made no other move.

"Hop," she repeated. "You know. I can't put much weight on my ankle, so I have to hop on my good foot. Hop into bed . . . get it?"

"I know what you said, Emma. And what you meant. *And* I'm still waiting for an invitation. A simple, honest invitation."

He deserved that, she thought, but her heart skipped into a nervous rhythm. What was she supposed to say? How were these things worded? *Alec, would you like to come inside and sleep with me?* Or maybe, *Please join me in a night of unbridled passion?* Or the more forthright, *Will you make love to me?* She summoned her courage. "Alec . . . will you stay? Please?"

He stood there, arms crossed, as if considering her proposition. He did nothing to eliminate the distance between them, and the waiting chewed on her fragile nerves.

"Is that a yes or a no?" she asked.

His lips slanted in a slow and wicked smile. "Give me a minute. I'm gathering my superhuman powers. As a hero, I have a certain standard to, uh, rise to."

Emma began to tremble. "God, I hope so."

He came to her then, pulling her up and into his embrace, taking her lips with pressure and promise. Her palms came away from the stucco wall behind her, tingling with anticipation and eager to explore a new texture…a male texture. Alec's texture. His shirt was coarsely woven cotton, nubby and soft to the touch, cool against the heat of his skin and cool, too, beneath her hand. She allowed her fingers to slip across the cotton weave to the few inches of flesh above his collar. There she discovered a faint sheen of moisture mixed with the smoothness of his skin and the fine feathering of hair that bordered the back of his neck. She slipped her hand beneath the collar and around to the contours of his throat, finding a smooth and masculine softness there, as well. She stroked the back of her fingers under and along his jaw, feeling the prickly beginnings of tomorrow's beard, the very maleness of his face.

He captured her hand in his and brought it slowly to his mouth, where he kissed each fingertip in turn before pressing to her palm a light and terribly tender kiss. Emma hadn't known he could be so gallant. She hadn't known she could be so easily swayed. *Easily swayed?* Who was she kidding? She was practically prostrate at his feet, committed to carrying out the worst idea of the century, and anticipating it with a truly appalling delight.

Her smile curved, effortlessly and slow. "We'll be cooler inside the house."

"I hardly think so."

Their eyes met, held, and the air thickened with excitement and a spark of escalating desire. Her heart took up a strong and sultry rhythm and she could see the accelerated throbbing of his pulse there in the tension of his jaw. She placed her hand over the pulse point and felt a tightening response in the pit of her stomach. He snared the fingers of her other hand and drew her closer.

"Do you want me to carry you?" he asked.

"Across the threshold?" She teased him with a smile. "Wouldn't that violate your principles?"

"You forget my heroic qualities. You're a damsel in distress, and it is my sacred duty to keep you from harm."

"If that were true, you'd say a gentlemanly goodnight and leave right now."

His breath moistened the corner of her mouth in a persuasive caress. "Would you let me go, Emma?"

Not a chance. Not even if she had to perform a slide tackle to stop him. He was a risky bet. A gambler. A man who enjoyed challenge for the simple thrill of mastering it. He was the type of man she most admired and most feared. Strong and self-assured and supremely confident. She was making a sucker's bet, a fool's wager, by beginning an intimate relationship with him. Her heart clearly was at stake, possibly her fledgling independence, as well. And still, without question, if he turned now to go, she would do everything in her power to make him stay.

"Alec," she whispered, "carry me to bed."

He kissed her, stroking her lips with deliberate languor and delicate promise. There was nothing urgent in the tender pressure, no manipulation in the soft movement of his mouth across hers, no coercion in the sensual motion of his hands over her arms. There was only sweet, delicious sensation and an unspoken assurance that they had time to discover, to explore, to enjoy one another. Even in the dry, arid heat of the desert night, her skin tingled with the cool breeze of expectation. When he released her mouth and picked her up in his arms, she buried her face in his shoulder and let her senses drown in his heady scent.

Alec carried her across the threshold and balanced her carefully as he closed the door with a well-placed kick. With a single glance, he oriented himself to new surroundings and made his way down the hallway to a bedroom. A floor lamp with a decorative shade spread a thin layer of light over a room that could only belong to the woman in his arms. It was as subtle and strong as she was, pastels mixed with a slash of bright accents, a love for tradition at peace with a flair for the unconventional. This was Emma's room, and he felt immediately as if he belonged in it.

Pausing beside the bed, he waited for her to overcome the sudden bout of shyness that had kept her face pressed into his neck during the brief journey across the threshold and down the hall. He kissed the top of her head, inhaled the fragrance of her hair and wanted her so badly he ached from head to foot. "Emma?" he whispered, not wanting to disturb the moment with a voice too loud in the quiet. "Are you asleep?"

He felt her sigh. "Dreaming," she answered. "Just dreaming."

"Me, too."

She lifted her head and looked into his eyes, and he knew he *had* to be dreaming. She was beautiful, a temptress and an innocent, guileless and irresistible, and he was suddenly aware that his heartbeat rose and fell with every curve of her smile. And when her dimple came into play... Well, he hadn't known his pulse could soar so high, so fast.

She kissed him, raising his pulse rate even more, cupping his face in her hands, enticing him with a tentative and seductive sweep of her tongue across his lips. A groan began deep in his throat as he laid her carefully, quickly, on the bed before pulling back for another long look into eyes as lovely and calming as a deep forest, as mysterious and fascinating as precious emeralds, as beguiling and dangerous as a fire's flames. "Join me?" she asked.

She was inviting him into her bed.

Remarkable thought. Not that he hadn't been invited into numerous beds over the course of his adult life. Enough, in fact, that he'd refused more than a few. But nothing had prepared him for Emma. She had gotten under his skin in a way no other woman ever had, and he knew of only one way to get her out of his system. Without taking his eyes from hers, he lowered himself onto the bed beside her.

He circled her with his arms and brought his mouth eagerly to hers. Embers of his banked and smoldering desire burst to full flame and he had to consciously dampen his eagerness and allow the fire to build at a safer pace. He kissed his way to her earlobe and savored the sound of her quickly indrawn breath. A sound he matched as her hands splayed at his back, moving in sensuous circles, giving pleasure everywhere she touched. Alec found himself bewitched by the silky softness of her skin beneath his lips, the press of her body against him. He felt the tentative brush of her tongue against his teeth and a slow, sweet heat swirled and spiraled within him. With measured movements, he nudged open her lips and found a way inside. She moaned softly as he claimed her wet surrender, then surprised him by matching the probing thrusts of his tongue with her own.

When her fingers worked the buttons of his shirt and slid beneath the fabric to tangle in the wiry hair of his chest, he was caught in a surge of desire. A shaky half gasp, half moan rushed from his mouth into hers. He couldn't suppress the convulsive thrust of his hardness against the softness between her thighs and, as she met his aggression with a satisfying resistance, he swallowed her ragged sigh.

His eagerness transferred itself to her and he thought she might tear the shirt from his back. But with some assistance from him, the shirt remained unscathed when she tossed it toward the chair, from which it slid like silk to the floor. He paused, then, forcing the first flames of passion into submission, allowing time for a gentler, more reasonable ardor. With the utmost patience, and a great deal of self-discipline, he rolled to his side, bracing his upper torso with his elbow and giving himself a pleasing view of his lover.

Emma. He allowed his fingers to stroke the shiny tendrils of her hair, allowed his memory to absorb the sight of her lying dewy-eyed and breathless beside him. She was such unexpected pleasure, such soft, sweet surprise. The scent of gardenias and roses clung to her skin, fragranced the bedroom, surrounded him, filled him with a steady crescendo of longing. The shallow swells of her breathing was mesmerizing music and all he could hear, save the thud, thud, thud of his own heartbeat.

The tiniest frown creased her forehead, as if she were wondering about his thoughts, or perhaps she was wondering at her own. Alec smiled and, with a roving finger, traced a line from her chin to the hollow of her throat. There, he placed a kiss, marveling at the hummingbird pulse he felt beneath his lips.

Emma lay still, dying a little with the slow deliberation of his hand as he unbuttoned first one button on her blouse and then another. When he nuzzled the material aside and traced the lace of her bra with his tongue, her stomach knotted with the intensity of anticipation. She knew she hadn't experienced this hungry ache before. Not at any time. Not for any reason. This, then, must be passion, the perfect chemistry of male and female, desire in its purest form, the sheer, undeniable thrust of need. And yet, how could this force of nature be content to move so slowly toward fulfillment? She felt as if her body might burst with the delay. At the same time, she exulted in his strength, savored the adagio rhythm of his movements.

Her breath caught as his mouth closed over her breast, wetting the lace that covered her and bringing her nipple to hardened arousal, saturating her body with sudden weakness. He seemed to know she had no strength as he removed the blouse and bra, and tossed them heedlessly over his shoulder. Then he looked at her naked breasts, gave a ragged sigh, and cupped one with a hand that trembled ever so slightly. With teasing nibbles, he lowered his mouth to her lips, and she drank deeply of his kiss. Desire tore asunder her inhibitions, and she reached for the waistband of his slacks.

Their clothes came off in random bursts of excitement, tempered by moments of slow discovery. Unnecessary items—and all were eventually deemed unnecessary—were discarded without consideration, abandoned and scattered in disarray about the room. Shoes, socks, stockings . . . anything that hindered the escalating rhythm of their lovemaking was disposed of in the most expedient manner at hand. Undressing became a game of sensual pleasure. But when Emma grabbed his silk boxer shorts and sent them flying across the room to land neatly on the lamp shade, Alec decided to change the rules.

He claimed both her hands in one of his and slid his palm over the contours of her breasts and the smooth, flat planes of her stomach. Once and then again. Caressing, exploring, he touched her, teased her with unmerciful kisses, and eventually removed her panties and bra in favor of a mutual and enchanting nakedness...a revelation that, of itself, demanded more intensive study.

She raised her head from the pillow and captured his lips in a slow and erotic kiss...a kiss that left him hard and hungry for more. He wanted to fill her, and to feel her all around him. With careful movements, he took time to protect them both, and then he slid over her satin skin, enclosing her within the prison of his thighs. Her fingers fanned across his hips, adding pressure to his undeniable need for her. With a deceptively simple and totally tantalizing maneuver, she opened her body to him in an invitation he had no power or desire to refuse.

For long moments he clung to her, locked in the first, physical sensations of the joining. And then he slowed the pace, taking long, seductive drinks of her lips. His tongue flirted with hers, dancing, tasting, tempting, until she opened her mouth wide to his invasion. Every hungering, secret place in her body accepted and delighted in his touch. Every hungering, secret yearning in his heart reached out to her. Like a sudden and furious storm, the passion broke over him and he plunged deeply, stroking her, filling her with his need, managing to restrain his own desires only until her cry of ecstasy released him.

He buried his face in the curve of her shoulder and held her close until their rapid breathing slowed to a common and steady flow. And then he kissed her, with all the tenderness at his command, letting his hands touch and quiet her fevered skin, allowing the moments to tick gently past while he shared with her the sweet afterglow of passion.

EMMA POSITIONED HER foot on the pillow Alec had thoughtfully, and unnecessarily, provided. She felt relaxed and so deeply satisfied, she thought her injured ankle might actually have mended in the past hour. Maybe Alec's kisses, too, had healing powers. Snuggling close to his side, she cushioned her head on his shoulder and sank into the sweet warmth of his arm cradled around her. "I'm convinced," she said lazily. "You *do* have superhuman powers."

He raised his head, looked at her, then frowned down at his naked and resting body. "I've always been reasonably satisfied with my, uh, special abilities, but I confess you're the first to comment on them." He paused. "With any degree of knowledge, of course."

"Of course." She traced the contours of his chest with a fingertip. "Actually, I was referring to the fact that my sprained ankle is miraculously better. It feels as good as new."

"And that makes me a hero?"

She smiled. "That . . . and a few other things."

"Ah, so you did notice my special abilities."

"I noticed." She pressed his skin with a light kiss. "But I'm not sure I fully appreciated the demonstration. Do you think you might be able to, uh, show me one more time?"

"What? You want me to rise to the occasion again?" He hugged her close to his side, his breathing a moist, warm stirring against her hair. "I think you should probably get some rest first, though. I don't want to exhaust your reserves."

"And to add to your other special abilities, you're amazingly considerate of my physical endurance."

"I hate to have to be the one to say it, but I'm modest, too."

She laughed and yawned at the same time, producing a purely musical and delightful little sigh.

"You know, Emma, being your hero could turn into an all-night job."

"I don't have a late date, do you?"

"No, but I wouldn't want to be accused of taking advantage of you. And without a specific invitation . . ."

She pressed a finger to his lips. "You're invited. Will you stay all night?"

"As you wish, dear distressed damsel. Unless, of course, you hog the covers."

"I don't think we'll have any problem, because frankly, I'm not moving. I'm not even sure I'll sleep."

He kissed the top of her head. "You'll sleep. If you have any problem, I'll sing you a lullaby."

He didn't have to take such a desperate measure. Emma's breathing grew even and deep within ten minutes, and when he shifted his arm from beneath her, she rolled onto her side and curled against him like a flower with petals folded and at peace with the evening. Alec smiled and watched her for a long time, mesmerized by the fascination she held for him, surprised by the protective feelings she aroused.

He dozed and finally drifted into soothing sleep, awakening when the sun streamed through the window, illuminating Emma's bare shoulder and the creamy curve of her breast. He tucked the sheet over her shoulder and lightly kissed the back of her neck. Taking care not to disturb her, he turned onto his back and was instantly aware that something was wrong. He lifted his head from the pillow—and came face-to-face with the disapproving stare of Big Julee Cates.

Chapter Eight

What's he going to do, Emma? Hold a shotgun to my head until I marry you? The words spilled from Alec's memory like machine gun blasts, and the idea of a shotgun wedding suddenly didn't seem so funny.

Julian Cates was a great grizzly bear of a man with big, beefy arms and handsome hands with long, blunt fingers. He had a square jaw, a dense mustache, and a patrician nose, green eyes like Emma's, and a head full of salt-and-pepper hair. He wore a double-breasted navy suit with wide lapels and a flashy print vest that would have labeled any other man a fat cat. But for all his size, Big Julee looked dapper and debonair, a triple-size Fred Astaire, a cultured and sophisticated John Wayne. He sat easily, if a trifle heavily, in the floral Victorian chair in the corner. His face was carved in the cryptic, unrevealing lines of a true gambler. He wasn't smiling, but he wasn't frowning, either.

Alec took that as a good sign. The fact that there wasn't a shotgun anywhere in sight seemed like a positive note, as well. Even so, as an alarm clock, Big Julee was one hell of an eye-opener.

"I'm Emma's father." He leaned slightly forward, piercing Alec's tenuous composure with his penetrating dark eyes. "Who are you?"

Alec pushed up on his elbow and felt Emma stir beside him. "Alec Sayre," he said, his voice as steady as a rock, despite the fact that his underwear was looped over the lamp shade and dangled not ten inches above Julian's head. "It's very nice to meet you in person. I've heard a great deal about you."

"Unfortunately, Emma hasn't told me anything at all about you."

"Julian." Emma groaned out her father's name as she pulled herself into a sitting position, pulling the sheet up with her. "What are you doing here? You scared me half out of my mind."

"I'm liable to scare you out of the other half if you don't give me a damned good explanation of why I wasn't invited to attend my own daughter's wedding."

Wedding. Alec felt the word crawl down his back. Julian thought he and Emma were...

Emma cleared her throat and pushed a strand of hair out of her eyes. "There wasn't a wedding for you to be invited to, Julian."

"Are you saying my eyes deceive me?"

"No, Julian. But the picture you saw was nothing more than a publicity photo."

"What? There's a picture of this?" Julian, clearly, wasn't pleased at the prospect. "You let someone take a photograph of you...in bed...with *him?* What kind of publicity is that?"

"You mean you didn't see the newspaper?" Emma asked.

"Newspaper! It's in the newspaper?" Julian clenched his hands on the arms of the chair. "You put a picture like *that* in the newspaper?"

Emma sighed and Alec wondered if he could make an unobtrusive exit without his underwear. "Can we discuss this later and somewhere other than my bedroom?"

"Oh, I see. It's all right to splash nude pictures all over the front page of the paper, but it's embarrassing to have your father see you in bed."

"Julian, this is none of your business. This is my house, my bedroom, and you were not invited into either."

"And *he* was? A man who doesn't have the nerve to marry you before he takes you to bed and ruins your virtue?" The gruff voice had picked up a nasty growl and Alec wondered if he could get out of this bed alive.

"You're being ridiculous." Emma's voice shook on the words. "I'm twenty-nine years old, Julian. It is absolutely none of your business if I have ruined my virtue. And it is none of your business if I'm in bed with Alec or with some guy I picked up on the street corner."

"*If?*" Julian nearly choked on the word. "This picture can't get much more focused, little lady. And for a man who's had the pleasure of my daughter's invitation, Mr. Sayre, you're not doing much of a job of jumping to her defense."

"I don't need Alec to defend me." Emma tugged on the sheet, nearly leaving him defenseless. "And I don't need you in my bedroom, Julian. Now, get out of here this instant!"

"Not without an explanation." Julian crossed his burly arms over his indignant chest and didn't budge. "And not without hearing that *his* intentions are honorable."

Feeling as if he was neatly caught between a Mack truck and a Peterbilt, Alec decided he had better think of something quick. "Mr. Cates," he said calmly, "Emma and I got engaged a couple of weeks ago. You might say it was just one of those . . . lucky things."

"Lucky, huh?" Julian tapped one sturdy finger against the chair arm, obviously considering the implications of an engagement. "And what's this about a nude publicity picture?"

"Julian. . . ." Emma's voice flagged a warning, which he ignored.

"We were wearing wedding attire." Alec slipped his hand behind his back and patted Emma's knee, hoping to calm the rising temper he felt breathing down his neck. "The photographer was a free-lancer. He made it look like a wedding portrait. A simple misunderstanding, really."

Julian's penetrating gaze swept to Emma. "If you were already in your wedding duds, why didn't you go ahead and get married? Considering that you were obviously hot to jump in the sack with him."

Emma's sigh was frustrated and angry. Alec knew her dimple was cast in stone. "There *wasn't* a wedding," she said tightly. "There *isn't* an engagement. And if you both don't get out of my bedroom in the next five seconds, I *am* calling the police."

"Ask for Stan," Alec suggested. "After last night, you're practically best friends."

Emma thumped him between the shoulder blades. "Out! Daddy, get out of here this minute! Both of you. Go on. Out!"

Alec held on to the corner of the sheet, hoping to be allowed to leave with his underwear, if not with some shred of dignity. Julian rolled slowly to his feet. "Me and your fiancé will continue our talk in the kitchen. Come along, son."

Alec managed a smile. There was a humorous side to this. Thirty minutes from now, he was sure he'd see it. "Give me a minute, sir. I'll be right there."

"I'm counting on you not to climb out a window." Julian laughed as if that were funny. "Stay and face up to your responsibility like a man. You like coffee?"

"Can't open my eyes without it."

"I'm glad to hear that." Big Julee ambled to the bedroom door. "Because I sure as heck want to be able to see your eyes."

The minute he was gone, Alec threw back the sheet and retrieved his scattered clothing. "How in the hell did he get in here?"

Emma pursed her lips and rested her arms across her bent knees. "You probably left the door unlocked."

"Since you customarily leave the key in a flowerpot, anyway, I don't see that as a relevant point." He stepped into his boxer shorts and jerked them into place. "Don't blame me, Emma, because your father showed up unexpectedly."

"I'm not blaming you, Alec. I'm embarrassed and I'm humiliated that my father treats me like a child. And despite the fact that I'm not a child, I feel terribly guilty because he found me in bed with you." She rubbed her forehead. "These parent-child relationships aren't easy to outgrow. And even though I have no qualms about being in bed with you, I wish to heaven *he* didn't know about it."

Alec zipped his pants. "Well, cheer up. With any luck, he won't feel it's necessary to inform my mother and get her over here."

"With any luck, he won't fill your boxers full of birdshot."

"Oh, thanks. If you'd given me a little warning that your father was a Peeping Tom, I'd have worn my bulletproof pair."

"There is no need to get nasty. As I recall, I did warn you that Julian is overprotective."

Alec laughed without humor. "Well, that's got to be the understatement of the decade. He probably already has the county sheriff and a justice of the peace waiting in the kitchen."

Emma hummed the first few bars of the "Wedding March" to irritate him. "And you're going to get to explain why our engagement—such a *lucky* thing—came about. I almost wish I were going to be there to hear you talk your way out of this one, Alec." She flipped aside the sheet and slipped out of bed. As she passed him on her way into the bathroom, her chin took on that annoying, impudent tilt. "But, of course, you'll want to talk to Julian alone, man to man."

He wanted to grab her and have a physical discussion, man to woman. Her hips swayed provocatively, and he was tempted to toss her attractive derriere back onto the bed and forget the rest of the world. As if that were a real possibility. How could he lure Emma back into bed when her father was in the next room? He'd have to be out-of-his-head, crazy-in-love with her to do such a thing. Either that or he'd have to have one hell of a death wish. "We'll talk later, Emma. Don't worry, I'll handle Julian."

She tossed a blithe smile over her shoulder. "Yes, of course you will. Shut the door on your way out, please. I hate having my shower interrupted by the sound of gunshots."

Annoyed that he'd ever gotten mixed up with Emma Cates in the first place, Alec retrieved his shirt from under the bed and pulled it on. Memory came with it. Emma...last night...pulling the shirt off, sliding her hands across his bare chest and down to the waistband of his slacks. Emma...naked except for a slash of moonlight across her breasts...eager, giving, pleasuring him in ways he hadn't imagined she might. Emma...sighing, satisfied, sleeping in his arms. It had been a beautiful night. One of the best he'd known. He'd felt like a hero.

Hell, he could face Julian Cates. And Julian would blink first.

Emma would be grateful. He'd be a hero again...and who knew what might develop from there. With a smile, Alec went out to slay the dragon.

THE COFFEE was thick, black, and scalding. One sip and Alec knew he was at a considerable disadvantage.

Julian drank half a cup in one swallow. "All right, son, tell me a little about yourself. Ever had a tattoo?"

Alec almost choked. "No. Never dipped tobacco, either."

"Smoker?"

"I gave it up for jogging."

"The health craze has ruined this country," Julian said sadly. "I used to enjoy a good cigar now and again. But those days are gone. Gone. Sucked right out of the American culture. A man has to feel ashamed of himself in order to enjoy the simple pleasures of life. And that, my boy, is a sad state of affairs. You got any other sins I need to know about before I give you my permission to marry my daughter?"

This conversation needed a fresh turn, Alec decided. If he hadn't felt he owed Emma some protection from her father's inquisition, he'd have taken a turn himself. Turned right at the front door and kept walking. "I've been drunk once or twice," he admitted.

"That's it? That's the best you can do? What are you trying to do? Make me think you're some kind of saint? I want to know the *sins*, son. The worst you got."

His sense of the ridiculous replaced Alec's annoyance. "Some people say they just can't tell when I'm telling the truth."

Big Julee swallowed that with a mouthful of coffee. "There are some who might call that bluffing."

Alec offered a nebulous smile as his only comment.

"Well . . ." Julian leaned across the table, crowding Alec. "I'm going to be straight with you, Alec. Emma is my only child and I will do everything in my power to make her happy. Now, you might not be the man I would choose for a son-in-law, but it's obvious that she's got her heart set on you. The question here is, will you make her happy?"

Yes or no? The clock was ticking. The world and Julian were waiting for the answer. Alec summoned his superhero powers and found they'd left him high and dry and facing the don't-lie-to-me-boy expression on Emma's father's face. There was no way out of this, he thought.

Luckily, Julian supplied one. "I know what you're thinkin', and I don't blame you one bit. It's old-fashioned for a father to look out for his daughter like I look out for Emma. But you'll discover, son, that I'm an old-fashioned guy. I believe in good morals and honorable intentions. I come from an era when men protected their womenfolk, body, soul and virtue. If I thought for one minute that you were taking advantage of my Emma...

Buckshot, Alec thought.

Julian got up and poured himself a second cup of sludge. "I'll be blunt, Alec. I prefer to have my grandchildren born the old-fashioned way—*after* marriage. So, tell me, when exactly is the weddin' going to be?"

Lifting his coffee cup to his lips, Alec took a courageous swallow. He set the cup on the table, in the center, where he could keep an eye on it and Mr. Old Fashioned at the same time. "You're a gambler, Mr. Cates. You should know that it isn't sporting to ask another player to show his hand before the bets are laid."

Julian frowned. "You know, son, it would upset me considerably if you were to tell me that even though you're engaged to my daughter, you're not going to marry her. I wouldn't regard that as being very sporting, myself."

Alec considered his options. If he denied the engagement, it would place Emma in an awkward and embarrassing position. If he said he did plan to marry her, he could be in a bit of a rough spot, himself. He decided, however, that if Big Julee Cates had a shotgun in his pocket, he would just as soon know now as later. "Emma doesn't want to marry me," he said. "Our engagement isn't a real commitment. It happened because ... well, it was—*is*—simply a matter of convenience. I needed a fiancée for a while. Emma needed my help with some publicity for her business. We never had any intention of getting married."

The big man's jaw clamped like a beartrap. "You compromised her virtue."

"I have to agree with Emma, sir. That is none of your business."

Julian shoved himself to his feet, frowned, and then sat back down. "Business? Did you say something about Emma's business?"

"Yes. The Golden Glow Wedding Chapel. She owns it."

"Lock, stock and barrel? What happened to Harry?"

"He still performs most of the ceremonies. And in between, he's polishing up his lounge act."

"And Emma bought that albatross? Did she pay cash?"

"I don't know the details. I met her after the fact."

"She wouldn't have told you, anyway. Stubborn, independent, bullheaded little thing. You'll have your hands full with her, Alec. I'll warn you right now. And you'll have the responsibility of runnin' the weddin' chapel, too."

"Emma manages quite well on her own."

"Don't let that Miss Independence act fool you. She needs a firm hand, I'm tellin' you. A firm hand and a firm man."

Alec wasn't about to comment on that.

"Well, of course you want to marry her." Julian pursed his lips and got lost in thought...but he found his way back. "I'd know you were lying if you said otherwise. Why there's a lot of men out there who would marry a woman just to get their hands on her business."

"I have my hands full, already," Alec said. "I run the Tuxedo Junction Hotel and Casino Complex."

Julian whistled. "I'm beginning to see the light. The gaming commission would probably take a dim view of your associating with the daughter of a professional gambler. Could raise some questions, huh? And that's why you and Emma are keeping things hush-hush."

Alec was beginning to share Emma's total frustration. "It isn't a hush-hush thing. There isn't any engagement to hush up."

"Ah, that's good. Real good. But I can help. Don't worry. We'll get this straightened out. I have contacts."

A groan of no small magnitude gathered in Alec's throat. Great. Just what he needed. Intercession with the gaming commission on his behalf by a notorious professional gambler *with contacts*. Alec pushed his chair. "I have to leave. It's getting late, and I need to get to my office."

"Don't fret," Julian advised. "I'll say goodbye to Emma for you. I'll handle the other little problem, too. Don't give it another thought. I'll take care of everything."

When Alec walked out the door, the words followed him like a doomsday prophet.

DESPITE HER RELENTLESS clench on indignation, Emma felt a stab of disappointment when she walked into the kitchen and realized Alec had left.

"Alec asked me to tell you goodbye. He had important things to do at his office." Julian rose, untouched by the bad vibes she directed his way. "Want some coffee?"

"That's crude oil, not coffee."

He sloshed the liquid in his cup, then swallowed it and poured more. "Alec liked it."

"Alec has the palate of a rhino." Emma got a glass of tap water, turned around, and leaned against the sink. "And you have the sensitivity of a buffalo."

Julian clicked his tongue as he resumed his seat at the table. "Sounds like you got up on the wrong side of the bed this morning, honey."

"That only proves my point, Julian. Did you expect me to be happy when I woke up and found you sitting in judgment beside my bed?"

"How was I supposed to know you had an overnight guest?"

"Ah," she said pointedly. "If you had called *before* you came over, none of this would have happened."

"If I'd called, you would have made up some stupid excuse about why I couldn't come to the house, and I might never have met my future son-in-law."

"Don't say that, Julian. There is no excuse for you coming into my house uninvited and absolutely no justification for your staying after you realized I wasn't alone."

"You're entitled to your opinion," he said stubbornly.

"I'm entitled to my privacy."

"You're my daughter. It's my responsibility to protect you."

"Dammit, Julian. Stop treating me like I was an eighteen-year-old virgin. I have a sex life." She sighed and tacked on a qualification. "Sometimes. But I'm quite capable of protecting myself."

"And who are you going to turn to if he refuses to marry you? That's what I want to know."

Emma closed her eyes and rubbed her forehead. "I am not going to discuss this with you. From now on, you call before you decide to drop in for a visit. I'm taking the key out of the flowerpot. You'll knock on the door. You'll wait for me to open it. And never, under any circumstances, are you to enter my bedroom. Is that clear?"

"What's clear to me is that you're not glad to see your old dad."

He was a master of expressions and knew how to play his cards. Despite herself, Emma felt the edge of her irritation begin to thaw. "It's not that I'm not glad...." What was the point? There never had been any reasoning with Julian. "I thought you were in Atlantic City," she said as a peace offering. "Did you get tired of the Taj Mahal?"

"I was lonesome for you. And I kinda had an itch to see what new casinos had sprung up on the strip since my last trip. Alec tells me he's in charge of Tuxedo Junction."

"If he said it, it must be true." Emma didn't want to talk about Alec. She wanted to think about him in private, recall last night, remember the feel of his lips on her skin, the taste of his mouth on hers. But of course, she couldn't do that now. Not under Julian's provincial eye.

"I was sort of hoping he was lying when he told me you bought the wedding chapel."

Her heart jumped. She didn't want to have this discussion. She wasn't going to have this discussion. Julian couldn't make her talk to him about the business. "Let's go out for breakfast," she suggested. "I'll buy."

"Don't be silly. You don't have any money. You bet it all on the Golden Glow. And don't tell me it's none of my business. You'll only waste your breath."

"Julian," she said firmly, "it is none of your business."

He smiled and got out of the chair. "Come here and give your old pop a hug. Then I'll take you to breakfast."

She hugged him. It was not the way she'd imagined this morning would begin, but it would just have to do.

Julian wrapped his arms around his little girl and wondered where the years had gone. She'd gone out on a damned limb of independence and mortgaged her life to the hilt to buy a stinking wedding chapel. She didn't need the worry of running a business. She needed to settle down and raise kids. His grandkids. He patted her back and gave her another affectionate squeeze before he let her go.

It would take some thought, but he could fix everything. Alec seemed like a nice guy. And he'd make Emma happy or Julian would know the reason why. It was obvious she was in love with him. She even blushed when his name was mentioned.

Julian smiled as he tipped up his cup and drank the last satisfying swallow of good coffee. Of course she wanted to marry Alec. And if that's what she wanted, by God, he'd make sure she had the man and the wedding of her dreams. Regardless of what she had to say about it.

Chapter Nine

"Good morning, handsome. It's about time you showed up for work."

Alec stood in the doorway of his office and frowned at Charity, who looked comfortable and composed sitting in his chair behind his desk. "Who let you in?" he asked as he closed the door with an irritable click.

Her eyebrows lifted in mild surprise. "Is that any way to greet a friend?"

He was in no mood to be friendly. "Let me rephrase that. What are you doing here?"

"Don't tell me you've forgotten me, Alec. I haven't even been away two weeks, yet." She offered a slow smile. "I'll bet you've missed me."

He took a seat opposite her, crossed one leg over the other, and watched her expectantly. "You bet wrong."

"Oh, Alec," she said easily. "You don't have to pretend with me. I know you better than that. We both got angry, said some things we didn't mean. I'm ready to forgive and forget."

"Charity, I fired you and I have no intention of reinstating you, if that's what you're here after."

The edge of her smile grew crisp. "This doesn't have to be difficult, Alec."

He stroked his freshly shaven chin with the pad of his thumb. "You're beginning to sound a lot like your father."

"I'm sure I don't have to tell you he isn't happy with your actions, Alec."

"And I'm sure I don't have to tell you that his happiness has never been one of my concerns."

She shifted, a slight and definite first sign of discomfort. "It isn't like you to be flippant."

"It isn't like you to beat around the bush. Lay your cards on the table, Charity, and let me see what you've got." The words brought a reminiscence of Emma, of her big, green eyes and her charming mouth, daring him to show her what he had. His lips curved with remembered pleasure... a smile that Charity immediately mistook and misinterpreted.

"There," she said. "I knew you couldn't stay mad. Not with me."

His smile fled, along with his patience. "Get out of my chair and get out of my office, Charity. I have nothing to say to you."

She jumped up like a jack-in-the-box. "If that's what you want, then so be it. I came here, in good faith, to try and negotiate a reasonable solution to our disagreement, but it is obvious you're in no mood to listen to reason."

Alec could see nothing to gain by arguing, so he pushed to his feet and waited for her to leave. When she simply stood behind his desk, her palms planted on his daily calendar like stubborn oak seedlings, her gaze an unblinking challenge, he decided he could either have the argument or call security. And since the security people would have reservations about evicting Sam McKimber's daughter...

This was turning out to be one hell of a morning. "All right, Charity, if you'll move out from behind my desk and let me have my chair back, I'll give you five minutes to *reason* with me."

"How generous."

"That's my best and only offer."

She took a moment to consider before she sauntered around the desk and stopped beside him. She stroked his sleeve with a fingertip. "Here's my offer. I want my job back. I want you to admit that your engagement to Ms. Lucky Emma Cates was a last-ditch effort to avoid making a commitment to me. And if I'm satisfied with what you say, maybe I won't foreclose on her mortgage."

Alec blinked. "Excuse me, but I could swear I just saw you twirl the handlebar of a Simon LeGree mustache as you hit me over the head with a rolled-up deed."

"Don't be silly," she said with a laugh. "I don't have a mustache. However, I do have the mortgage on the Golden Glow Wedding Chapel." Her eyes and lips combined to deliver the challenge. "My father, you'll recall, has friends in high places."

"A few low ones, as well," Alec murmured as he battled a wave of white-hot anger. "What do you hope to accomplish with this bit of extortion, Charity? My undying devotion?"

"I've told you. I want to be reinstated in my position. I want a confession that your engagement was phony right from the beginning. And I want to hear you say that you did it all because of me."

Alec put some distance between them and met her belligerent gaze with cool indifference. "I did it all because of you. You drove me to the edge and pushed me over . . . right into another woman's arms. That's quite a theory."

"It's fact. I know it and you know it. You were afraid of your feelings for me, Alec, so you pushed me out of your life, hoping that would end it. But it hasn't."

"No, I can see that." He looked out the window, regaining control of the furious words he wanted to fling at her. "Why did you drag Emma into our fight, Charity?"

"You did that, Alec. Not me. I could hardly buy up *your* mortgage, now, could I?"

He smiled without humor. "No, your father's friends aren't placed quite that high."

"Luckily for you."

"I want the mortgage, Charity. Name your price. In dollars, not blood."

She crossed her arms and shook her head. "My terms or no terms."

Alec eyed her for a moment before he reached for his phone. "I'm giving you fair warning. If you're not out of my office by the time I've dialed three digits, you'll find yourself facing charges for trespassing."

She laughed. "It will never stick, Alec. Give in. You need me. The Wedding of Your Dreams contest must be in shambles by this time. I'm the only one who can fix it. *She* certainly can't."

"*She* certainly can." He slapped the desk with his palm. "And has. The contest is under control, despite your best efforts."

"Sorry," she said with unfaltering confidence. "But that isn't possible. I canceled the state contests. Not even one bride and her groom will be showing up at the wedding conference, Alec, much less *one hundred.*"

"You can't cancel a contest you've advertised."

She smiled, excessively sure of her facts. "I'm very good at my job. I would never commit to a publicity contest on that big a scale without a protective clause. You know, 'if there isn't sufficient number of *acceptable* entries, contest may be null and void,' something like that."

"What about all the play you gave this contest in the wedding conference brochures? You promised these people a minimum one hundred brides and grooms and at least one fabulous wedding giveaway."

"Hmm. Now, that could be a problem. But as I see it, Alec, it's your problem. Unless, of course, you're asking for my expertise?"

Alec picked up the receiver and punched the first number. "Don't make this difficult," he said.

The resolve in his voice must have reached her, because she visibly wavered. "There's no need to exert yourself. I'll leave. I'm staying at the condo. You can reach me there whenever you're ready to talk. You know the number."

He punched the second number and she grabbed her purse and headed for the door. "Don't wait too long to call," she said over her shoulder. "I may get lonely and decide to visit Lucky and my investment property. You know I like to handle small details personally."

Alec stabbed the third number with such force that his finger slipped and buckled against the hard plastic. He refrained from wincing until the door had closed behind his uninvited guest. Then he sank into his chair and assessed his injuries.

"GOODNESS GRACIOUS, Harry, will you please go outside and play in the street!" Emma's head pounded with the incessant rhythm of a Jerry Lee Lewis hit. She'd be singing "Great Balls of Fire" in her sleep. "You've been practicing that song for hours."

"Can't do this outside, Emma." Harry flexed his nimble fingers. "Pianos don't have the right-of-way. I'd get run over by a limousine and you'd be short one very important employee."

"Humph! What does Emma need with an over-paid employee like you, anyway?" Julian paced to the doorway of the chapel and batted the gauze curtains until the bells in the centerpiece gave out a tinny chime. "There hasn't been anybody in here wanting a wedding for over an hour now. She can't afford you, Harry."

"Don't start that again," Emma warned. "And get away from that doorway. You're making Sanchee nervous."

Julian poked his head past the curtains and into the consulting area where the florist was hard at work. "You've got enough bouquets there to cover every damn horse in the Kentucky Derby, Sanchee. Why do you have to have so many of those expensive flowers, anyway? They're just going to wither and die. Couldn't you make up some of those fake flower things? Use the same ones over and over? Save my daughter some money—"

Emma flipped him with a rubber band. "Julian, I mean it, if you say one more word to that poor woman, I'm going to make you leave."

He pulled back inside the chapel room, dragging one end of the curtain with him. "Now, Emma, you know I was only trying to help."

She met that lame excuse with the silence it deserved. "Sanchee doesn't need your help and neither do I. Find someone else to hassle. Go play a duet with Harry." She brushed past him into the other room, hoping it wasn't too late to soothe the florist's frazzled nerves.

"Hey, Harry," Julian demanded. "Play 'Misty' for me."

His laughter rumbled like a bowling ball heading for a strike, and Emma rubbed her forehead. What a morning. She'd had other plans for the day, had hoped to spend a first leisurely hour or two with Alec. He had had important business, though. Too important to stay long enough to help her stare down her sanctimonious and inconvenient papa. Ha! As if Alec Sayre would stay in any place where words like "When is the blasted wedding?" and "Marry my daughter, please" were being tossed around like BBs from a double-barreled air rifle.

Okay, so he had a phobia about weddings and marriage and commitment and all things traditional, but he could have phoned. He'd left early this morning. It was now afternoon. Hours since Julian had awakened them. Hours and hours since they'd made long and passionate love.

He should have called.

He should have sent flowers...or candy...or a card.

He should've done something, anything, to let her know that last night hadn't been just any night and that she wasn't just any woman. They were engaged...sort of. Didn't that count for something?

"The bouquets are beautiful, Sanchee." She reassured the woman by complimenting each arrangement in turn. "Don't listen to Julian. He doesn't know a thing about flowers."

Sanchee sniffed. "He doesn't know a thing about wedding chapels, either."

"If only he knew that he didn't know," Emma said sadly. "But, never mind. You know how busy we are on Saturday. We'll need all of these bouquets and more. Just ignore him, if you can."

"I can." Sanchee jerked a strip of florist tape from the spool and snapped it taut between her hands. "But if he says one more word about my bouquets, I'll jump him and fix it so he can't complain."

Emma wanted to say she'd help, but thought she probably shouldn't. For better or worse, Julian was her father.

The phone rang and she started down the hallway to her office to answer it.

"Let me answer that," Julian shouted, the sound of his rapid, rolling walk as he approached the front extension reaching her with a whisper of alarm.

"No, I'll get it." She turned to intercept him. "It might be a customer."

"Well, I certainly hope so. Doesn't do you any good to own a wedding chapel when you don't have any customers wanting to get married."

She reached for the phone, but he was faster. "Golden Glow Wedding Chapel," he announced into the receiver. "You pitch 'em, we hitch 'em. Weddings are our business, our only business. We do the job right. We tie the knot tight. For a nominal fee, the Golden Glow is the place to be."

As she tried to cut off his salesmanship by slicing her hand across her throat, Emma tried not to dwell on the daunting thought that Julian had only been in town a few hours. "Give me that phone," she said through clenched teeth.

He shrugged and handed it right over. "It's for you." Then he waggled his eyebrows. "It's Aaaal-lleccc."

She eyed her father, who made no effort whatsoever to move out of hearing range, but lounged comfortably, like a permanent fixture, against the wall beside Sanchee's station. It would be courting disaster to leave the florist and her father alone in the same room. Emma lifted the phone to her ear. Score two for "Make Room for Daddy," zero for privacy.

"Hello?"

"Emma." *Alec.* His voice was like midnight, and she felt its dark, sultry syllables slide over her like a gown of soft chiffon.

"Hi," he said. "Long morning?"

"Need you ask?"

"The Caped Crusader is still there, obviously."

"Only his mission has changed. The threat to my virtue is now secondary to my financial status."

"Financial status?" Alec's tone took a sharp turn. "What's wrong with your finances?"

"Nothing that I know of," she said with a slight frown. "But Julian believes that five minutes without a wedding is revenue lost. He's doing his best to increase my odds of success, as he puts it."

"What's he doing? Trying to round up customers with a shotgun?"

"The only weapon in evidence is his big mouth." She made sure Julian heard that, but he didn't seem even slightly concerned as he sidled a little closer to the work station and a ribbon-tied bouquet of white carnations.

"Did he mention that I asked him to say my good-byes this morning?"

"He said something important came up and you had to leave."

"I had to leave because he wanted to set a wedding date." Alec's tension traveled the phone wire and told her better than words that he had had to escape while he was still single. A thread of her earlier annoyance returned. "But," he continued, "as a matter of fact, something has come up."

His voice conveyed distraction, discomfort and distress, and Emma could well imagine the reason. "Something very important, no doubt."

"We have to talk, Emma."

She should have expected this, she thought. She'd known from the beginning that Alec jumped and ran at the first hint of the word "commitment." Now he was going to make some excuse for why he couldn't see her, why they shouldn't see each other. Well, she was in no mood to find herself relegated to being just another notch on his belt, another notation in his diary.

"We're very busy right now, Alec."

"But this is important."

"It will have to wait." Her change of mood must have struck paydirt, because his pause was sudden and wary.

"Emma," he said slowly, as if testing the water. "Charity's back."

That did it. The return of the old girlfriend. Just what she needed to complete her disastrous morning. "Then why are you talking to me?"

She slammed down the receiver just in time to see Sanchee jerk the carnations from Julian's hand and place them out of reach.

"I was only counting how many flowers you put in that one bouquet." Avoiding Sanchee's murderous glare, Julian turned his attention on Emma and chastised her with a parental frown. "Did you just hang up on my future son-in-law?"

Emma motioned to Sanchee. "Give me some of that tape."

HE DID NOT HAVE time to chase around like this. What had gotten Emma going, anyway? He'd only wanted to talk to her. Five minutes, maybe less. And she'd snapped at him and then slammed the phone in his ear. Okay, so Julian was no picnic first thing in the morning. Hell, Alec had been the one to bear the brunt of his disapproval. But Emma apparently had no appreciation for his effort. So instead of a few minutes on the phone, he now faced a trip to the chapel to explain to Emma that they had to do something to salvage the damn wedding contest. Her contest, as a matter of fact. He was only trying to help her, for Pete's sake. As if he didn't have better things to do than to worry about the contest, worry about Charity's threat, worry about coming face-to-face again with Big Julee Cates and his insistent suggestions regarding marriage.

"Call Benjamin and postpone our meeting until tomorrow." Alec issued instructions to his assistant as he strode to the elevator. "Get Harris to give you this month's tally for the hotel restaurants. Tell Jacques that he has to clear any change on the menu with Benjamin. And don't let him give you any of his famous French sweet talk, either. If Benjamin doesn't okay it, it doesn't change."

He adjusted the black cummerbund at his waist as he stepped inside the glass elevator. There were days, like this one, when he wished the hotel and casino were named Casual Junction and he could wear jeans, sneakers, and a knit shirt as his uniform instead of this pristine and stiff tuxedo. He waved to Sheryl as the doors began to close. "Put everything else on hold, take two aspirin, and I'll call you later."

The elevator slid seamlessly through the shaft, allowing Alec a view of the hotel atrium. As always, he looked for potential problems—employees out of pocket, guests in need of assistance, any detail that might detract from the overall appearance or efficiency of the hotel. Usually, he delighted in keeping a close watch over his small empire, loved to walk the length and breadth of the casino, noting the enjoyment, testing the comfort level of the guests. But today his thoughts were with Emma, and he waited impatiently for the elevator to release him so he could leave Tuxedo Junction and head blindly for the last place he wanted to be—the Golden Glow Wedding Chapel.

"WELL, WELL, WELL, the prodigal bridegroom returns." Julian greeted Alec with a booming welcome that cleared the boogie-woogie beat of the piano to echo through the chapel. "Emma, look who's here."

She didn't look pleased to see him, Alec thought as he hesitated in the archway. She was in the aisle, helping the florist drape pink netting over the chairs. Pink netting covered the altar and the dais, looped over the backdrop, and camouflaged the ceiling in a rolling wave. Pink flowers adorned the white candelabra that had somehow escaped the flood of pastel color. The piano, too, remained unchanged by the deluge, but behind it, Harry was dressed in a flamingo pink leisure suit that made Alec wince. "Let me guess," he said. "The bride's favorite color is blue."

"Blue!" Julian let loose a hearty laugh. "Now, that's funny. Come on in here, son, and help Emma get this place pinked up."

He received no such encouragement from the lady, but decided he couldn't just turn and walk out without talking to her. "If it gets much pinker in here, the pigment police will have to issue a color violation."

"That's all right," Julian declared. "The happy couple is paying extra for all this tinting. I told 'em we were happy to do whatever they wanted . . . for a small fee."

"Of course." Alec offered Emma his sympathy in a smile. A smile she didn't return. He approached her with caution, remembering the first time he'd walked into the chapel, swept her into his arms and kissed her. Something sure as hell had changed. "You look pretty in pink," he said.

"Don't we all." She rolled her eyes and tucked a length of net under the chair legs. "Sanchee, keep it loose on your end. We don't want people to sit down and rip this bower of pink bliss. As you can see, Alec, we're very busy. If you came to help, get Julian out of here. If you came because you want to talk, go away—and take Julian with you."

There was no mistaking that signal—cool, crisp, and green as a traffic light. *Go.* There was more to this than being busy. He touched her arm and felt her stiffen. His suspicions were confirmed. Now, if he could only figure out exactly what those suspicions were.

He unbuttoned his tuxedo jacket. "When is the wedding and what else needs to be done?"

"I have everything under control." She went down the row of seats, tucking the netting around the chair legs. "And I'm sure you have much more important things to do."

"Alec!" Harry waved from the piano. "Any word on my performance last night at the Silk Stocking? Did you bring a contract for me to sign?"

"Haven't had a chance to follow up on that, Harry." Alec kept his eyes on Emma. "I'll get back to you as soon as I can."

The first boisterous notes of "Let Me Entertain You" filled the chapel, and Emma cut an accusatory now-see-what-you've-done glance at Alec. "Don't let us keep you," she said.

He pursed his lips, considering his alternatives, then waded through the pink surf, and scooped Emma up into his arms.

"Put me down!" She cuffed his shoulder with her fist.

"We're going to talk, Emma. Right now. Either here or in your office. Do you have a preference?"

"I would like to be left alone to manage my own business, thank you very much. I don't have time for your nonsense. We have a wedding to do in fifteen minutes."

"This won't take five."

She protested by kicking her feet and hitting him in the ribs with her heel. With a sigh of frustration, he shifted her position, slinging her over his shoulder like a sack of unruly potatoes. "I think we'll have our discussion in your office, if you don't mind."

"I mind! I don't want to talk to you."

Julian walked over and bent to look at his daughter's face. "Emma, sweetheart, this is the man of your dreams. The least you can do is listen to him."

"One more word out of you, Julian, and I'm putting myself up for adoption. Do you hear me? Do not defend this idiot. He's always picking me up and putting me down against my will. What is it with the two of you? Do you think I'm incapable of standing on my own two feet?"

Julian straightened and patted Emma's dangling arm. "Don't worry about a thing. Harry and Sanchee and I can handle this pink wing-ding of a wedding. You just go talk to your fiancé." He looked at Alec. "I told you she needed a firm hand."

Alec frowned and strode from the chapel, ignoring Emma's furious silence, but not untouched by it. He didn't know what he'd done to deserve the cold reception he'd just received, but he realized he hadn't helped his cause much by playing the part of the caveman. At the moment, an apology was bound to sound insincere, but he forced one forward the moment he closed the door of her office.

"I'm sorry. I handled that poorly."

Her continued silence was an indictment. He set her on her feet, grateful that her tiny office provided an intimacy he couldn't provide for himself, wanting to kiss her more than he cared to acknowledge. But kissing, undoubtedly, would do nothing to expiate his error in judgment, so he tucked his hands in his pockets and pressed his lips into a determined-not-to-offend line.

She made a hand-sweep of her now rumpled, two-piece linen suit and managed to look terribly desirable as she straightened the skirt. A couple of irritable swipes put her honey-shaded hair in place and made Alec curl his fingers into tight fists of control. She walked behind her desk, a gesture of distancing that he hoped meant she was as bothered by his nearness as he was bothered by hers. But when her lashes lifted to reveal cool emerald eyes, he couldn't detect any hint that she was anything other than angry. "Your five minutes is now four," she said. "Talk fast."

He did, repeating Charity's remarks that the contest was in jeopardy. "She says there's no way we can salvage it without her assistance."

"The conference is only a week away." Emma's anger disappeared in the wake of new concern. "If she did cancel the state contests, we don't have time to conduct new ones. And without contestants, how can we give away the Wedding of Your Dreams?" She looked at Alec with a frown. "Do you think she could be bluffing?"

He shook his head. "Not Charity. If she isn't holding a winning hand, she doesn't bet."

Emma pondered that and a 1950's photograph of the Golden Glow Wedding Chapel that hung in a cheap frame on the wall. "So, what are the stakes, Alec? What is it she intends to win?"

He couldn't tell her, couldn't bring himself to say that Charity had obtained the mortgage on the chapel, couldn't dangle one more worry over her head. Especially not when he was responsible. He had brought Emma into this war with Charity, and he would find some way to keep her from becoming a casualty. "I don't think that's the point, Emma. We have to salvage the contest. If Charity can do it, then there's a way. We'll just have to figure out what it is.''

''Do you have a suggestion on how we're going to come up with one hundred couples in just a few days? Julian's been doing everything but dragging total strangers in off the streets, and he's only managed to book one ceremony in several hours.''

''We'll think of something,'' Alec promised.

Emma sank to the edge of her chair. ''So speaks the man who hates everything to do with weddings.''

He took his hands out of his pockets. ''Not everything.''

She didn't acknowledge his soft protest, if she even heard it. ''I've spent a lot of money advertising in the conference brochure. I had coupons printed to be distributed to the contestants. The Golden Glow Wedding Chapel is listed as a sponsor in every article, every promotional flier that's gone out during the past month. What if we get sued for nonperformance? What if someone accuses us of false advertising? Maybe the casino can afford a lawsuit, but I certainly can't.''

''There won't be a lawsuit. I spent half the morning with a company attorney. He's checking into the liability, but he feels the protective clause will hold us blameless against any claims. Whatever her motives, Charity would never leave Tuxedo Junction open for a lawsuit.''

''She wouldn't mind if the wedding chapel were open for one, though, would she?'' Emma pushed herself up from the chair. ''And since the Golden Glow wasn't included in the first few months of advertising, the protective clause probably doesn't apply to me."

"I'll make sure you're not harmed by this, Emma. Besides, we're going to have the contest even if I have to hit the streets with Julian to round up a hundred brides and grooms."

"That's it, Alec! We'll make a game of it. A massive, mammoth, no-holds-barred scavenger hunt. We can divide the conference participants into teams and each team will have to come up with a preset number of engaged couples. That would work, wouldn't it?"

He tried to wipe the skeptical look from his face. "We're going to scour Las Vegas for brides and grooms?"

"Where else could you do something like this? Las Vegas is the mecca of the quickie wedding. We'll have a hundred couples in no time. Everyone will have fun. We'll generate more publicity than I ever dreamed of, and Charity will be sorry she didn't think of it."

Charity. Alec knew her better than he wanted to, and he knew she wouldn't be sorry. She'd be furious. And the brunt of that fury would be directed straight at Emma. "I'll handle Charity," he said with more determination than confidence. "You handle the scavenger hunt."

She nodded. "This will work, Alec. I know it will."

Watching her, he didn't see how it could fail.

"Alec? Em?" Julian's voice preceded his staccato knock. "We've got problems out here. That crazy woman you call a florist is ranting and raving and tossing flowers all over the place. And the bride is mad because they're not all pink flowers. And the groom *hates* pink. You probably ought to stop talking now and come out here and tend to business."

Emma rolled her eyes. "He's ruining my life, and the day isn't even over yet."

"At least you know he cares about your happiness."

"In his own blundering way." She sighed and reached for the doorknob.

Alec stopped her with a touch and then couldn't stop his lips from claiming her kiss. The embrace was light and all too brief, but Julian kept knocking and there was no time to say the things Alec wanted to say. So he settled for a moment's kiss and a few words that would have to suffice. "Last night was . . . special."

Her smile squeezed his heart.

She opened the door, interrupting Julian in mid-knock. "I heard you," she said. "Now, what is going on?"

"It's that Sanchee. She's nuts. All I said was—"

"*Don't* tell me, Julian. Just stay back here until I get things calmed down."

Emma walked briskly toward the chapel, but when Alec moved to follow her, Julian took his arm. "Wait just a minute. You're coming with me." With surprising agility, Julian turned on his heel, pulling Alec with him. "You and me got some planning to do, son. We're going to plan ourselves a wedding."

Chapter Ten

"You've got class, Alec." Julian spread-eagled his arms across the top of the seat and settled back against the plush upholstery of the Tuxedo Junction limousine. With amiable grace and a big grin, he made himself right at home as he faced Alec, who was in the seat opposite. "Not every man would be so accommodating as to offer his own vehicle for a command performance like this one." Julian chuckled. "I guess there's some folks who might call this a kidnapping."

"With some justification," Alec agreed. "On the other hand, there might be some who would say *I* kidnapped you. It is my limo and my driver."

"True, true." Julian nodded his concession of the point. "Emma would say it was good riddance no matter which one of us was shanghaied and which one did the shanghaiing."

"She seemed a little put out."

"Been testy all day long. No matter what I did to try to help her, it was the wrong thing. I accused her of getting up on the wrong side of the bed this morning."

Alec wasn't going within fifty yards of that remark. "She takes her business very seriously," he said.

Julian's head bobbed in agreement. "You got that right. Emma works too hard and worries too much. Why she wanted to burden herself with that blasted wedding chapel and a mountain of debt, I can't tell you. She's got a college degree, you know. I made sure she went to one of the best colleges in the country. I thought she'd meet some nice young medical student or a law school graduate—somebody who could take care of her. And what did she do but come out of there with a business administration degree, some crazy ideas about owning her own business, and not a prospect for a husband in sight."

"Most fathers would be proud to have a daughter like Emma."

"Well, hell, I never said I wasn't proud of her. I just know she'd be happier if she didn't have to work so hard. Women are fragile, you know. They need a man's protection."

Alec had to smile. Emma needed protection the way she needed another overbearing man in her life. "She seems satisfied with her independence."

"Sheesh, son. That's just a front." He gave Alec the once-over. "Haven't you figured that out yet? All this talk about not wanting to marry you is just her way of flirting. I know my daughter. You can take my word for it, she wants to marry you . . . no matter what she says."

The possibility that Emma had discussed this with Julian—and given a negative answer to an unasked question—didn't set well. "Did she *say* she doesn't want to marry me?" Alec asked.

"Doesn't matter what she said," Julian maintained. "I'm telling you the truth, here. Her heart is set on you. That's why you and I are ridin' around in this limousine right now plannin' the wedding.''

"You can't force two people into marriage. Not in this day and age."

Julian made eye contact and wouldn't let go. "Is there something I need to know? Any reason you can't marry Emma? Like, maybe, you're already married to some other woman?"

"I'm as free as the wishful thinking that every gambler brings along on a trip to Las Vegas." Which wasn't exactly true. Charity had a hold on him, a piece of paper that rightfully belonged to Emma, and now was being used to blackmail him. "But there are other considerations."

"Like what?" Julian wasn't about to let this discussion stray from his purpose. "Be straight with me, son, and I'll help you any way I can. If it's the gaming commission that worries you, I can fix that. I'm not and never have been mixed up with any 'unsavory elements,' if you know what I mean. I've got friends who'll testify that my character is unblemished and my reputation as squeaky clean as a deck of unopened cards. I love to gamble, I admit it. I play because it's just so damned much fun. I won't kid you. I've won my share of fortunes and lost 'em again, sometimes all in the same twenty-four hours. And once or twice, I've cut the deck with some pretty unscrupulous individuals. But, and here I'm telling you the gospel truth, I've never done anything I considered dishonest and I've never spent a single night in jail. You got nothing to worry about from an investigation into my background."

"I know."

Julian looked surprised and then amused. "Had me checked out, did ya? Smart boy. No one can accuse you of taking foolish chances."

Alec's smile faded. "I don't know about that, Julian. I'm getting ready to do something I think may be very risky."

"Will it affect my Emma?"

He might as well confide the whole thing, Alec decided. Julian was never going to let him out of the car otherwise. Besides, at the moment, he needed a sounding board and Julian was as good as any. "Charity McKimber is the daughter of my business associate. She has had her mind set on marrying me for years, and when I introduced Emma as my fiancée, Charity believed I'd gotten engaged to keep from making a commitment to her."

"Did you?"

"Does that really matter?"

"If I was Emma, it would matter."

"Emma had her own reasons for wanting the engagement. But that's not the problem. Charity has obtained, by fair means or foul, the mortgage on the Golden Glow Wedding Chapel."

Julian pursed his lips as that sank in. "So, buy it from her. If I had the cash on hand, I'd do it myself."

"Charity wouldn't sell it for twice what she paid. Not now. Not to you, not to me, not to anyone. She's using it as a means to punish me for not falling in with her plans. She'd rather lose every dime of her investment than to let me rescue the wedding chapel's future for Emma."

"Well, what are you going to do?"

"Make a wager. Emma's contest against the mortgage. If the Wedding of Your Dreams contest is successful, if a hundred brides and grooms participate, then she'll sell me the mortgage for the same amount she paid."

"And what if the contest fails?"

Alec turned to look out the window. "I'll resign as manager of Tuxedo Junction and suggest to the board that Charity be my replacement."

The ensuing pause stretched into a pregnant silence. A silence Julian eventually broke by clearing his throat. "You'd do that for Emma?"

It was an admission Alec wasn't ready to make. "It's my fault she's involved in this, and it's my responsibility to make sure she isn't the one who's hurt."

"I see." Julian was obviously reading all kinds of meaning into the words, but Alec didn't care. He had to do this because…well, because he had to. "Let me get this straight," Julian continued. "You'll wager your job against Emma's mortgage and the outcome hinges on a contest."

"A scavenger hunt, actually."

"What are the odds?"

Alec rubbed his thumb across his jaw. "Hard to calculate. The odds of finding one hundred brides and grooms in this town on any given day are decidedly good. The odds of persuading those same couples to participate in a scavenger hunt are a little less favorable."

"Luck is always the unknown factor." Julian tapped one beefy finger against the leather seat. "If you win, will you give the prize to Emma as a wedding present?"

The man had a one-track mind, Alec decided. "I certainly have no interest in owning a wedding chapel. Emma can do whatever she wants with the mortgage once I get my hands on it. All I have to do is figure out how to convince Charity to take the wager."

"You're going to have to put on your best kid gloves," Julian stated. "A proposition bet like this one has to sound like a no-lose deal with the odds stacked heavily in her favor. She's got to think she's holding a royal flush, even before the cards are dealt."

Alec waited, knowing that Julian was working toward the conclusion he, himself, had already reached.

"And since you're the payoff she's planning to win, you're going to have to break your engagement to Emma. This woman, this Charity, she's got to believe she has a real shot at winning you back. Because if she gets so much as a hint that you're double-dealing . . ."

With no trouble at all, Alec could follow the scenario to its disastrous conclusion. "Charity isn't an easy person to bluff."

Julian rolled his shoulder in a shrug. "I'm here to tell you, son, that whether you've got five bucks riding on the outcome, or five hundred thousand, you play with all the skill you got and hope Lady Luck is sittin' on your shoulder. When it's over, win or lose, you walk away. But while the game is in play, you don't think about winning or losing. You think only about the cards on that table."

Alec shook his head. "I only hope Emma will understand that."

"She will when it's over, and that's all you can make book on at the moment." Julian leaned forward, resting his elbows on his knees, clasping his hands in genuine concern. "Okay, son, deal me into this game and tell me how I can help."

HARRY RAN a set of melancholy chords and answered them with a trill of random notes. He played the first few bars of "Love Me Tender" and then switched to "People Will Say We're in Love."

"You know, Emma," he said over the song, "I've been thinking I might spend a couple of months in Lake Tahoe. See if I could land a gig in one of the clubs there."

Emma stopped trying to fold the mountain of pink netting and looked across the room. "You wouldn't actually leave Las Vegas, would you? You've always said this is the one place in the world where a man can see everything without ever having to step outside the city limits."

Harry kept the music coming, softly but with persistence. "I'm quite a talker, sometimes. I don't know that I've seen everything, but I know I can play the piano, sing a couple of tunes, and have the crowd sitting in the palm of my hand. And that's what I want to do. It's not that I don't like the chapel or that I don't enjoy doing the weddings, it's just..."

With a smile, Emma bent to tackle the netting again and renew her effort to reduce it to a manageable heap. "You haven't gotten to enjoy your retirement much, have you? I'll bet you've worked harder since I took over the running of the chapel than you ever had to before."

He gave her a grin. "I haven't had the worry, though. That's worth a lot. And I've had time to get my act together... literally. You've done a good job with the place, Emma. I'm proud of you."

"I have a lot of ideas, but until we're in a little better financial position, they'll have to stay on hold." She smoothed a length of pink net, folded it, again and again and again, and still the end of the fabric was buried in the pile at her feet. "Of course, if Julian stays in town very long, we'll be bankrupt in a couple of days, anyway. He must have bought five hundred yards of this stuff."

Harry laughed and swung into "It Had To Be You." "I thought Sanchee was going to kill him today."

"I thought she was going to quit. Then I would have murdered him, myself."

"He's a good man, Emma. He just doesn't want to admit that you've grown up and are no longer his little girl."

"And I, for one, am grateful she isn't." Alec walked into the chapel and straight to Emma, casting Harry a casual wave. "Harry, we need someone to fill in at the Silk Stocking tonight. Are you available?"

Harry was on his feet in a flash. "I'm halfway there. Any requests?"

"'Goodbye, Tootsie, Goodbye'?"

"Consider it sung. See you tomorrow, Em."

"Lock up the front as you leave, please, Harry."

"Done! Hey, Alec, thanks."

"You're doing me a favor." Alec turned his full attention to Emma as Harry hustled from the room.

She took a backward step. "If you're planning to pick me up and carry me off someplace, Alec Sayre, tell me right now and save us both a lot of trouble."

His slow, sure, and terribly sexy smile nearly knocked her over. "Emma," he said, "do I have to sweep you off your feet every time we meet?"

She wanted to say yes. "Don't be silly. Am I not the woman who is constantly saying 'put me down'?"

"You certainly sound like her. All right, tell me this . . . if I don't pick you up in my famous two-arm carry, will you have dinner with me?"

She smiled. "That sounds like a trick question to me."

"No trick to it. Jacques is preparing your favorite dishes even as we speak."

"Really? And how does Jacques know my favorites?"

Alec lifted his brow in teasing surprise. "He's a French chef, Emma. He assures me that whatever he prepares for your dinner *will* be your favorite."

"Another overconfident male."

"Yes, and we mustn't keep him waiting. He can get ugly over delays."

Emma knew a protest was pointless, mainly because her heart wasn't in it. But Alec didn't need to know how easily he had won her forgiveness. "It's a little late for dinner," she said.

"In this town, it is never too late for anything."

She made another fold in the pink netting. "What did you do with Julian?"

"I lost him somewhere between the blackjack table and my office. With any luck, he won't surface again until late next week."

"If he stays lost for the next twenty-four hours, you'll have my deepest, most heartfelt gratitude."

Alec lifted his hand and brushed the side of her face. "I'll be happy if he isn't anywhere in sight when I wake up in the morning."

Emma didn't have an answer for that, although her heart leapt in response. She looked down at the pile of pink surrounding her feet. "I should put this away before I leave for the night."

"I'll help." Alec bent, scooped the netting into his arms, and asked the question of where to put it by the simple arching of his eyebrow.

"The back room," Emma suggested, leading the way. "On the couch."

Alec had fond memories of Harry's apartment and of the bed with its abundance of scattered pillows. It looked the same, except that Emma had looked much prettier lying on the peach-colored comforter than the pink netting was going to look. He dumped the bundle on the bed and watched as it rolled to the floor like a big lump of bubblegum. "Wouldn't it be easier to toss the whole wad into the nearest Dumpster?"

"Easier, but not efficient. We're going to be needing rice bags for our scavenger hunt and for our one hundred brides and grooms. I'm just being thrifty."

"And who is going to cut this stuff into little squares, Miss Thrifty?"

"You and Julian." She gave him a saucy smile as she turned to leave the back room.

He stopped her with a touch of his hand and a smile of his own. "Just a minute. I think you may be operating on the assumption that I can be had for next to nothing."

"Oh, no." She tapped a finger against his chin. "I think you've already been had for a lot less."

Her laughing eyes and the appearance of the dimple proved more than he could resist. He pulled her against him. In the space of a heartbeat, his lips were on hers, milking the sweetness she offered, returning the pleasure she gave. The tender flesh of her lips became firmer as her arms slipped around him in an embrace that matched the growing absorption of his kiss. His heart stepped up its rhythm, until the blood raced like quicksilver through his veins. He gathered her closer and felt a tingle of new excitement as her hands stole about his neck.

When she pulled away, he was too hungry to let her go. "I missed you today," he murmured into the fragrance that wove through her silky hair. "I did not want to leave you this morning."

Emma raised on tiptoe and brushed a light kiss across his jaw. "Julian has a way of making you do things you don't want to do. I believe I warned you about that."

"He is the last person I want to talk about tonight."

"I'm in complete agreement with you."

"Good, then that means you're having dinner with me."

She turned toward the door. "Did you ever, actually, entertain any doubt?"

"The pink netting caused me a moment's concern. There's so much of it."

"It may be reproducing. We should probably get out of here while we can. Otherwise, we may spend the rest of our lives in this storage room, fighting for survival, cutting pink netting into four-by-four squares."

"It could engulf the entire chapel."

"You know, you're right. Let's move. You lock the back door. I'll double-check the front."

He took a step into the hall. "Have you got everything you need?"

"And then some." Emma's wry smile captured his heart, and he knew he would have had a better chance of winning a battle with the whimsical alien army of pink netting.

JACQUES HOVERED like a nosy mother-in-law as Emma took first one bite and then another of the special entrée he had prepared. "You like?" he asked in a thick accent. "Yes?"

She swallowed the bite of crabmeat prepared in a sauce straight from heaven. "It's wonderful."

The chef nodded his pleasure. "Good. So, *ett,*" he ordered motioning with his hands. *"Ett."*

"We'd like to eat, Jacques." Alec laid down his fork. "And we will just as soon as you go back to the kitchen."

Jacques clapped his palms to his cheeks. "The kitchen! I must prepare the dessert!" He spun on his heel and made tracks, leaving Emma and Alec to *ett* in peace.

However, they were no sooner alone at the secluded table than Emma's appetite vanished under a delicate and pervasive awareness. It seeped into her like a caress as she looked across the table and caught Alec watching her. On the table, a candle flickered in a crystal hurricane, casting his face in dramatic relief. The expression in his blue eyes was unreadable, and as he speared a piece of crabmeat and carried it to his mouth, Emma thought he had never appeared more dangerously attractive. The angles of his face were cut sharply by the candle's flame, and the slash of his dark brows seemed at once unfamiliar and very seductive. He seemed suddenly distant, mysterious and desperately desirable.

As he chewed, the strong lines of his jaw claimed her attention. And when he raised his wineglass and drank, she followed the action, staring in fascination as the wine slid between his lips and down his throat in a swallow. She could barely breathe, so captivated was she by the thought of where this night could end.

"Is it too much for you?" His voice was deep and resonant, an intimacy in itself, and she wondered if this was a trick question.

"Too much?" Her reply shimmered with the awareness she couldn't escape.

"The food," Alec clarified. "Jacques is very fond of rich sauces."

"Oh." Emma glanced at her plate and then found her gaze pulled inexorably back to his. "No," she said. "It's not too rich. It's very good."

"But you're not eating. Or should I say, you're not *etting?*"

His smile only made her more conscious of him, and she made a deliberate effort to ignore the erratic thunder beat of her pulse. She picked up her fork, pierced a tender bit of crab, and lifted it. He watched, the smile lingering on his lips, in his eyes. Without tasting the food, Emma laid the fork on the edge of her plate.

"I think you need some assistance." Alec leaned forward, lifted the fork with its bite of crabmeat and repeated the journey, bringing the food against her mouth, urging her to part her lips and accept the offering. Without taking her eyes from his, she took the food, allowing her mouth to slide over the tines of the fork in a smooth, succulent sweep. The taste of the crabmeat might have been delectable or as dry as sawdust. She was only and completely conscious of Alec, seated so near, but too far away.

As he cocked an eyebrow, she chewed, sure that he was equally aware of the tension, of the sensual intimacy of the meal they shared. His gaze didn't waver as he dipped her fork into the dish and returned to feed her another bite. "I adore rich sauces," he said softly.

"Yes," she replied in a throaty whisper. "I can see how you would."

"Jacques makes superb desserts, too."

"I won't be having dessert."

"Oh, yes, you will." His affirmation was as quietly delicious as any concoction from Jacques's kitchen, and Emma savored the sweet taste of anticipation.

She sighed at the tempting movement of Alec's perfect mouth. "I suppose it will hurt his feelings if I don't."

"Yes, Jacques will be devastated." Alec's smile was slow and sexy. "And so will I."

"But what about all those calories?"

"We'll burn them off."

The possibility made her breathless. She ran the tip of her tongue across her lips. "We're going to dance until dawn?"

"And if dancing doesn't do it, we'll think of something else."

She allowed a provocative smile to reach him across the candlelit table. "In that case, bring on the dessert."

"'CALL ME IRRESPONSIBLE...'" Harry crooned into the dusky ambience of the Silk Stocking Lounge. A long-legged waitress leaned against one end of the counter and kept an eye on her tables while talking to another long-legged woman who tended the bar. The outline of a lady's high-heeled shoe shimmered in relief on the polished marble back wall, and muted spotlights cast the small dance floor in shadows.

"'Throw in unreliable, too...'" Harry's voice lingered over the words, and Emma laid her head against Alec's chest as they danced. The evening couldn't have been more perfect. From Jacques's delectable meal to Alec's delicious and intermittent kisses, the hours had floated past like the iridescent and irrepressible bubbles in champagne. She half expected to awaken and find she'd dreamed the entire evening.

"Stay awake for this," Alec teased, his lips grazing her temple with the softest of touches. "You know what a scene it would create if I had to pick you up and carry you upstairs."

She tipped her head so she could see his face. "I'll keep my eyes wide open."

His smile caressed her spirit, and she cradled her head, again, in the pillow of his shoulder.

"'I'm irresponsibly in love with you...'" Harry sang, and Emma sighed.

"I am, you know," she whispered into Alec's pocket, the one that rested over his heart. His cheek brushed the top of her head, almost as if in answer to the admission he could not have heard. It was true. She was irresponsibly in love with a man who stuttered and turned pale at the mention of marriage, who had demonstrated effectively that the word "commitment" wasn't in his vocabulary. If Charity McKimber hadn't pushed him so hard to make a commitment, Emma would not be dancing in his arms at this very moment. She knew that without a doubt and, as much as she hated to feel any kind of obligation to Charity, Emma couldn't be but grateful for this one evening....

"That's it for tonight, folks." Harry played a scale, a chord, and a soft tootle-doo on the piano keys.

"Thanks for stopping by the Silk Stocking to hear Harry Lukinbill, the keyboard magician. We'll see you again real soon." Then, as if he hated to quit, Harry launched into a reprise of the last song.

Alec let his arms slide from Emma's waist, catching hold of her hand with his. "Shall I take you home?"

"I don't think I want to go home."

His lips curved in a languorous and dangerous smile. "That sounds like my cue to invite you up to view my etchings."

"I was hoping to be invited to see something a little more personal."

"My sock drawer?"

Her mouth assumed a wanton slant. "Any pair of drawers will do."

Alec laughed softly. "Let's get out of here." He turned and started for the door, but Harry was lying in wait and delayed their retreat.

"What did you think?" Harry asked. "Was there enough variety in the act? I can energize or slow it down. I'll put in new songs every night, change the rhythm here and there, put a different spin on an old favorite, play more requests.... You name it, Alec, I'll do it."

Alec clapped the older man on the shoulder. "Relax, Harry. I'll see you in my office tomorrow. We'll talk to Bruno, iron out a few details, see what kind of schedule we can work out. Okay by you?"

Harry's grin occupied half of his face. "Okay. And don't worry, Emma. This won't affect my duties at the chapel. I can do both jobs. And if the schedule gets tight, I know this Presbyterian minister who's retiring from his church. The wedding chapel business will be right up his alley. He can fill in for me whenever necessary and—'' Harry grabbed Alec's hand and pumped it vigorously ''—thanks for giving me this opportunity. I appreciate it more than you know.''

''I'm not giving you anything, Harry. You're good. If you weren't you wouldn't be here.''

Harry nodded. ''Yeah, well, I'm grateful, anyway.''

''Good night.'' Alec placed his hand at the small of Emma's back and guided her away from Harry's effusive thanks. ''Still in the mood to see my bedroom?'' he whispered in her ear.

''Only if you're in it.'' She smiled at him, but the moment was interrupted by an employee of the casino. The man spoke softly to Alec, listened to the response, then slipped quietly into the crowd.

''Sorry,'' Alec said, but no sooner had he taken two steps toward the elevator than another employee, a woman this time, approached and quietly asked a question. Emma watched the ease with which Alec handled the interruptions, admired his smooth, self-assured manner, and was ashamed to feel a little jealous of the attention he gave to others.

It took several starts and stops before they stepped inside the elevator and, even then, another couple intruded on their privacy. Emma stood beside Alec, pretending an interest in the view of the atrium, but so aware of him that she could hardly breathe.

The elevator glided to a stop. The other couple got off, leaving Alec and Emma to travel alone to the floor above. But the tension didn't ease. It vibrated like a tightly wound cable, ricocheting from him to her, from her to him. Her arm brushed the sleeve of his jacket. His fingers were no more than a half inch from touching hers. The longing to be closer was like an unslaked thirst . . . a slow, steadily increasing need.

When the elevator doors opened again, neither Emma nor Alec moved. They simply stood, caught in one another's gaze, steeped in the accumulation of the evening's delights, aware that the best was yet to be. As the doors began to close, Alec put out his hand and stopped them. "You may have to carry me the rest of the way," he said softly. "I'm feeling suddenly weak in the knees."

"You probably should lie down." Emma lifted her hand and made a shaky sweep through her hair, letting it tumble in disarray about her shoulders.

Alec watched it fall and wanted her more than he could ever remember wanting any other woman. And still he made no move in any direction.

A buzzer sounded, signaling that the elevator doors would close automatically within the next few seconds, replacing the hesitation with new motivation. Emma started at the sound of the buzzer, then stepped out and into the hallway. Alec was right behind her, catching her elbow and turning her around and into his arms. His mouth met hers in a compelling kiss, seeking satisfaction for the hunger burning inside him. He tasted the sweetness of a yearning as strong as his own and knew, without conceit, that the intensity of her desire more than matched his. And he fervently prayed that, after what they would share tonight, her feelings would be strong enough to help her survive what was to happen the next morning.

Her hands splayed at his back, clutching and releasing the fabric of his jacket in quick, uneven movements of her fingers. Spirals of pleasure coursed down his spine. He pulled her against him, cupping her hips and positioning the rigid thrust of his body in the hollows of hers, so that she could have no doubt that he wanted her. He could feel her rapid heartbeat challenging the persistent tempo of his own. Her body pulsed a thousand messages to his, confessing her need, rousing his animal instinct.

With little effort, he could have forgotten where they were and let the passion overpower them. His suite and privacy lay no more than a few feet away, but it might as well have been miles. His body responded to no commands but hers. His need left no room for other considerations. He moved his hand to her breast and encircled the rounded peak. Her quick intake of breath stole what little reason he had left, and he renewed the assault on her lips with rough possession.

Somewhere, far below them, the elevator chimed a warning. Emma gathered her senses and realized that she was out of control. Just like the night before, with one kiss Alec had reduced her to a hotbed of physical yearning. She had slid from a kiss directly into the fire of wanton desire, from a spark to a white-hot blaze, in less time than it took to strike a match. She pressed her palm flat against his chest, and the quick, throbbing rhythm pulsed into and around her until she wasn't sure if it was his heartbeat or hers. His hand at her breast was exquisite torture. Too much fabric separated them and suddenly Emma was determined to get out of the hallway and into his bedroom.

"Come with me to the Casbah," she whispered, her voice a mere ruffle of sound in her throat. "Otherwise, you're going to be very embarrassed the next time those elevator doors open."

He placed a line of kisses at her throat and then, with a sigh of reluctance, stepped an arm's length away. "I've forgotten which room is mine."

Her laughter caressed him, renewed the anticipation, and paved the way to the door of his suite. Once inside, they reached for each other and intimacy flooded the softly lighted room. Passion returned with a fierce and urgent demand, a demand hungry kisses couldn't begin to satisfy. There was a grasping of hands, the throaty murmurs of a mutual desire, emptiness and achiness and the shared knowledge of the one way to assuage both. Yet the intensity grew too powerful and too fast, and with a common will, they banked the fire and let the kisses diminish into soft, sweet pledges.

Emma was surprised at the sudden shyness that seemed to envelop them when they finally drew apart. They stood in silence, trying to catch their breaths, sharing a look that bespoke their longing, waiting for the tension to ebb and allow them time to fully enjoy the moments ahead. Just looking at him made her hot all over. His jawline was strong, masculine, and her palm tingled with the need to stroke it. The corners of his sensual lips tipped up, inviting her participation in his smile. His dark brows defined his expression and his eyes—those infamous bedroom eyes—promised her worlds she had barely dreamed of. She wanted him. She would have him. Tonight she would surrender her body, her heart, her soul, into his keeping and sleep at peace in his arms. There was no question, not so much as a whisper of protest, and yet she felt oddly shy and uncertain.

As if he recognized her hesitation, Alec extended his hand and let a slow smile curve his mouth. It was easy to match his effort. The shape of her lips was intimate and inviting, the pressure of his touch a request for trust and surrender. A request she granted with a happy heart. Together they walked, hand in hand, into the bedroom and Alec closed the door.

Shut inside, with the glitter and giddiness of Las Vegas going on unnoticed below, the world expanded to a universe. He became her center, the sun and source of her existence. For a woman of independence, it was a sobering realization. She had thought herself immune to Alec's take-charge charm. But she had fallen in love, anyway. And worse, she was beginning to hope that he was falling, too. The look in his eyes, the smile on his lips, the gentle possession in his touch, all whispered of deeper feelings, of a thousand tomorrows, of caring and... of commitment.

As he claimed her kiss once again, she left her daydreaming for another dawn and responded to his embrace without hesitation. Tomorrow held little importance when she was in his arms. Her fingers wove into his hair, holding him close. Her breasts lifted and molded to his chest. She stepped out of her shoes and, with one foot, she stroked the muscles of his calf, creating a static resistance on the fabric of his slacks. Alec broke the embrace with a shaky sigh.

"If you don't mind," he said, "I'm going to get out of these clothes."

"And slip into something more comfortable?"

A sexy grin edged onto his lips. "Yes... you."

Her stomach curled into a silky knot of anticipation and she reached for the buttons of her blouse. "I'll be out of these by the time you get your cummerbund undone."

"You underestimate my eagerness." He shed the jacket and bow tie in one motion. The cummerbund and shirt were nearly as easy. And Emma was still working on her buttons.

"Wait a minute," she said. "You're getting ahead of me."

"I promise not to start without you." He leaned down and unbuttoned the middle two buttons on her blouse, then slipped his hand inside the opening.

She stopped breathing as he pushed aside the material of her bra and moved his thumb in excruciating circles across her breast. He watched as the teasing movement took its toll on her composure, reducing her to a trembling mass of insistent need. "Sorry," he said softly. "Now, I'm letting you get ahead of me."

She reached for the fancy buttons on his shirt, but he caught her hands and held them tightly within his grasp. "Would you care to make a little bet on which one of us can get out of our clothes and into that bed first?"

Tilting her head to one side, she pursed her lips and casually unfastened the rest of her buttons. "Sounds like a sucker bet to me."

He stripped off his shirt, tempting her to break rhythm and run her hands across his chest. "It's a legitimate proposition. The odds are not stacked in my favor."

She laughed then as her blouse skimmed from her shoulders and floated to the floor. Her bra was next and she relished the knowledge that the sight of her bare breasts hampered his efforts to get his pants off. "No, definitely," he said hoarsely. "If any stacking has been done, it is all in your favor."

With a smile, she reached for the back zipper of her skirt. And then the teasing subsided, replaced by an urgency that could no longer be held at bay. The skirt listed to the side and then slipped over her hips and to the floor. Her underclothes were vanquished with a push and a twist and she stood before him, wearing only her desire.

Alec caught his breath and stepped away from his own discarded clothing, only to pause and gaze at her in tormented wonder. Their eyes clung, pledged, and he became lost in the fascinating certainty that she wanted him as much as he wanted her. He reached for her then, slowly, purposefully, cupping her face between his hands, stroking the velvety softness of her cheeks with his thumbs, holding her gaze with tender insistence. "You are very beautiful, Emma."

His thumbs moved down and guided her chin up as he lowered his face to hers, breathing in the gentle gardenias and roses fragrance he had come to associate with her. His lips touched hers lightly, with a heart-stopping reverence, and the tip of his tongue tasted the bow of her mouth.

Emma thought she might die with the gentleness of his touches and the crushing weight of her own desire. He opened her lips with a docile nudge and then deepened the kiss with a consuming pressure. He moved and the pressure traveled, along the curve of her throat, down to the heavy, hungering ache in her breasts. He nuzzled her, nursing a new and empty sensation deep in her belly. An unmistakable craving swirled and spun within her, and the only truth she recognized was that it could only be satisfied by Alec. He gathered her into his arms, and his lips seared a return trail to her mouth, which he captured with a kiss. She swept her arms around him, exulting in the smooth texture of his skin, caressing the tangible evidence of his muscular strength, trembling at the exquisite conjunction of her body aligned with his. Her breasts were crushed against his chest, and an arc of electric longing sailed through her at the touch.

He tore his mouth away from hers in sweet torture and looked at her with eyes that promised a bit of heaven. "So beautiful," he whispered. He lifted her up, holding her taut against him, and she cradled him between her thighs as he carried her to the bed.

They went down together, sinking into the softness, tumbling within the bed's embrace, kissing, touching, kicking aside the satiny coverlet to roll on top of the finely woven sheets. Nothing mattered but the taste of him. Nothing reached her ears but the sound of his quickened breathing—or maybe the rushing gasps she heard were her own. Nothing existed beyond the feel of his body against her. Behind her closed eyelids, desire seared the darkness with the impression of light and fire and the too dear image of Alec's face.

Her passion flared like a flammable liquid reaching flashpoint after being too long exposed to heat. He stroked her with his body, investigating every sensitive point of contact with his mouth, his hands, his tongue. In a tangle of legs and arms and mouths, she discovered pleasures she had never known before and opened herself, heart and soul, to his possession.

Passion spun a seductive web as he moved to cover her, to steal her heart in a hundred, or perhaps a thousand, exquisite moments. Taut with tension, trembling with need, he entered her and then his heat was inside her, meshing body with body, emotion with sensation, combining, blending, becoming one with her in the fever pitch of a single yearning.

Release came like sunrise, exploding on the horizon in an explosion of light and bringing with it the magnificent awe of morning, breathtaking and ever new. Emma thought no dawn had ever come with such splendor, with such wonderful promise, and she slept in Alec's arms, satisfied, sated, and very much in love.

Chapter Eleven

Alec checked his watch three times on the way down in the elevator.

"Are you late for an appointment this morning?" Emma asked—and was completely surprised by his guilty start.

"Uh, no." He covered the watch face with his hand. "No. No appointment." His smile was hardly convincing.

"I can get home by myself, Alec. You don't have to walk me through the hotel lobby and outside just to see me settled in the limo."

"It's the gentlemanly thing to do."

The contented feeling that had graced her morning took a direct hit. "Is something wrong?"

"No," he answered too quickly, and then more slowly added, "No, what could be wrong?"

She didn't know, but something certainly seemed to be. She attempted to ease the tension with some light humor. "You can relax, Alec. I don't think Julian and his shotgun are anywhere around."

His expression changed, but not for the better. "I'm not worried about your father." Turning, he sent his gaze across the atrium and away from her. "Look, we had a nice evening together. Let's not spoil the memory by talking about what's going to happen next."

The elevator reached the lobby and, with the smooth opening of the doors, Emma hid her frown. Maybe Alec was tired. Maybe she'd kept him up too late. She smiled to herself at the thought as he took her elbow and guided her from the elevator bay into the hustle and bustle of a Friday morning in the hotel lobby. Maybe she should think positive. Alec could be making his last stand against the sobering concept of a lifetime commitment.

"You know, Alec..." She raised her voice slightly because of the general noise around them. "This time next week, we'll be giving the final 'ready, set, go' to the Wedding of Your Dreams contest. This place will be full of wedding consultants and florists and photographers and caterers. And they'll all be taking part in our scaveng—"

He squeezed her arm so tightly, she looked up and followed his line of vision to Charity McKimber, who stood a few dozen feet away in front of the reservation desk. The cuss word Alec uttered under his breath was unmistakably heartfelt.

Emma couldn't help but notice the confidence of expression and the possessiveness of the secret smile Charity directed at Alec. Her throat tightened with uneasy suspicion, but before she could turn to measure Alec's response, she heard a familiar voice behind her.

"Emma!" Julian was too close. There wasn't a prayer of outrunning him. "Emma! Where have you been all night?"

This time Alec's cuss word wasn't even faintly sotto voce, and he dropped his hand from her elbow as if he were a worn-out oven mitt and she, the hot potato.

And then Julian was upon them, his face a spectacle of conjecture as he greeted them each in turn. "Emma. Alec."

"Good morning, Julian." Emma sighed as her heart dropped like a leaden weight. "I'm just on my way to the house. Would you like to go with me?"

Julian scraped his hand across his chin as he looked from Emma to Alec. "She spent the night here with you, didn't she?"

"That, sir, is none of your business."

"Well, I think it is. She is my daughter!"

"She's also a consenting adult, old enough to do whatever she pleases without asking your permission."

"I know she never gave you permission to take advantage of her."

This could not be happening, Emma thought. Not in a hotel lobby. Not after one of the most wonderful nights of her entire life. "Julian," she said sharply. "This is not the place or the time. Let's go."

He shrugged off her persuasive pressure on his arm. "This man has taken advantage of your innocence and, by God, he's going to marry you."

Alec's laughter was not kind. "You're a stupid old man. I told you before, I have no intention of marrying your daughter. Not even if you hold a shotgun to my head."

"But you're engaged!"

Alec shrugged. "A matter of convenience, nothing more. I never intended to marry Emma. She's always known that. You're the only one who seems to be having a problem understanding."

"I understand you're an ignoramus who has trifled with my daughter's emotions."

"Emma is a grown woman and we've had some good times together. She never expected more."

Julian stepped to within inches of Alec, a grizzly bear facing off with a panther. "The hell she didn't."

"That's it." Alec's expression turned frosty. "I want you out of here. Take your ridiculous threats and your daughter and get off of my property."

Emma struggled with the double whammy of embarrassment and disillusion. Alec didn't want to marry her. Her time with him had been just that. Time. Not a commitment. "Julian," she said in a hoarse whisper. "Please."

"Let me handle this, sweetheart." He never even looked at her, directing all his disapproval at Alec. "You owe my daughter an apology, and I'm not leaving until I hear it."

"You're leaving." Alec's voice was deadly calm. "There are security people standing all around you, waiting for my signal. Don't make this any more embarrassing for Emma."

"You dog!" Julian said for all to hear. "You're the one who's embarrassed my Emma. Not me." He lunged forward, grabbing for Alec's lapels, but losing his grip when his target stepped nimbly aside.

The security officer was at Julian's side in a split second, restraining him from further displays. "I'll see you to the door, sir."

"I'll see myself *and* my daughter out, thank you." Julian shrugged aside any attempt to harness his massive arms, and gave Alec a nod that seemed oddly satisfied for a man who was being thrown out on his ear—along with his daughter.

Emma made a futile attempt to swallow what remained of her pride and apologize for her father's actions, but her throat was too dry. She looked at Alec, wanting some acknowledgment from him, some small gesture that would let her know he regretted his part in her humiliation.

But he was sharing his gaze with Charity McKimber and didn't seem to realize anyone else was in the world.

"WE'LL SUE HIM for breach of contract."

"There was no contract, Julian." Emma tied silky knots in the ribbon streamers of a bridal bouquet and tried not to think about her headache. "You mean, breach of promise."

"Yeah, breach of promise, we'll sue him for that, too." Julian slammed his fist on Sanchee's worktable, scattering carnations and baby's breath across the countertop. "No one is going to treat my little girl that way and get by with it. Not in this town."

Emma took a deep and painful breath. "Julian, he told you the truth this morning. Our engagement was a matter of convenience. Marriage was never our objective. I'm not unhappy. My heart isn't broken. My virtue is intact. Please, please, don't talk about this anymore."

"But, Emma, he should do right by you. You're in love with him."

She lifted her chin. "*That* is the silliest thing you've said today. Now, either find something useful to do around here or go to the strip and bury yourself in a game of blackjack or something. And don't think that I've forgiven you yet, either, because I haven't."

Looking unduly pleased with himself, Julian reached across the florist's bench and chucked Emma under the chin. "You will, darlin'. You will."

THE PICTURE made the paper the next day.

Marry My Daughter, You Dog! the caption declared. And there, for the scrutiny of the curious, was a fulsome photograph of Julian glaring at Alec, like a bull ready to charge the red flag in moral outrage. Alec looked particularly composed and generally unperturbed by the menace staring him in the face. And in heartbreaking humiliation, Emma stood between the two, looking for all the world like a virgin about to be sacrificed.

It was a grainy, black and white record of the most embarrassing moment of her life. The only thing missing was the shotgun, and Emma could only wish now that she had been able to get her hands on one then.

"Not a great shot of you, sweetheart." Julian pored over the paper as he drank a cup of his awful coffee. "But they did spell your name right."

She stared at the empty mug in front of her and wondered why she had ever given Julian her address.

"And they mentioned the Golden Glow Wedding Chapel." He nodded agreeably. "Spelled that right, too."

"Well, I can certainly count my blessings this morning." Scraping her chair against the floor, she pushed herself up from the table, took a wide path around the counter that held the coffeepot, and got the milk from the refrigerator. Returning to the table, she eyed the photograph from an omniscient, overhead view. "You know, if that reporter hadn't been in a blackjack game with you the night before, he wouldn't even have been in Tuxedo Junction at that precise and opportune moment."

"True statement." Julian took a long swallow from his coffee cup. "On the other hand, if you hadn't been horsin' around all night, you wouldn't have been there, either."

An irrefutable observation, which did not improve her morning. "In my opinion, it was an incredible bit of bad luck that the man had his camera with him. Honestly, Julian, couldn't you have won it from him or something?"

He looked up and frowned. "Have some coffee, darlin'. You're not thinking straight." He tapped the newsprint with a blunt finger. "What you got here is publicity. There's no such a thing as *bad* publicity. Good, bad, true, false... you get your name in front of the public and presto-chango, your business booms. If I've heard you say that once, I've heard you say it a hundred times."

She answered with a hostile glare. "Don't tell me you got into a yelling match with Alec to give me publicity."

He took a swallow of coffee. "Hmm, this is good. You should have some, Emma. It's the stuff that dreams are made of." He offered a salute to the sludge he called coffee and then set the cup on the table. "No, darlin'. I am not responsible for this bit of promotion. You must just be lucky."

Lucky. Oh, yes, that was her. Lucky Emma, who owned her own business. Lucky Emma, who had secured her independence. Lucky Emma, who didn't need the man she *did have* in her life, much less the man she *didn't have.* "Lucky," she said. "Yeah. That's me."

Being lucky wasn't going to get her through the next few days, though. She'd have to work with Alec, organizing and completing the details for the scavenger hunt...unless he wanted Charity to take over now that she was back in the picture. Emma's heart hurt at the memory of the way he'd looked at the other woman, and she quickly pushed the thought aside.

What Alec wanted was not her problem. The contest had been her idea from the beginning. She wouldn't allow Charity to steal it away from her again. She would see it through to completion, no matter what the effort cost her.

With sudden determination, Emma pushed aside the carton of milk and got up to pour herself a cup of coffee.

"Changed your mind about my brew?" Julian asked.

She looked at the liquefied muck in her mug and sighed as she raised it to her lips. "Just practicing self-discipline."

"GOT TIME for another quick question?" Alec's voice was friendly and efficient as it reached her through the phone lines. "I won't take up too much of your time."

That was certainly true, Emma thought as she perched on the edge of her desk and fixed her gaze on one of the several wedding photos on the wall. Alec hadn't taken up much of her time since that morning in the lobby of Tuxedo Junction. A few phone calls. A couple of drop-in visits. A brief meeting over an even briefer lunch. All pertaining to the Wedding of

Your Dreams contest and the organization of the rapidly approaching scavenger hunt. No explanation for his sudden change of heart was offered. None asked for. Emma knew what was going on. Or more accurately, who. Charity was back in Alec's life. What else was there to say?

"I have a few minutes before the next wedding," she said, matching his tone exactly. "What's up?"

And he told her. A little detail gone awry. Nothing to agonize over. Together, they worked out a solution in less than two minutes. "We work well together," he said with a smile she could only imagine.

"Yes, we do." Her voice was a replica of his, cordial and carefully screened to remove any hint of deeper meaning. Light, impersonal conversation. As if they'd never kissed or made love. As if Lucky had never existed. "If I ever decide to do another publicity campaign, I'll enlist you as my partner."

"Thanks for the warning." His laughter was gentle and gave her heart a painful twist. "Right now, it seems like this contest will never be over. And once it is, I don't ever want to do this again."

"Only a couple more days." After that she probably wouldn't even have this brief contact with him on the phone anymore. "The conference attendees will arrive in town tomorrow, and by Sunday, you'll be a free man again."

"If I survive that long. I wish the scavenger hunt were taking place today."

So she'd be out of his life completely? So he could devote even this small amount of his time to Charity? Emma swallowed a bitter lump of heartache. "I'm sure you'd rather be doing almost anything else."

"Not—" He broke off the words and muffled the phone, but in the background, she could hear Charity's voice.

"Hello, darling. Jacques is on his way up with our lunch. Can you take a break?"

Alec's reply was just as audible. "Give me five seconds to get off the phone."

The connection became clear again and his tone became distant. "I'm sorry, but we'll have to talk again later. I've got to go."

"Me, too," she said nobly, pretending she didn't care. "Keep your fingers crossed. Remember, we want this scavenger hunt to be a success."

There was a pause in which Emma longed for the touch of his hand.

"It has to be," he said. "It simply has to be."

The Top Hat Room was filled to overflowing. A wedding consultant from Lincoln, Nebraska, stood at the podium and told a well-worn anecdote about a rooster and his hen who planned a wedding with all the "egg-stras" and then flew the coop when they found out the justice of the peace was a weasel.

Emma stood to one side, the scavenger hunt rules and prize list hugged tightly to her chest as she awaited her turn at the microphone. Her rehearsed instructions seemed suddenly as dry and dim-witted as the chicken story. What if no one wanted to participate in the game? What if they all chose to play the slot machines instead of scouring Las Vegas for brides and grooms?

This was going to be a disaster. It was a bad idea to begin with. Why, oh, why, hadn't she let Charity take full responsibility and credit for this fiasco? Why had

Charity sabotaged the contest in the first place? What did Alec see in the woman, anyway?

There was a spattering of laughter as the speaker plugged in the punch line, a round of applause as he left the podium, and a rustle of noise as a handful of people slipped through the door and left the conference room. Taking courage in hand, Emma walked up the steps to the stage and positioned the mike. "Hello," she said. "I'm Emma Cates, owner of the Golden Glow Wedding Chapel here in Las Vegas and one of the sponsors of the Wedding of Your Dreams contest."

No one yawned. So far, so good.

She held up the papers in her hand. "This is the list of prizes which will be given to the winning team. All the rules, restrictions, and conditions are spelled out, but if you have any questions, ask me or any one of the sponsors, those of us wearing red ribbons. Starting time is midnight tonight and the contest ends at the Golden Glow Chapel in exactly twenty-four hours, at midnight tomorrow."

Only one person had left the room since she'd started talking. Emma began to hope this might turn out all right. "You'll notice that your name tags have a number typed in the bottom left corner. That number designates your team. Your team leader will be the sponsor whose name tag bears the same number. You'll meet in this room at midnight and from there you can go anywhere within the city limits. The panel of judges will be at the Golden Glow Wedding Chapel throughout the twenty-four-hour period to authenticate that a team has secured a legitimate item on the hunt list, answer questions, or to rule on any alleged violation. Any questions?"

A hand in the middle of the audience flew up. "How will we know if we have a *legitimate* item as opposed to an *illegitimate* one?"

There were a couple of smart-aleck remarks from the audience, but Emma ignored them. "The hunt list is very specific and the team leaders are well versed on the rules. You shouldn't have any trouble. Other questions?"

A spirited murmur rippled through the crowd, but no one else voiced a question. Emma sighed with momentary relief. "All right. I'll pass out the prize list now and let you see what you can win. Good luck and have fun."

The murmur turned into full-fledged enthusiasm as she moved away from the podium. No sooner had she stepped from the platform than people crowded around, eager to acquire a copy of the prize list and contest rules. Several times she heard people comment on what fun they thought the scavenger hunt would be, and one person even told her he was passing up a few hours at the baccarat table to participate in the contest. In a matter of minutes, the flyers were distributed and the crowd began to disperse.

Emma looked up and saw Alec. He was at the back of the room, chatting with a group of people. As always, he was dressed in a traditional black tuxedo and couldn't have looked better if he'd spent days preparing for this one appearance. Her heart pumped out a quick-step rhythm of unwelcome emotion, and she wished she had the moxie to walk straight up to him and give him a well-planted kick in the seat of his well-pressed pants. She couldn't think of anyone who deserved it more, with the possible exception of Julian.

Charity slipped into the group and placed her hand possessively on Alec's arm. She smiled at him. He smiled back. The other people wandered away, but Alec stayed and talked to her. He looked interested— no, not interested, *entranced*—by whatever she had to say.

Emma's heart slogged back to the lackluster, heavy cadence of loneliness. As she recalled, he'd been running from Charity the first time she'd met him, that first time he'd kissed her. It was obvious he wasn't running anymore, and Emma reminded herself to keep that in mind during the next twenty-four hours. She'd be friendly, easy to work with, gracious, charming, witty, self-assured, carefree, and, under it all, totally, utterly miserable. Not that she'd let him see. Not that he'd notice. But at least she'd have the satisfaction of knowing that she'd played out the game and left the table with the wild card of pride still tucked inside her sleeve.

"I DON'T SEE WHY I can't be a team leader with you." Charity traced the shape of his fingers with her fingertip. "Just because we have a bet on the outcome seems like a silly reason to exclude me from the fun."

Alec shored up his eroding patience and from somewhere found a smile. "Conflict of interest, Charity. Remember our agreement?"

"As if I'd want to forget it." Her smile was pure conviction. "As if I wasn't going to be the big winner tomorrow night at midnight."

A familiar anxiety kicked Alec in the stomach, but he didn't let it show. "Haven't you heard, Charity? It's bad luck to count your money before the cards have left the dealer's hand."

Charity laughed, unperturbed. "I think I'm safe. It's obvious Little Ms. Lucky doesn't have any aces up her sleeve."

Irritation overshadowed the anxiety, but he hid that, too. "How do you know Emma doesn't have the best poker face this side of the Grand Canyon?"

"Oh, please, Alec. Look at her. I can read her expression from here. The silly thing is desperately in love with you."

Alec had been trying not to look at Emma, but at Charity's declaration, he couldn't help himself. *Love?* Was that the emotion she disguised by turning her head the moment he glanced her way? He'd embarrassed her, humiliated her, hurt her. Wasn't it more likely she was simply averse to being in the same room with him?

Love? Was it possible Charity could perceive a truth he hadn't been able to see? Emma's gaze swung back to his unexpectedly, catching him in mid-ponder. The curve of her lips was faint, but imminently kissable. She lifted her hand in a casual wave, and his pulse rocketed as if she had given him a come-hither signal. Not that he could go to her, if she had. The game was still in play. Charity was still a force to contend with.

He turned, reluctantly, to the woman at his side and hoped Emma would understand.

Twenty-four more hours, he thought. Twenty-four hours and one hundred brides.

"HEY, YOU! Number Eight!" Julian elbowed his way into the middle of a group of contest participants. "I see you hiding in here with the Threes." He pointed to another section of the Top Hat Room. "Get over there with your own set of numbers."

A skinny man in a Hawaiian print shirt went sheepishly to join the Eights. Julian dusted his hands and checked his watch. "Hey, Harry," he yelled across the room, "what time have you got?"

Harry checked his limited edition, fourteen-carat-gold, Elvis-in-Concert watch and yelled, "Minus ten and counting! Emma! You'd better get those envelopes passed out."

She felt a little like passing out, herself, but there wasn't time for that. It seemed as if she'd been in the Top Hat Room for hours, waiting for the stroke of midnight, and now, suddenly, it was almost upon her. She hurriedly handed the sealed envelopes, along with last-minute instructions, to each of the team leaders.

"No peeking," she said. "Everyone will find out what items are on the scavenger hunt list at the same time. Wait until you're given the okay." She repeated the same directions to each group and answered questions and comments as she moved around the room. At the podium, one of the judges rattled off a few words and then, all too quickly, the countdown began. *"Ten, nine, eight..."*

On the other side of the room, Julian, Harry, and Alec had their heads together. By the time Emma felt the first stray stirring of suspicion, Julian was waving for her to join them.

"Seven, six..."

"We've got a problem." He put his arm around her shoulder and pulled her into the huddle. "The Sevens just lost their leaders. You and Alec will have to fill in."

"We can't do that." She shared one brief panicked glance with Alec. "I planned this whole contest. I have to be at the Golden Glow to make sure the judges..."

"Five, four, three..."

"Don't argue." Julian pushed her toward Alec. "Harry and I will take care of the judges. We'll handle everything."

The kiss of death. "But—"

Alec grabbed her hand, and his touch spilled through her like melted butter. She couldn't think of an intelligible thing to say, a coherent protest to make, as he pulled her into the group of eager Sevens.

"Two, one... Go!" The sound of envelopes being ripped open preceded by half a second the voices that raised in a chorus of questions and laughter and the spirit of fun.

"What's on the list? Let me see."

"Oh, that's easy."

"I know where to find those."

"Wait, how are we supposed to find *that?*"

Alec quickly opened their envelope and showed the contents to the other team members. There were murmurs and a few giggles as everyone huddled close to read the list.

"Ten brides?" a man said. "We have to find ten *brides?*"

"And grooms." A woman pointed to the item. "See. It says right there, ten brides *and* grooms. I guess they have to go together. Not one bride and someone else's groom."

"Where does it say that?" Another person edged in for a closer look. "I mean, isn't it possible to have a bride without a groom? Does that count?"

"It might not. Hey, I've got an idea."

"Let's canvass the casinos first and get the other items."

"No, we've got to get to the courthouse. We ought to be able to bag ten couples in half an hour there."

"Great idea!"

"Se-ven! Se-ven!" The chant began as the group, list in hand, ideas bouncing back and forth like Ping-Pong balls, headed for the door. Alec smiled at Emma as their team took charge of having fun.

"Come on, Team Leader Seven." Alec held out his hand to Emma. "I have a feeling this is our lucky night."

Chapter Twelve

"There's one, now! Get 'em!"

With a militant shout, Team Three converged on the startled couple who had just emerged from the courthouse. In seconds, they were surrounded, and the members of Teams Five, Nine and Seven commiserated among themselves on their lost opportunity.

A limousine from a wedding chapel eased to the curb. Another young couple stepped out and, hand in hand, entered the courthouse to get their license...all under the wishful and watchful eyes of the hunters.

"Keep an eye on those Nines," Alec whispered to Emma. "I think they're getting desperate."

"Desperate or not, they can't steal a couple away from the chapels. That is strictly against the rules."

"Not to mention just plain bad manners."

Emma glanced around at the mixed bag of teammates. "I'm not sure they'll have any manners by the time this is over. I never dreamed a scavenger hunt would stir up such competition."

"Obviously, the prizes are better incentive than we thought they were."

Emma nodded and checked the item list. "We're not doing so well. In eight hours, we've only managed to find one bride and groom who were willing to take part in our little game."

"We have half a dozen of the other items on the list, though. I think we're doing just fine. And there's still sixteen hours to go. No need to worry at this point."

She certainly hoped he was right.

"I say we go back to the strip." One team member gave the jubilant Threes a dirty look. "We're wasting our time, here, trying to beat out these other guys."

"Yeah. Let's head for the casinos. We can come back here later, when there's more activity."

"I think we'll have better luck at the hotels."

"What are we going to do?" a disgruntled Seven asked his cohorts. "Go room to room, pounding on doors, waking people up to find out if they want to get married?"

"Don't be stupid. This is Saturday in Las Vegas. No one's asleep."

"I have an idea." A young florist from Texas shyly offered a suggestion. "Why don't we ask the hotel employees to help us? I'll bet couples always ask them for information on wedding services."

"Hey, that's right."

"Yeah, they'll know."

"Let's go."

And like a field of racehorses released from the gate, Team Seven headed for the strip.

"WHICH WAY did they go?" Emma caught up with Alec and stopped a minute to catch her breath. "The team is supposed to stay together. How did they get away from us?"

"I don't know. One minute, they were three steps in front of me, right outside Harrah's and the next minute, I'd lost them."

"I looked in the casino, but you know what that's like. I could look for days and might never find them."

"I checked the hotel lobby. No luck there, either."

"They're bound to turn up. I mean, we're the leaders. They have to have us in order to win, right?"

Alec shrugged. "That's what the rule book says. I got the idea they wanted to talk to the bellhop in, uh, private."

Emma's frown deepened. "They know better than to offer him a bribe, don't they?"

"Oh, I'm sure they do." He took her arm. "While we're waiting, let's have some coffee."

"But what if they come looking—"

"Don't worry. I'm sure they'll find us."

OVER A MIDAFTERNOON breakfast, Team Seven rehashed the night's collections. "Did we get any garters?"

"We got three, but we still need two more. And we have the wedding veil, already. How about the ruffled shirt?"

"No. Hey, Alec? Have you got a ruffled shirt?"

Caught with a fork in his mouth, Alec quickly swallowed the bite of food. "I have one at the hotel. Someone will have to pick it up."

"We can do that after we get through here. Did we get our justice of the peace authenticated?"

Someone down the table waved. "I did that. We're okay on that item."

"Then all we have left is a wedding ring with an inscription, a recording of 'We've Only Just Begun,' and four brides-to-be with their corresponding grooms and we're finished."

"Except for the two garters."

"Yeah, except for those. And the ruffled shirt."

"We'll be done long before midnight. I vote we all take a nap, spend a few hours and a few bucks in the casino, and meet again around seven."

"Then we'd lose for sure."

"Oh, we've got this thing sewed up. We can get those last items, easy, in an hour or two. And with the money Alec slipped those bellhops, we'll have more bridal couples than we can use."

Emma let her gaze slide sideways along the table to Alec, who was suddenly busy stuffing his face. "Did he just say that *you* bribed the bellhops?"

"Me?" Alec tried for a look of utter astonishment and fell somewhat shy of the intended result. "Why would I do something like that? I've already spent more money on this contest than it can possibly be worth."

Emma decided she wasn't going to pursue this. The judges could deal with him...if he got caught. "I must have misheard," she said.

"I should say so." His voice was replete with injury. "I think you owe me an apology."

"Don't push your luck."

"LADY, WE'LL BRING IT back. I swear." Troy, the ringleader of Team Seven's assault on Las Vegas, tried to pull a woman's gold wedding band from her finger. "We just need to borrow it for a couple of hours."

"Let go of my hand, you lunatic!" The woman, a matronly type, brought down her purse squarely on the top of his head. "Do you want me to call the police?"

"I just want your ring." He dropped her hand to rub his head as Emma hurried forward to break up the fight. "You didn't have to get nasty about it."

"I'm sorry," Emma apologized sincerely to the woman. "We're participants in a scavenger hunt and some of us are becoming a little overenthusiastic."

The woman snapped the purse into safekeeping beneath her arm. "*He* told me he was doing a survey."

"Well, we're trying to locate a wedding band with an inscription that has the word 'love' in it," Emma explained. "You're the first one we've found."

"Humph." The woman cast a clear, disapproving gaze over the assembled group. After twenty-two hours, the Sevens were showing signs of desperation. "If you continue to accost people on the street, you'll all end up in jail."

"Please forgive our high spirits, ma'am." Alec walked to Emma's side and made a slight but extremely courteous bow. "We're very close to winning the grand prize in this contest and if you could see your way clear to loaning us your ring—"

With his hand at the small of the woman's back, Alec took her for a short stroll down the boulevard. Emma knew he was promising the moon, offering something of monetary value in exchange for the ring, and by rights, she ought to put a stop to it. But before the thoughts came to a determination, she was surrounded by team members and propelled away from the scene, and away from any chance of interfering.

"All right, you guys," she complained. "You know we're not supposed to coerce people into cooperating."

"Are you saying we're attempting to *coerce* that woman?" Troy's mouth fell open in pretended dismay. "You know we wouldn't do a thing like that, Emma. Why, old Alec is just talking to her."

Alec was actually shaking the woman's hand. And smiling so charmingly that it was a wonder the woman was still standing. Emma knew if he'd shone that smile on *her*, she'd have gone down like a burning bridge.

The woman walked away, and Alec turned his smile on the assembled Sevens. He held his hand over his head, and—on the tip of his index finger—the ring sparkled like a new promise.

"THERE'S BEEN SOME strange activity going on around town tonight." Officer Stan crossed his arms over his uniformed chest and leaned against the hood of his cruiser. "You two know anything about it?"

Emma refrained from glancing at Alec, who was stationed on the other side of Stan.

"No idea. It's been kind of a quiet night for us." Alec lied with the simple finesse of a toddler caught with his hand in the cookie jar. "We're just out with a bunch of people from the hotel."

Stan nodded, as if he believed that. "No nursing home runaways, huh?"

"No, sir. Not tonight."

"Saturdays are busy days for the wedding chapel business, Ms. Cates. Kind of an odd time for you to be out running around, isn't it?"

"We're celebrating," Alec explained.

"What's the occasion?"

"Hey, Alec!" The team members were growing restless. "We've only got forty-five more minutes and we're still short a bride!"

"Be right with you," Alec called, and waved his hand in response. "It's sort of a, uh, wedding party. Isn't that right, Emma?"

She swallowed her reservations about misleading the police. "I think a, uh, 'wedding party' just about covers it."

Alec stepped away from the car. "If you don't mind, Stan, we need to be moving along. Emma and I have a midnight date with our wedding party."

"Okay. I'll let you get on with it. But let me offer you a piece of advice. If I receive any more complaints about attempted kidnappings, people losing their ruffled shirts in a rigged poker game, or a wedding cake getting swiped right out from under the chef's decorating tube, I might not be so understanding."

"If we see a trail of cake icing, Officer, we'll report it immediately." Alec grabbed Emma's hand and pulled her away from the police car.

"One more question."

They turned back to Stan, ready to give him any answer he wanted. Within reason.

"Which one of you had the brilliant idea of having a scavenger hunt, anyway?"

Without hesitation, Emma pointed at Alec, only to find to her chagrin that he was pointing the accusing finger at her.

"OKAY. WE'RE GOING IN. Cover us, boys." Crystal, a wedding consultant from Denver, and Fred, a limousine salesman from Upper New York State, entered the courthouse on the heels of another couple.

"Go get 'em." A member of the team whispered the hoarse encouragement as the doors closed, shutting the rest of the Sevens outside.

"We haven't got much more time."

"This will be the couple. I have a good feeling about these two."

"That's what you said last time."

"I had a good feeling about them, too."

Emma leaned against the courthouse wall and wished the temperature would drop. She wondered how an early-to-bed, early-to-rise person such as herself had managed to wind up in an all-night party town like this one. She wondered what mischief Julian and Harry had created while "taking care of everything" at the chapel. But mainly, she wondered if she'd see Alec at all after tonight.

Not likely. Not even remotely possible, given Charity's penchant for being possessive. Emma sighed. She'd adjust. Her heart might be patched and pieced together, but she would live to tell the tale.

Alec turned his head and smiled at her.

And her heart broke all over again.

Crystal and Fred ran from the building, a bewildered but smiling couple attached to their outstretched arms. "They're ours!" Fred shouted.

"We did it!" Crystal danced a little jig. "This makes ten couples for Team Seven!"

"Don't just stand there. Let's get to the chapel while there's still time."

"I knew we could do it!"

"Se-ven! Se-ven!" The chant accompanied them as they rushed to a waiting limousine, bridal couple in hand, and headed for the finish line.

"COME ON IN!" Julian stood at the entrance of the Golden Glow Wedding Chapel issuing invitations with the exuberance of a game show host. "There's champagne punch and wedding cake being served inside. Check in with your team and then join the party!"

Emma took one look at her father and knew that he was having a wonderful time. From the sound of the ragtime piano inside, Harry wasn't exactly a wallflower, either. The small front lawn was covered with people, the crowd spilling out of the chapel and overflowing onto the street, where someone had thoughtfully placed orange safety cones to divert the traffic. Which was a good thing, in Emma's first five-second assessment of the party. There was enough champagne being passed around that Officer Stan could probably hear the resulting gaiety clear across town.

"If our policeman friend gets wind of this party, we're going to have some tall explaining to do," Emma said.

"We should have invited him." Alec stood with his hands on his hips, surveying the good time being had by all. "He would have lent this affair a little dignity."

"Too late for that." She pointed out a man who was wearing blue jeans, cowboy boots, a T-shirt with the slogan On Earth As It Is In Texas, and a wedding veil. "We're going to be lucky if no one gets arrested."

"Look at it this way, Emma. At least no one's trying to climb on top of the sign and kiss your neon bride and groom."

"Yet."

"Emma! Alec! You're needed inside, a-s-a-p!" Julian bellowed the command, easily traversing the party chatter. Beside him at the doors, Troy waved his arms frantically, trying to get their attention.

"We've got to check in," he explained when they reached him. "We're the last team. Everyone else has already been cleared."

Julian leaned close to Emma's ear. "Harry and I have done our part to keep the judges well supplied with champagne punch ... my own special recipe."

Emma knew there was no point in scolding him, so she simply kissed his bulldog cheek. "Thanks for taking care of everything, Dad."

"My pleasure," he assured her, which was undoubtedly true. "And if you don't double your business with this bit of publicity, I don't know what it's going to take."

Emma glanced over her shoulder at the rowdy party going on outside the chapel and the equally raucous bunch inside and hoped the resulting publicity wouldn't bury her. And then, she was captured by Troy's urgency on one side and Crystal's buoyant good spirits on the other and borne through the thick crowd to the judges.

"Team Seven reporting." Troy snapped a salute. "All members present and accounted for. Here's our shopping list. You'll notice that every item has been authenticated except this last bride and groom." The couple from the courthouse were presented like royalty to the panel of judges, asked to show their marriage license, and declared legitimate. Team Seven cheered—a reaction that rippled through the building and beyond like tumbling dominoes. The party barometer climbed another notch.

"Need some more champagne punch?" Julian magically appeared at the judge's table. "Need any help tallying the winners?"

Alec pushed his way to Emma's side. "What's the total? Have we got one hundred brides?"

She looked up at him, surprised to see his jaw stretched tight and his mouth locked in an uncompromising line. "What difference does that make?" she asked. "I mean, we're close enough. We had the scavenger hunt. And by the look of this place, I'd say it was successful beyond our wildest expectations."

He didn't seem in the mood to agree. Catching Julian's eye, Alec cupped his hands to his mouth and yelled, "What's the count?"

Julian shook his head and tried to see over the hunched shoulders of the judges who were tabulating scores with fast pencils and fierce frowns. He looked back at Alec and shrugged. A skein of concern began to thread its way around Emma's smile, pulling down the corners of her mouth along with her sense of humor. Something was amiss. Something that was known to both Alec and her father, but that she couldn't quite grasp.

And then she saw Charity McKimber standing to one side of the dais and the judge's table. She smiled when she caught Emma's gaze. A cat with a mouthful of feathers couldn't have looked more satisfied.

Alec's hand closed over her upper arm and gave her a painful squeeze. "Emma, we've got to have a count before midnight. This is your show, can't you get them to hurry?"

She turned an inquiring look on him. Was he that anxious to be rid of all obligation to her? Wasn't the rest of his life enough time to spend with Charity? Did he have to have these last few seconds, too? But then, it wasn't her place to ask for more. She had never been his fiancée, not in truth. Why should a few measly moments more or less make any difference? "I'll see what I can—"

"One minute to midnight!" The shout came from somewhere in the back of the chapel and excitement rustled through the gathering.

Alec stepped onto the dais with the judges. "How many couples?" he asked. "How many brides and grooms altogether?"

Two of the three judges afforded him a glance, but quickly resumed their duties, clicking off the count with a checkmark. "Ninety-seven, ninety-eight, ninety-nine..."

"How many?" Alec demanded.

Confused by his terse manner, Emma stepped up onto the dais beside him and found herself face-to-face with Charity. Emma fought the impulse to play tug-of-war and dropped the hand she had placed on Alec's forearm. Charity made no such concession, however, linking her hands in an acquisitive loop around his arm. "There are ninety-nine couples," she said in a tone of supreme confidence. "I've been keeping track all evening. It's been close, but you came up one couple short."

Alec spun to face her, knowing the truth of her statement even before he saw the triumphant gleam in her eyes. And then the judges were confirming it, shouting to the contestants, quieting the hubbub of noise to announce the results.

"Team Three is hereby declared the winner of the Wedding of Your Dreams scavenger hunt. And the goal of one hundred brides and grooms falls short by one couple!" The crowd didn't seem to mind, but Alec couldn't believe it. Lose by one lousy bride? Not a chance!

"There's been a mistake," he said to the judges.

Charity laughed. "Don't be ridiculous, Alec. Your time is up. You wagered and lost. Be gracious about it."

He ignored her. "There's been a mistake," he repeated. "There are one hundred engaged couples in this room. You failed to include me and my fiancée in the final count. I believe that will put us over the top."

The judges exchanged puzzled looks. Alec reached behind his back, groping for Emma's hand. He knew by the surge in his heart rate when he'd found her and, with a slight tug, he pulled her close. "This is my bride-to-be, and I am hereby giving our consent to participate in this contest. We will be the one hundredth couple."

"You can't do that," Charity shouted over the increasing volume of sound in the chapel. "Your time is up!"

Alec pulled back his sleeve to show her his watch. "It's thirty seconds until midnight. We're in the clear."

"But you're not really engaged. Not to her." Charity's finger swung accusingly to Emma. "She's not even real. You made her up."

Alec laughed, feeling suddenly very free. "Oh, she's real, all right. And so is our engagement."

One of the judges posed a question. "Do you have some proof of the engagement? Some way we can authenticate your intentions?"

"Ask that man right there." Alec indicated Julian, who was watching with interest.

"Hell, yes, they're engaged." Julian lifted his glass of champagne punch in a toast. "You think I'd let my daughter marry just anybody? I handpicked this fella, myself."

Alec turned a triumphant smile to the judges. "There. My future father-in-law vouches for me."

"Ms. Cates?" The judge moved closer to Emma. "You haven't said anything one way or the other. Do you want to participate in the contest?"

Emma lifted her lashes to reveal eyes shadowed with confusion and doubt. When she looked into his eyes, Alec knew it was a mortal blow and that no matter what happened next, he would never recover. "Alec?" Her voice was so soft, he was surprised he heard her so clearly. But he knew the question she asked, just as he knew the answer came straight from his heart.

"I love you, Emma. Will you marry me?"

"Isn't that going a little too far to win?"

"Winning isn't my objective, Emma. You are."

"But what about Lucky?"

"You're all I ever imagined her to be and more."

"Ten seconds to midnight!" Someone began a countdown in the back of the room and it was taken up by a plethora of voices.

"Emma," Julian pleaded, "for Pete's sake, say yes."

"Six, five, four..."

"Emma?" Alec squeezed her hands. "Marry me, Emma. For real."

"Three, two, one..."

"Yes."

Alec swept her up into his arms as the party exploded into a New Year's Eve type celebration. People shouted and laughed and kissed and hugged. Harry pounded out a sentimental version of "Auld Lang Syne."

Emma hardly noticed. Under the pleasurable pressure of Alec's kiss, she could barely breathe, much less get her thoughts in order. His touch was so tenderly loving, she wanted to be in his arms forever. Her desire for him so intense, she thought she would drown in it. Would he have said he loved her to win the contest? Would he actually go through with a wedding for the same reason? She didn't know, but it seemed prudent to put some distance between them until she did know. Alec, however, wouldn't let her get too far away.

"May I have your attention?" One of the judges called for quiet. "The goal of one hundred engaged couples has been met. The grand-prize winner—the couple who will be given the wedding of their dreams—will be selected by a random drawing at the last session of the conference. Other prizes will be awarded in accordance with the printed guidelines.

We, the appointed judges, declare the Wedding of Your Dreams contest closed and all conditions satisfied."

"Wait a minute." Charity stepped forward. "There's no way I'm going to stand back and let you cheat me out of what is rightfully mine—"

"Hold it right there, miss." Julian elbowed his way to the dais. "There ain't no *rightfully mine* to it. You made a wager and you lost. That's the tall and the short of it."

"But it wasn't a fair contest."

"Those are fightin' words," Julian said. "And, as I happened to be present when you made your little wager with my future son-in-law, I consider any claim of cheatin' to be a slap in my own face."

Julian was a big man and Charity, obviously, wasn't eager to provoke him.

Emma, however, had no such compunction. "Julian. Alec. Will someone tell me what this is all about?"

"A wager," Charity snapped. "As if you didn't know. You conspired to get your hands on Alec since the first minute you saw him. And this is just another one of your tricks. Pretending to be engaged to him so that I lose the bet and the mortgage on this chapel. My father didn't raise a fool."

"That is a matter of opinion." Julian's face was turning red, not a good sign. "And to prove it, Emma and Alec will get married right here, right now. You can be the witness."

"Hold it!" Emma slipped free of Alec's hold and re-established her independence. "I want an explanation. Right here, right now. Julian, don't say another word. Alec, please tell me what kind of wager you made with Charity and what it has to do with my chapel.''

Her chin was up, the militant sparkle clear in her eyes, and the dimple was nowhere to be seen. Alec couldn't stop the love that nudged the corners of his mouth into a smile. "Will you kiss me if I tell you?"

"Alec...." It was as near as she could get to threatening him, and he thought it was close enough.

"All right," he said. "If I tell you, will you marry me now? Here?"

"Don't joke about that."

His expression softened. "I would never do that, Lucky. I love you. I want to marry you. Not because of Charity. Not to win a contest. Not even to save your wedding chapel." He took her by the shoulders and fixed her gaze with his own. "Charity pulled a few strings and got her hands on your mortgage. So I made a little wager with her to get it back."

"A *little* wager?" Emma asked. "On the outcome of a crazy scavenger hunt?"

He shrugged. "We won, didn't we?"

"And what if we hadn't?"

"I would still be crazy sick in love with you and absolutely positive my life isn't worth living without you in it."

"And you're not saying this to avoid making a commitment to Charity?"

"Marrying you to keep from marrying her would be overkill, even for me."

Emma's slow smile sent shivers of delight coursing down his spine. "You're a smooth talker, Mr. Sayre."

"And that isn't my only virtue, either. I have lots more. Trust me, you have years of pleasant discoveries ahead of you."

She tipped her head to one side, assessing his meaning, taking time to accept his love. "You meant what you said."

"Every blessed word. I love you. I want to be married to you every day for the rest of my life. Will you marry me, right here, right now?"

"I thought you hated weddings."

"I'm sure I'll make it through this one. And after that, who knows? I may learn to love them."

"I feel sure you will." With a smile, she went into his arms and gave him her answer in a long and expressive kiss.

"Can we get on with this?" Julian interrupted. "Too much of this kissin' can lead to trouble. So before this goes any further, I want to hear a few simple words exchanged, a couple of promises, et cetera, et cetera."

Alec released his bride-to-be and adjusted his bow tie. "I think we better get married before he brings out the shotgun. Harry? Will you do the honors?"

"Be glad to. Got the license?"

Alec looked stricken. "I didn't think of that."

"Hold it!" Julian stepped forward. "I have a special license in my pocket. I have a few contacts in this town, you know." He produced the document with a flourish. "Been carrying it around, just in case the opportunity arose to see my daughter safely and happily married."

"More deadly than a shotgun," Alec commented as he took the license and handed it over to Harry. "Your father has a way of smoothing the path, doesn't he?"

"I warned you." She awarded a smile of thanks to Julian. "And he's about to become a very present part of your life. Are you sure you don't want to reconsider?"

"Not a chance. We'll give him a couple of granddaughters to take care of. That will keep him too busy to interfere in our lives."

"I wouldn't count on that," Emma cautioned.

Alec leaned down to kiss her, sweetly, tenderly, and with a lifetime of promises.

Harry cleared his throat. "Have you got a ring?"

With a smile, Alec produced his grandmother's engagement ring from his pocket. He held it out to Emma. "Want to wrestle me for it, champ?"

"Later," she promised. "I should warn you, though, I'm a professional body slammer."

His smile lit up her world. "I'm an amateur at this wedding business, but if you'll hold my hand, I think I can get through this without stuttering."

"I'll hold on and never let go."

He dropped the ring into Harry's outstretched palm and then took both of Emma's hands in his. "I'm betting on that, Lucky."

"Dearly beloved," Harry began, then stopped, frowned, and yelled, "Hey! Quiet down out there."

The noise dimmed, but only slightly. Julian turned around and cupped his beefy hands around his megaphone mouth. "Qui-iiii-etttt!"

A stunned quiet descended like Christmas snow. Julian smiled and gave Harry a nod.

"Dearly beloved, we are gathered here..."

Emma looked into Alec's eyes and felt a rush of excitement. As Harry's voice cascaded over her, she gave Alec her silent pledge of devotion. The slight and sober curve of his mouth affirmed his acceptance of her vow and returned it to her in a look that bespoke an emotion older than time and as new as the Sunday dawning around them.

"Repeat after me," Harry said. "I, Alec..."

Alec squeezed her hands, and his voice flowed through her like a deep and powerful river as he took the words and made them his own. "I, Alec, take you, Emma, to be my wedded wife. To have and to hold, from this day forward, for better, or worse...for richer, for poorer...in sickness and in health...for as long as we both shall live. And thereto, I pledge thee my troth."

Emma's hands shook as Harry instructed her, but her voice was strong and confident and filled with an unshakable love as she offered her promise to Alec in return. "I, Emma, take you, Alec, to be my wedded husband. To have and to hold, from this day forward, for better, for worse...for richer, for poorer...in sickness and in health... for as long as we both shall live. And thereto, I pledge thee my troth."

Harry placed his hand over their clasped ones. "Take this and place it on the third finger of her left hand."

Alec took the ring and slipped it over her finger. It felt cool and precious and solid. A mist of emotion glistened in the beautiful blue of his eyes as he softly said, "With this ring, I thee wed."

She blinked away a shimmering teardrop as she let Alec's love encircle her heart. From somewhere behind her, Emma felt a nudge at her elbow.

"Here," Julian said, "take this."

Turning, she saw her father, a fat, gold wedding band in the palm of his outstretched hand, a fat, happy teardrop glistening at the corner of his eye. "Use my ring," he whispered. "Give it to your young man."

She leaned away from Alec for the briefest of moments to take her father's offering and to kiss him on the cheek before she turned back to her love. "With this ring, I thee wed." She slipped the gold band onto Alec's third finger and trembled with a strange and wondrous sentiment as she raised her eyes to his. He looked at her for a long moment before a shared smile of pure happiness stole through the sobriety of their vows.

"I now pronounce you husband and wife. You may kiss the bride."

The crowd burst into riotous applause as Alec took his bride into his arms and kissed her. Without missing a beat, the party resumed in full force, as if the newlyweds embracing on the dais deserved a noisy honeymoon send-off. Somewhere, above the noise in the chapel, the cork of a champagne bottle blew off with a joyous pop. Emma, fresh and tingling from her husband's kiss, thought it sounded like a shooting star. She made a wish, knowing that her heart's desire had already been granted . . . granted amidst the chaos of too many people having the time of their lives on too many glasses of champagne punch . . . granted as

Alec smiled at her with a love that caught at her heart and robbed her of all reason.

Mrs. Alec Sayre.

She was one very lucky lady.

Harry began to play an old love song on the piano. " 'I'll be loving you... always...' " he sang. " 'With a love that's true... always...' "

Julian wiped away a tear for the sheer beauty of it all. And for years afterward, he told everyone who would listen how he'd moved heaven and earth—and a good part of Las Vegas—to give his daughter the wedding of her dreams.

Where do you find hot Texas nights, smooth Texas charm and dangerously sexy cowboys?

Crystal Creek reverberates with the exciting rhythm of Texas. Each story features the rugged individuals who live and love in the Lone Star State.

"...Crystal Creek wonderfully evokes the hot days and steamy nights of a small Texas community." —*Romantic Times*

"...a series that should hook any romance reader. Outstanding."
—*Rendezvous*

"Altogether, it couldn't be better." —*Rendezvous*

Don't miss the next nook in this exciting series.
PASSIONATE KISSES by PENNY RICHARDS

Available in April wherever Harlequin books are sold.

Take 4 bestselling love stories FREE

Plus get a FREE surprise gift!

HARLEQUIN®

A M E R I C A N ◆ R O M A N C E®

THE BABY IS ADORABLE...
BUT WHICH MAN IS HIS DADDY?

Alec Roman: He found baby Andy in a heart-shaped Valentine basket—
but were finders necessarily keepers?

Jack Rourke: During his personal research into Amish culture, he got close
to an Amish beauty—so close he thought he was the father.

Grady Noland: The tiny bundle of joy softened this rogue cop—and
made him want to own up to what he thought were
his responsibilities.

Cathy Gillen Thacker brings you TOO MANY DADS, a three-book series that asks
the all-important question: Which man is about to become a daddy?

Meet the potential fathers in:
#521 BABY ON THE DOORSTEP
February 1994
#526 DADDY TO THE RESCUE
March 1994
#529 TOO MANY MOMS
April 1994

If you missed any titles in this miniseries, here's your chance to order them:

#521	BABY ON THE DOORSTEP	$3.50	☐
#526	DADDY TO THE RESCUE	$3.50	☐

TOTAL AMOUNT $
POSTAGE & HANDLING $
($1.00 for one book, 50¢ for each additional)
APPLICABLE TAXES* $ _____
TOTAL PAYABLE $ _____
(check or money order—please do not send cash)

To order, complete this form and send it, along with a check or money order for the
total above, payable to Harlequin Books, to: *In the U.S.:* 3010 Walden Avenue,
P.O. Box 9047, Buffalo, NY 14269-9047; *In Canada:* P.O. Box 613, Fort Erie, Ontario,
L2A 5X3.

Name: _____

Address: _____ City: _____

State/Prov.: _____ Zip/Postal Code: _____

*New York residents remit applicable sales taxes.
Canadian residents remit applicable GST and provincial taxes.

DADS2

HARLEQUIN®

Don't miss these Harlequin favorites by some of our most distinguished authors!

And now, you can receive a discount by ordering two or more titles!

HT#25409	THE NIGHT IN SHINING ARMOR by JoAnn Ross	$2.99 ☐
HT#25471	LOVESTORM by JoAnn Ross	$2.99 ☐
HP#11463	THE WEDDING by Emma Darcy	$2.89 ☐
HP#11592	THE LAST GRAND PASSION by Emma Darcy	$2.99 ☐
HR#03188	DOUBLY DELICIOUS by Emma Goldrick	$2.89 ☐
HR#03248	SAFE IN MY HEART by Leigh Michaels	$2.89 ☐
HS#70464	CHILDREN OF THE HEART by Sally Garrett	$3.25 ☐
HS#70524	STRING OF MIRACLES by Sally Garrett	$3.39 ☐
HS#70500	THE SILENCE OF MIDNIGHT by Karen Young	$3.39 ☐
HI#22178	SCHOOL FOR SPIES by Vickie York	$2.79 ☐
HI#22212	DANGEROUS VINTAGE by Laura Pender	$2.89 ☐
HI#22219	TORCH JOB by Patricia Rosemoor	$2.89 ☐
HAR#16459	MACKENZIE'S BABY by Anne McAllister	$3.39 ☐
HAR#16466	A COWBOY FOR CHRISTMAS by Anne McAllister	$3.39 ☐
HAR#16462	THE PIRATE AND HIS LADY by Margaret St. George	$3.39 ☐
HAR#16477	THE LAST REAL MAN by Rebecca Flanders	$3.39 ☐
HH#28704	A CORNER OF HEAVEN by Theresa Michaels	$3.99 ☐
HH#28707	LIGHT ON THE MOUNTAIN by Maura Seger	$3.99 ☐

Harlequin Promotional Titles

#83247	YESTERDAY COMES TOMORROW by Rebecca Flanders	$4.99 ☐
#83257	MY VALENTINE 1993	$4.99 ☐
	(short-story collection featuring Anne Stuart, Judith Arnold,	
	Anne McAllister, Linda Randall Wisdom)	

(limited quantities available on certain titles)

AMOUNT	$ _____
DEDUCT: 10% DISCOUNT FOR 2+ BOOKS	$ _____
ADD: POSTAGE & HANDLING	$ _____
($1.00 for one book, 50¢ for each additional)	
APPLICABLE TAXES*	$ _____
TOTAL PAYABLE	$ _____
(check or money order—please do not send cash)	

To order, complete this form and send it, along with a check or money order for the total above, payable to Harlequin Books, to: **In the U.S.:** 3010 Walden Avenue, P.O. Box 9047, Buffalo, NY 14269-9047; **In Canada:** P.O. Box 613, Fort Erie, Ontario, L2A 5X3.

Name: _____

Address: _____ City: _____

State/Prov.: _____ Zip/Postal Code: _____

HBACK-JM

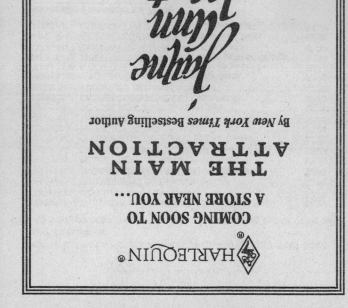

HARLEQUIN®

MARRIAGE By Design

Harlequin proudly presents four stories about *convenient* but not *conventional* reasons for marriage:

◆ To save your goddchildren from a "wicked stepmother."

◆ To help out your eccentric aunt—and her sexy business partner.

◆ To bring an old man happiness by making him a grandfather.

◆ To escape from a ghostly existence and become a real woman.

Marriage By Design—four brand-new stories by four of Harlequin's most popular authors:

CATHY GILLEN THACKER
JASMINE CRESSWELL
GLENDA SANDERS
MARGARET CHITTENDEN

Don't miss this exciting collection of stories about marriages of convenience. Available in April, wherever Harlequin books are sold.

MBD94